D1544855

WITHDRAWN

A Garland Series

Foundations of the Novel

Representative Early

Eighteenth-Century Fiction

A collection of 100 rare titles
reprinted in photo-facsimile in 71 volumes

Foundations of the Novel

compiled and edited by

Michael F. Shugrue
Secretary for English for the M.L.A.

with New Introductions for each volume by

Michael Shugrue, *City College of C.U.N.Y.*
Malcolm J. Bosse, *City College of C.U.N.Y.*
William Graves, *N.Y. Institute of Technology*

The Adventures of Lindamira, a Lady of Quality

Anonymous

The Jilted Bridegroom

or London Coquet

Anonymous

with a new introduction
for the Garland Edition by
William Graves

Garland Publishing, Inc., New York & London

1972

Library of Congress Cataloging in Publication Data
Main entry under title:

The Adventures of Lindamira.

(Foundations of the novel)
Reprint of 2 anonymous works separately published in
1702 and 1706, respectively.
I.   The jilted bridgegroom. 1972
PZ3.A2455 1972 [PR3291]   823'.5   79-170506
ISBN 0-8240-0517-1

Printed in the United States of America

Introduction

The Adventures of Lindamira, A Lady of Quality *and*
The Jilted Bridegroom: or, The London Coquet, *published anonymously in 1702 and 1706 respectively,
represent the efforts of English authors to provide
romantic epistolary fiction devoid of many of the
extravagances of contemporary French romances. Both
works, with generally reasonable plots and realistic
characters, examine the plight of lovers caught in the
snares of a hostile world. In the first, the heroine
Lindamira undergoes a series of misadventures before
she finally enjoys the love of the misled but ever-
constant Cleomidon. The lover in* The Jilted Bridegroom
*is less fortunate; his tale is a public exposure of the
wrongs done him by a cruel and fickle woman.*

The Adventures of Lindamira, *edited but apparently
not written by Thomas Brown, appeared in at least
three editions in the first part of the eighteenth century.
In the first, which is reproduced here, page numbers
63-96 are repeated. The second edition, titled* The
Lover's Secretary: or, The Adventures of Lindamira, A
Lady of Quality *(1713), and the third (1734), with the
original title, correct the error in pagination. Benjamin
Boyce has provided an authoritative, scholarly introduction to a twentieth-century edition (Minneapolis: University of Minn., 1949).*

INTRODUCTION

Less notable for the excellence of the epistolary techniques employed than for its interesting plot and characterizations, The Adventures of Lindamira *consists of an unsigned "Preface" and twenty-four letters from Lindamira to her friend Indamora. In effect a first person narrative divided into chapters described as letters, the work lacks but looks forward to skillful interaction of self-revealing characters that marks the best, later fiction of Samuel Richardson, the greatest eighteenth-century English master of the epistolary novel. It does, however, offer a carefully worked and sustained picture of the emotional life of a woman of sensibility and spirit.*

The "Preface," possibly by Thomas Brown, reflects a characteristic eighteenth-century preoccupation with the moral worth of a work of fiction. Against the accusation that "Amorous Intrigues" *promote* "Vanity and Folly," *the author insists that* "All vertuous Readers must needs be pleas'd to see the Vertuous and Constant Lindamira carry'd with success thro a Sea of Misfortunes, and at last married up to her wishes" *(p. i). The work ought to be acceptable because it is concerned with matters of truth,* "manag'd according to the humours of the Town, and the natural temper of the Inhabitants of this our Island. . ." *(p. ii). Moreover,* "the weight of truth, and the importance of real matter of Fact, ought to over Balance the feign'd Adventures of a fabulous Knight-Errantry" *(p. ii).*

Lindamira's suitors, with the exception of Colonel Harnando and Cleomidon, are foolish, egotistical men who serve only to annoy the heroine with their pretensions. *Philander and Sir Formal Triffle, derivative from characters on the Restoration Stage, are representative. With a touch of scorn, Lindamira summarizes Philander's flimsy proposal:* "That he was become the most Amorous of Men, since he saw me, and was not able to drive my fair Idea out of his mind" *(p. 7). Through an elaborate and entertaining ruse, Lindamira then rids herself of Sir Formal Triffle, whose deceitfulness is matched only by his arrogance.*

The first of the serious lovers in Colonel Harnando, a brave, well-bred soldier who attracts Lindamira but must be held off because he is a married man. By the time that the death of his wife has made Harnando an eligible consort, Lindamira has become passionately attached to Cleomidon, a gentle, honest man of good sense. The enthusiastic ending comes only after a number of painful misfortunes caused by malicious enemies: "... my Constancy is rewarded with the best of Husband's, whose Affection to me, makes me infinitely happy.... no Jealousie or Suspicion, is able to dissolve that Union that is betwixt us" *(p. 194).*

The Jilted Bridegroom, *of which only one edition is recorded, reveals that men also can suffer from the cruelties of unfaithful lovers. The recipient-editor of the letter offers it to the public to counteract the scandalous tales the flirt Floria, her father Hortarius, and her mother have spread against the spurned lover Amintor. He also wishes women in general to learn from Floria's errors, for if they do not* " 'tis morally impossible any

INTRODUCTION

Man can be secure of his Safety. . ." *(p. iv).*

The work itself is a single long letter from Amintor containing several shorter letters between Amintor and Floria. Amintor describes the progress of his suit for Floria and his subsequent betrayal by her and her family. Even though Amintor has received permission from Hortarius to court his daughter, the willing Floria, he becomes an object of scorn and deceit after Floria's mother has persuaded her husband and daughter that a more wealthy suitor can and should be found.

The Jilted Bridegroom *is filled with parenthetical observations on the nature of love, the capricious qualities of woman and the tyranny of ungenerous parents over their children.*

The Adventures of Lindamira *and* The Jilted Bridegroom, *significant examples of early English epistolary prose fiction, helped contribute to a realistic presentation of the highly structured relations between middle class men and women.*

William Graves

The Adventures of Lindamira, a Lady of Quality

Anonymous

Bibliographical note:

This facsimile has been made from a copy in the Rice University Library (*PR 3291 A1 A255)

THE
ADVENTURES
OF
LINDAMIRA,
A Lady of Quality.

Written by her own hand, to
her Friend in the Country.

In IV. Parts.

Revised and Corrected by
Mr. *Tho. Brown.*

London, Printed for *Richard Wellington,*
at the *Dolphin* and *Crown in* St. *Paul's*
Church-yard. 1702.

THE

PREFACE.

'TIS needless to make out the usefulness of performances of this nature. Tho Amorous Intrigues are commonly charg'd with Vanity and Folly; yet, when they are calculated according to the measures of Vertue and Decency, they are equally instructive and diverting. To expose Vice, and disappoint Vanity; to reward Vertue and crown Constancy with success, is no disserviceable aim. All vertuous Readers must needs be pleas'd to see the Vertuous and Constant Lindamira carry'd with success thro a Sea of Misfortunes, and at last married up to her wishes. Not to mention the stroaks of Wit, the agreeable and innocent turns, and the just characters of Men and Things, that drop from her artless Pen.

If the Histories of foreign Amours and Scenes laid beyond the Seas, where unknown customs bear the greatest figure, have met with the approbation of English Readers: 'Tis presum'd, that Domestick

A   Intrigues

The PREFACE.

Intrigues, manag'd according to the humours of the Town, and the natural temper of the Inhabitants of this our Island, will be at least equally grateful. But above all, the weight of truth, and the importance of real matter of Fact, ought to over balance the feign'd Adventures of a fabulous Knight-Errantry.

We have taken care to correct the Style, where the rules of Grammar and the humour of the English Language requir'd an alteration : But so as not to disguise the natural passion, or to depart from the natural softness of the Female Pen.

THE
ADVENTURES
OF
LINDAMIRA,&c.

LETTER I.

BElieve me, this is the greateſt Proof I can give of my ſincere Friendſhip to my dear *Indamora*, that I comply with her in a requeſt ſo diſagreeable to my own Inclinations, as to make her a Narrative of my Adventures, being ſo unfit to pen a Hiſtory, altho my own. But if you can excuſe the Inaccuracies of my Language, as things offer themſelves to my Thoughts, I will impart them to my deareſt Friend, in whoſe diſcretion I ſo much Confide, as to be ſure ſhe will not expoſe my Follies; and ſince her goodneſs has made her ſo much imbrace my Intereſt, as to give her ſelf the trouble to be better inform'd of the Particulars of my Life, I ought not to deny her ſo ſmall a ſatisfaction; and I am fully perſwaded ſhe has Indulgence enough to excuſe the indiſcretion of my Youth, therefore ſhall not ſcruple to advertiſe her of the moſt ſecret Thoughts and Movements of my Heart.

B   I ſhall

I ſhall paſs over thoſe little Occurrences of my Life, till I arriv'd to my 16th Year, during which time nothing remarkable hapned unto me. I was then bleſs'd in a good Mother, who never fail'd me, to give me all the neceſſary Inſtructions of Vertue and Honour, and after what manner I ought to Comport my ſelf in all Companies ; ever telling me that Pride in young Women, was as injurious to their Fortune, as an eaſie believing Temper might prove on the other hand, and whatever Addreſſes might be made to me, that I ſhould give no encouragement, till I had firſt acquainted her with them. The great Eſteem I had for my Mother, and the high opinion I had of her Vertue, and the extraordinary Affection ſhe ever expreſt for me, extorted from me this Promiſe, that I would always be govern'd by her Advice, and that my Will ſhould Center in hers. But at the ſame time I made my Requeſt ſhe would not force my Inclinations, out of any Conſideration of Eſtate or Intereſt of Alliance, and I gave her this ſolemn Promiſe, never to Marry without her Conſent and Approbation. My Mother being well ſatisfied in what I promis'd her, as freely granted my requeſt, and this Recriprocal Promiſe having paſt between us, my Mother was very eaſie in her Thoughts about me, and the Affection ſhe had for me, made her conceive a very advantagious Opinion of my Conduct, which eaſed her of thoſe Fears that uſually attend a

miſtruſtful

miſtruſtful temper in Mothers, that their Children muſt be guilty of great Indiſcretions, if out of their ſight: but on the contrary ſhe never debar'd me of the Liberty of ſeeing ſuch Friends as were moſt agreeable to my own temper. As for publick Diverſions I never was much addicted to 'em, and that which confirm'd me in this humour, was for the ſake of two Young Ladies of Fortune, of indifferent Beauty, but very Gentile and Sparkiſh; who were of a humour to be at all publick places of Rendevouz, as Plays, Balls, Muſick-meetings, *Hide-Park*, St. *Jame's* and *Spring-Garden*. One Day being at a Friends Houſe, who had a Young Daughter near my own Age, in whoſe Converſation I took much Delight; I went thither to ſpend my Afternoon, taking with me a new Piece of Work, wherein I wanted her Ingenious fancy to aſſiſt me in the Contrivance. Whilſt I was there came in two very Beauiſh Sparks to viſit my Dear Companion *Valeira* (for ſo was ſhe call'd) they entertain'd us with the News of the Town, and of the laſt Comedy, and pleaſantly reproach'd us for being at home, when all the fine Ladies of Beauty and Quality were at the Play; as for my own part, I told 'em I took more pleaſure in looking on my Work than others did in beholding all the Pagentry of the Operas; to this one of 'em reply'd whoſe name was Mr. *W*—— that 'twas pitty we were not of the humour of the two Ladies I have already mention'd, that were at the

B 2   Play

Play almoſt every Day. The Devil take 'em
ſays t'other, all places are fill'd with their
ugly Faces, I'de as live ſee a Toad, as their
two long Noſes appear. To this *Valeria* reply'd, That if ſhe and I were of the ſame humour, he wou'd ſay as much of us : but Mr.
S—— excuſed himſelf for uſing ſo courſe an
Expreſſion, and to attone for his Crime, he
told us both very obligingly, that our Faces
would Command an Univerſal Reſpect, and
that the Criticks in Beauty, would go with
pleaſure to thoſe places, where they could
delight their Eyes in beholding two ſuch
Miracles of Nature. The large Encomiums
he made on this occaſion, I aſcrib'd to the
Merits of *Valeria*, and the too well grounded
Admiration he had of her Beauty, for ſhe was
certainly a Perſon infinitely Charming.

And to deal ſincerely with you *Indamora*,
that Afternoons Converſation was the occaſion that I reſolv'd with *Valeria* not to be ſeen
in publick places, and that our Faces ſhould
give as little offence as poſſible. We concluded upon this Expedient, not to go often
to our own Pariſh Church, but change our
place as often as the Week came about. This
humour we perſued a good while : for my
Mother not being very well, ſhe kept her
Chamber for two or three Months, for ſhe
knowing I was in *Valerias* Company, remain'd
very well ſatisfied, ſo that I had the opportunity of gratifying my own fooliſh humour :
but after we had continued our rambling fancies

cies for fome time, an accident befel me, for
a punifhment of my Folly.

It hapned one *Sundday* we went to *White-
Hall*-Chappel, where I obferv'd a Gentleman
had his Eyes perpetually fix'd on me, and
when ever I look'd that way, I found him ftill
in the fame pofture ; this I muft confefs put
me extreamly out of Countenance , fo that I
was forc'd to rife up in my own defence, and
turn away my Head. The Confufion I was
in, made me give little attention to what the
Minifter faid, whom I thought very tedious,
but at laft there was a general Releafe, and
Valeria and my felf were the firft that made
an attempt to go out; the Croud being fo
great we could not without much difficulty
difengage our felves : but when I was at Lberi-
ty, and that I could breath, the frefh Air, I
turn'd about to *Valeria* to tell her I never was
in fo much Confufion, as at the Spark that
ogled me, whom it feems fhe had obferv'd as
much as my felf : I doubt not (faid fhe) but
you have made a Conqueft of that Beau, for I
dare fwear for him he was more intent on
you, than the Minifter that Preach'd.

Now is your time *Lindamira* (continued
fhe) to do full Execution with your Eyes, and
I hope you'll ufe your Victory with Moderation. She rally'd me exceedingly for being
fo concern'd for being look'd on, and as we
were on our way home, I obferv'd an Ordinary Man that pull'd off his Hat to me ;
and without looking him in the Face I return'd

turn'd his **Civility**, but *Valeria* knew him to be a Porter I ufed to imploy upon bufinefs, and as by accident fhe turn'd her head fhe perceiv'd the Spark a talking to this Fellow and told me of it, which extreamly vex'd me, for I concluded this Ignorant Blockhead would not have the Senfe to Evade any Queftions that might be asked by *Philander* (for that is the name I gave him) and that he would certainly know by his means who I was,

Valeria did fo unmercifully Teeze me, that I could hardly pardon her Railery, which fhe continued till we got home : at which place I think moft convenient to take leave of you, and to give you fome Refpite after fo long, and fo ill Pen'd a Narrative; but let the Acknowledgments I have made of my Difabilities plead for me; for nothing but your Abfolute Commands could prevail with me, to give under my own Hand, how Indifcreetly I have govern'd my felf. But am in all Sincerity my Deareft *Indamora*,

Your moft Faithful
Friend and Servant

Lindamira.

LETTER

LETTER II.

My Dearest Indamora,

ABout two Days after, my Maid (whom *Valeria* call'd by the Name of *Iris*) brought me a Letter which the said *Roger* the Porter gave her, tho' I knew not the Hand, I open'd it, and soon perceiv'd it came from a Lover tho' unknown to me. The natural Curiosity that attends our Sex, prevail'd with me to Read it, and tho' I have not the Letter by me, to the best of my remembrance it was to this effect.

That he was become the most Amorous of Men, since he saw me, and was not able to drive my fair Idea out of his mind, he beg'd I wou'd permit him to wait on me, that he might tell me with his own Mouth, how great an Admirer he was of me, and much to this purpose.

I sent for *Roger*, demanding of him, from whom he had the Letter, and from what place: he told me from a brave Gentleman of the *Temple*, I enquir'd his Name which he readily told me, adding that he was a very familiar obliging Gentleman, and had a notable Head-piece of his own, and as I knew *Roger* was none of the best Judges of a Man's Sense and Breeding, I had not a better opinion of *Philander* for the Character he gave

him

him, when he had anfwered all my Queftions, I bad him return this Anfwer to the Gentleman; that had I known from whence the Letter came, I wou'd have return'd it to him, if it had not been open'd, and that I was highly difpleas'd at his boldnefs, and abfolutely forbad *Roger* bringing me any more Letters; but before I difmift him, I added one Query more, which was, how he came to be imploy'd by this Gentleman, knowing that he plyed a great way off from the *Temple*: he then told me, that as I pafs'd by, he putting off his Hat to me that Day we had been at the Chappel, *Philander* who had followed us, enquir'd of him my Name and the place of my Aboad, to which Queftions he having anfwered the Gentleman Commanded him the next Morning to come and receive his Orders.

In the Afternoon *Valeria*, according to her ufual Cuftom, came to pafs with me a few Hours; I accofted her with the wonderful News I had to tell her, confcerning the Letter I receiv'd from *Philander*, fhe laugh'd at me extreamly, telling me I was rightly ferv'd for being fo offended at his looks, but fhe hoped his Letter had not given me fo much offence. I recounted to her all the Difcourfe I had with *Roger*, whom I had charged to bring me no more Letters: But have you forbid him bringing me any reply'd *Valeria* pleafantly? at the fame time produc'd a Letter from the fame Hand, and to prevent my asking
ing

ing how she came by it; she told me that *Roger* had brought it to her from a Gentleman, who was very Ambitious of her Acquaintance, but she might reasonably imagin it was for *Lindamira*'s sake. I was very impatient to know what answer she return'd; which was that she would not permit of his coming to wait on her, till she knew the sentiments of her Friend, which she did believe would not incourage his Visits, without her Mothers Knowledge, and then she laid her Commands upon the Porter not to bring her any more Letters. I gave my Dear *Valeria* a thousand thanks for the good office she had done me, believing this would blast all his Hopes, and that I should be troubled no more with the importunity of a fluttering Beau; whose Genius only lies in dressing and saying Amorous things: But said *Valeria* to me, Prithee tell me my Dear *Lindamira*, what sort of a Man wou'd be most agreeable to your Humour; for *Philander* seems to be a Person very deserving, he has a good Presence and seems to have Wit, and yet you hate him, only because he is become your Admirer? What Accomplishments must he, or any one have, to render him worthy of your Affections? I told her it was not a delicate shape, or a fine Face, that cou'd Charm me, but a Person of a tender and generous Soul, one that was not capable of a disingenious Action to his Friend, that was Master of a sound and solid Judgment, and had Wit enough, but not too much least

he

he fhould difcover my Ignorance. In fine
(faid I) *Valeria*, I think that my Happinefs
would confift in having an abfolute Empire
over the Heart of a Vertuous Perfon. You
have given fo good a Difcription of an Accomplifh'd Perfon, reply'd *Valeria*, that I
wifh it may be your Fortune to Reign Abfolute
in the Heart of fuch a one : but 'tis not ufual
to meet with thofe that can excite true Love
and Admiration at the fame time ; and I fear
added fhe, that you may keep your Heart long
enough, if you don't beftow it, tell you meet
with one who is owner of all thefe Perfections. In fuch fort of Difcourfe we pafs'd that
Afternoon, but I never thought the Day long
enough when I was in her Company, fuch
pleafure there is to Converfe with thofe one
delights in, but *Valeria* was a Perfon that was
extreamly pleafing, having abundance of Wit,
and no Affectation, but much Difcretion, and
I ever prefer'd the fweet injoyment of her
Company before any Diverfions of the Town;
but fince 'tis not her Hiftory I am to Write,
I will perfue my former Narration, and acquaint you with the Fopperies of *Philander*.

The *Sunday* following, after Evening Prayer,
came the Minifter of the Parifh to wait on my
Mother, and *Philander* a long with him; my
Mother fent for me into her Chamber, and
bid me go and Entertain Mr. *G*—— till fhe
came, I obey'd her, but never was I more furpriz'd than when I beheld *Philander* in the
Room, I was in difpute with my felf if I
fhould

fhould advance or retreat, but being oblig'd
to be Civil to Mr. *G*—— I acquitted my felf
as well as I could, and made my Complement
to him. Mr. *G*—— who was an Ingenious
Man wanted not for Difcourfe to pafs the
time till my Mother came, and then I was oblig'd to change my Seat, and could not avoid
fetting by *Philander*, who all this time had
not fpoke one word, but figh'd heartily whilft
Mr. *G*—— entertain'd my Mother, (which
feem'd to be about bufinefs of Confequence
for fome times he fpoke low) *Philander* took
the opportunity to difcover the weaknefs of
his Soul, and his intolerable Foppery; he was
very Loquatious, yet he often complain'd he
wanted Rhetorick to exprefs his Sentiments,
which he did in fuch Abominable far-fetch'd
Metaphors, with Incoherent fragments out
of Plays, Novels and Romances, that I thought
he had been really diftracted. 'Tis impoffible
to reprefent to you, the feveral Grimaces,
the Geftures of his Hands and Head, and with
what eagernefs he ply'd his Nofe with Snufh,
as if that would have infpir'd his fhallow
Noddle with Expreffions futable to the occafion. I faid all to him that my Averfion
could fuggeft, which I thought was enough to
put a Young Lover out of Hopes, and frighten
my Parchment Hero from making a fecond
affault at my Heart, which I was fure was
proof againft any impreffion he cou'd make.
But *Philander* was refolv'd to perfift in tormenting me, and in a Foppifh Impertinent

way,

way, told me he wou'd wait on me, whether
I would or no, for he could not live without
the fight of me. At length Mr. G —— took
leave of my Mother, and I was deliver'd from
the Converfation of one of the moft Ridiculous, Fantaftical Fops the Town ever bred.
When they were gone my Mother asked me
how I liked that Gentleman; as well Madam
(faid I) as 'tis poffible to be pleas'd with a
Conceited Coxcomb, who has only a fair
out-fide, but has neither Senfe nor Brains to
recommend him. You are very Satyrical faid
my Mother, for methinks he is a very pritty
well bred Gentleman, I told my Mother that
Appearances were often falacious, that I
cou'd difcover no Charms he had, but the
Gentile tofs with his Wigg, and the grand
flur that indeed was handfome enough, yet
he was my Averfion, for I cou'd never have a
true efteem for any one fo monftroufly Fopifh:
but reply'd my Mother, he has a good Eftate,
and is a Counfelor at the *Temple*; and is very
much taken with you, as Mr. G—— tells me,
and in my opinion ought not to be flighted.
But as my Mother had promis'd not to force
my Inclinations, I did not apprehend much
trouble from Mr. G——'s Interceffion on
Philanders behalf, who made me a vifit three
or four Days after, and came in a drefs fuitable to his Defign, if fine Cloaths, well chofe,
and well put on, would have altered my
opinion of him. My Mother Commanded me
to go into the Parlour to him, and to fhew
                                        fome

fome Complacency to a Gentleman that had
an efteem for me. I obey'd my Mother, but
with all the Reluctancy imaginable, which
was eafily difcover'd in my looks, and gave
Philander fome reafon to fear, that my Heart
was not fo eafie a Prize as he imagined after
the firft Ceremonies, he asked me the Caufe
of that Chagrine that appear'd in my Eyes,
and did hope that his Prefence did not Contribute to it. I took the opportunity to
affure him I was furpris'd to fee him after the
Repulfes I had given him, for I was not of the
humour to encourage the Affection of any
one only to add Trophies to my Victories,
and that I thought it more for Reputation to
have no Lovers at all, than fuch as I cou'd
have no efteem for. Then Madam (faid he)
I perceive I am not of that Number, that are
blefs'd with your efteem on Friendfhip, and
retreating back a ftep or too, as if he had
been Thunder-ftruck, he Curft his Stars for
Loving one (as he faid) fo fair, and yet fo
cruel; and fighing faid, when I reflect on the
feverity of my Deftiny, and what Difpair
you drive me to, I am of all Men the moft
unhappy : but cou'd I reprefent to you the
Torments of Love, the Hopes, the Fears,
the Jealoufies, that attend a violent Paffion,
it wou'd certainly work upon your generous
Humour, and wou'd prevent thofe Miferies
that accompanies a defpairing Lover. I
hearkned to his Harangue without interupting
him, and when he had fqueez'd out his laft
Sentance,

Sentance, I took upon me to reprefent the unhappinefs of a Precipitate Inclination, and that the effects of it, were nothing but fighs, and a fruitlefs Repentance, and however re-fin'd his Paffion might be, I had not fo much good Nature as to favour it : and being not willing to give way to the freedom of thofe thoughts I had of his Foppery, I refolv'd to confider him as he was, and to treat him with refpect, and Ingenioufly to confefs I had fo great an Indifferency for him, that it was im-poffible for me to vanquifh it, whatever Vio-lence I ufed upon my Inclinations, and that if he was truly generous, he wou'd not give himfelf the trouble of coming any more to me. At thefe words the Poor Lover feem'd much concern'd, and ftrugling between Love and generofity, he at laft faid ; that he wou'd obey me, and bannifh himfelf from my Pre-fence, for he did believe the fight of him was odious to me, and fince I was fo Niggardly of my favours, his Life wou'd be fil'd with nothing but difafters, and out of my Prefence it would feem a dull infipid Being : and added alfo that he would take a Voyage at Sea, and Travel for fome time, in hopes that Abfence wou'd work the effect I defir'd. I confirm'd him in his pretended Refolution, reprefent-ing to him the Advantages that young Gentle-men receiv'd by Traveling, that they might improve their ftock of Wit, their Judgment and whatever their Genious led 'em to : and that in *France* Love and Gallantry, was fo

much

much practic'd, and incourag'd, that I believ'd he would be esteem'd in the first Rank
of the most Gallant Men of *Paris*, since he
knew so well how to admire our Sex, and to
extol Imperfections for Excellencies, and that
Flattery was a bait so easily swallow'd, that
none would question his Judgment.

Some more discourse we had upon this subject, wherein he accus'd me of too much
Cruelty, and that I was guilty of great Tyranny that would see him languish in Dispair;
but the Pious resolution he had taken of Traveling, I told him wou'd prevent my seeing
an object that cou'd raise no Compassion in
me.

He then perceiv'd I rally'd him, and not
being willing to be the subject of my Contempt, he beg'd leave to take his last farewell
of me, that pleasing found so charm'd my
Ears, that I was ready to receive his Salute,
before he was rose from his Chair, which
confirm'd him more in the opinion of my
Aversion to him. And according to the ancient Dialect of Lovers, he blam'd his Fate,
and deplor'd his misfortune, and then took
his last Adieu.

When he was gone I gave an account to
my Mother of what had past, I believe my
proceedings did not agree with her Judgment,
but she said little to me of it, and thought me
very difficult to please.

But

But my *Indamora*, my time was not yet come, that the little God of Love, took a Revenge for my Infenfibillity; my next Tormentor was an old ftiff Ceremonious Knight, to whom I gave the Name of Sir *Formal Trifle*, but having fpun out this Letter too long already, I fhall defer the Recital of his Addreffes till the next opportunity I have of conveying my Thoughts to my dear Friend, with whom I wifh my felf daily, and that I cou'd make you a Vifit in your Charming Solitude, which you have fo ingenioufly defcrib'd, that I long to partake of your pleafure in your folitary Walk of high Elms, which brings into my Remembrance fome paffages of my Life, which you fhall be acquainted with in the fequel of my Story, Farewel my Dear *Indamora*, I am

Your *Lindamira*.

L E T-

LETTER III.

I Shall, my deareſt *Indamora*, ſuccinctly run over the accident that brought me acquainted with Sir *Formal Triffle*, that I may the ſooner come to that part of my ſtory that has occaſioh'd the curioſity of the cauſe of that great misfortune that has coſt me ſo many ſighs and tears.

And I think two months had ſcarce paſt over after *Philander* had left me at liberty, but my Mother and my ſelf were invited to dinner by an Uncle of *Valeria*'s; where was to be only a ſelect number of Friends, and knowing *Valeria* wou'd be there, I went with more pleaſure than I ſhould have otherwiſe gone, if my pleaſant Companion had not been one of the number. At dinner, according to Cuſtom, all the Ladies Healths were drank, and at laſt it came to my turn; and as the Fates wou'd have it, it fell to Sir *Formal*'s lot to begin it. Madam (ſaid he) my fair Oppoſite, 'tis ordained by the Stars above, that I ſhou'd be that happy Man, that has the Honour, (tho' undeſervedly) to begin the moſt amiable *Lindamira*'s Health, this long Herangue was ſo ſurpriſing to me, and ſo uncommon that if I had not been under ſome Reſtrictions I ſhould have diſcover'd my ill breeding by

C   laughing

laughing in his face : But this dignified Fop
for fear I did not apprehend his Compliment, repeated the same words again, that
he might have more efficacy upon my mind,
and oblig'd all the Gentlemen to follow
his example. Now that you may know him
the better, I will send you his Portraiture
drawn in as lively colours as ever *Titian*
or *Tintoret*, represented any one to the Life.
This Knight was about the age of Forty
Five, Tall, Lean, and ill Shaped, but I
could not difcover the leaft Reliques of a
good face : He was flow of Speech, mightily Opinionated of his own Wit, one who delighted in hard words, and admir'd himfelf
for his Difcourfes, his fuftian way of ex-
prefling his wretched Thoughts ; which he
was pleas'd to mif-name Oratory, and Eloquence, at the fame time he was infupport-
ably impertinent in all Companies, he wou'd
be giving his advife when he was never ask'd ;
and, to the mortification of all that convers'd with him : He had a prodigious long
memory, which made him never to omit
the leaft Circumftance, that ferv'd to enlarge his ftory ; fo that all his Auditors
ftood in need of what patience they had,
to fupport 'em under the fatigue (if I may
fo exprefs it) of being oblig'd to give attention to him.

Thus

Thus my *Indamora* have I given you a
moſt exaɛt deſcription of this Sir *Formal*,
without either magnifying or detraɛting from
his merits. As ſoon as dinner was over,
Valeria and I withdrew from the Company,
and went into a Cloſet, where we had our
fill of laughing, for all dinner time he threw
his eyes about, as if he wou'd have thrown
'em at me, and ſent me ſo many Amorous
glances, and made ſo many wry faces, that
one wou'd have imagin'd Convulſion Fits
had ſeiz'd him. I was particular in my Enquiry, whether he was Batchelor or married Man, if the latter, I had good nature
enough to pity his Lady, but if the former,
I rejoyc'd to think that no Woman was ſo
unhappy to be ſubjeɛt to his humours, which
to me ſeem'd inſupportable, eſpecially the
everlaſting penance of hearing his impertinencies. But ſaid *Valeria* what if the Knight
ſhou'd become your Lover, how wou'd you
receive him, for I am of opinion you have
made a Conqueſt of his heart already, and
he never makes his application but to young
Ladies. Is it poſſible (ſaid I) that he ſhou'd
have Confidence to make Love with that
forbidding face? 'Tis moſt certainly true,
reply'd *Valeria*, and you need not doubt but
he will make you a Viſit, which will laſt
you ſix long hours by the Clock, his diſcourſe you'll find worſe than his name-ſakes
in the Vertuoſo; he'll perpetually teize you
with long Narrations of his Intrigues with

young Ladies, of Favours receiv'd, of his Compendious way of ftorming of hearts, and the infenfibility of his own, for he pretends 'tis his greateft diverfion to draw the fair Sex into his fnares. When *Valeria* had done fpeaking, I cou'd not help admiring that any thing that went on two legs, and pretends to Reafon, could be fo vain, fo conceited and fo abandon'd to folly. The Character fhe gave of him, made me entertain a mortal averfion for him; and I heartily wifh'd I might never fee the face of him more. But for the punifhment of my fins, no Queftion, *Valeria* and my felf were call'd down to the dining-room, and the firft Object I caft my Eyes upon was Sir *Formal*, who came fmirking towards me, and offer'd me his hand to lead me to the other end of the room, which I cou'd not civily refufe him, he then began a long Harangue upon the fecond Chapter, (as he expreft himfelf) of my Incomparable Perfections.

Madam (faid he) have you not heard of the Robbery that was committed within thefe few hours at noon-day? The Party that was robb'd loft his beft Jewel in his Cabinet, and continued he, the pretty Thief that ftole the prize is within ear-fhot of me. I could not comprehend his meaning as being utterly unacquainted with his figurative way of fpeaking, and innocently told him, I was altogether ignorant of the ftrange news

news he told me, and that I did not know how
I ought to apply his Simile, to your felf, faid he,
for you are the Thief above-mentioned, and
'tis my heart that is loft, and fo with this
thread-bare, fulfom, weather-beaten Simile,
he perfecuted me at leaft an hour ; telling
me that when he met with Ladies of Wit,
he chofe to entertain them with Allego-
ries. What I have related to you was not
fo foon fpoke as you may have read it o-
ver, for he drew out every Syllable with
as much Grace, as the floweft *Spaniard* in
Caftile, and this fo effectually tired me, that
like Prince *Pritty-man* in the *Rehearfal*, I
was ready to fall afleep. But my Mother
releas'd me from his tirefome Converfation,
by telling me it was time to be gone, becaufe fhe defign'd to make a vifit to a friend
before fhe went home.

I leave you to judge, my dear *Indamora*,
of the Joy I felt in my Soul, when I was
fummon'd to be gone, for tho' I made a
thoufand little excufes, yet all this while I
was not able to difingage my felf from his
Company. When we were arriv'd at this
place I made my complaint to a young Lady of what pennance I had undergone for
an hour, and related to her all the Difcourfe, and fhe frankly told me, that the
condition I was in wou'd rather provoke
Compaffion than Envy; but fhe referv'd her
pity for the future, for fhe forefaw my unhappinefs would not end prefently ; for

Sir

Sir *Formal*, according to his method having given me a taſte of his Wit, wou'd certainly purſue me with his Favours. I took this preſage of the Ladies for an ill Omen, and as I had already receiv'd the true marks of the Beaſt from *Valeria* it poſſeſt me with ſo invincible a hatred to his Perſon, that I believe all the perſwaſions in the World could not prevail with me to be Civil to him if he came to viſit me; which he failed not of doing in two days after. It happen'd to my great Conſolation, that *Valeria* was with me when he came into the Room; he ſaluted us both with his uſual Parade of Ceremonies, and applauded us for our Ingenuity, and great Wiſdom in employing our ſelves in Work, for (ſaith he) it diverts young Ladies from thinking on the Town Intrigues, which ſo much corrupts the youth of our Age; and my adviſe is Ladies (ſaid he) to continue in this method you have ſo happily begun. This Methodical old Coxcomb, that always went as regular as a Pendulum, I imagin'd all the World either were or ought to be of his unpleaſant humour, but he was much miſtaken in us, for tho we never pleaded for a Criminal Liberty, we hated form, and ſlaviſh obſervations of old Cuſtoms, and what our inclination led us to, that we generally gratified our ſelves in.

But

But to return to Sir *Formal* (who fail'd
not of making his Character good) he made
Love to me in a manner quite different from
other Men, for he much inlarg'd on his
own Vertues, Merits, and upon the Conquests
he had made, and mightily extoll'd his good
Humour and Moderation : Giving us to understand he was a great Philosopher, had stu-
died Self-denial the most of any Man. I
heard him with much Patience, for the
Knight being taken up wholly with his own
good Qualities, I found I had nothing more
to do, than to hearken to him, and this
first visit was the only diverting one I e-
ver had from him, for his Entainment was
absolutely new. My Mother was gone a-
broad when he first came in, but his Visits
being of the usual Longitude of 6 hours,
he was not gone before she return'd home:
He no sooner saw her but began a long
winded Discourse of his own Excellencies,
and after he had entertain'd her thus for
some time, he ask'd my Mother, if she had
no design to marry her Daughter, saying that
he knew a Man of Quality, and of a great
Estate, without Incumbrances, was fallen
desperately in Love with her. My Mother
reply'd, that I being very young, she had
no thoughts of disposing of me yet ; and
besides, so few were happy in that case,
that she could not perswade me to alter my
Condition, for the observation she had made
(by the sad Experience of some of her Friends,)

that

that few Men lov'd their Wives fo well as
their Miftreffes, and that Marriage quite
alter'd the Conftitution of their Souls, and
as Saint-like, Complaifant and Obliging as
they appear'd during their Courtfhip, they
became Tyrants inftead of Husbands, and
did fo ill ufe their Power, that they treated their Wives like Slaves, and had not
that Tendernefs and Affection for 'em as
might be juftly expected.

Sir *Formal* thought my Mother Entertained too fevere an Opinion of the ill treat-
ments of Men to their Wives ; and did
aflure her that this Perfon he mention'd,
had thoughts too tender and generous to
ufe a Wife like a Slave: And to be fhort,
gave her to underftand, that himfelf was
the individual Perfon that wou'd render
me happy. But my Mothers Sentiments
were fo conformable to my own, that fhe
gave him no Encouragement to hope, that
his Love wou'd be agreeable to my Inclinations. At laft he took his leave with
thefe comfortable words, that he wou'd often wait on me. Sir *Formal*, to fhew himfelf a Man of his word, came often indeed
to fee me, tho' he was as often told, I was
not at home, or had Company with me ;
but his fuccefs was the fame, for my A-
verfion increas'd by his continual importunity of perfwading me to Marriage, the
very thoughts was enough to make me
fwound ; and his fulfom Letters compleat-
ed

ed my Hatred; for never was so soft a
Paſſion as Love so ill expreſs'd as what came
from the Pen of Sir *Formal.* This mortification continued at leaſt three months, notwithſtanding the frequent denials he had
both from my Mother and my ſelf. But one
day it came into my mind to put a trick
upon him, for he had often told me, that
Ladies of the beſt Quality were in Love
with him, and that every day he receiv'd
Billet Deux from 'em, but ſlighted their kind-
neſs for my ſake. I had no ſooner contriv'd
a way how to fathom him, and try how
real his Love was to me, but I went to
Valeria, and acquainted her with my deſign,
who was so kind as to approve of it, ſaying he deſerv'd to be us'd ſcurvily, tho'
ſhe made ſome few Objeƈtions at firſt for
fear we ſhou'd injure our own Reputation
in it, but I alledg'd so many reaſons, and
so well ſatisfied her, that we ran no hazard
in this matter, that I brought my friend to
comply with me.

I have not leiſure to continue my Narration, by reaſon of ſome buſineſs that o-
bliges me to go out; but if *Indamora* is
not ſurfeited with the recital of Sir *Formal's* Amour; I can aſſure you I am, and ſhall
make all the haſt I can poſſible to diſingage
my ſelf from so natious a ſubjeƈt. I am

My dearest *Indamora*

Your Friend and Servant,

Lindamira.

LET-

LETTER IV.

Immediately I fet my felf to compofe a
Letter, my dear *Indamora*, as from a Lady, much Charm'd with the Eloquence of
Sir *Formal*, who being under fome Reftrictions, cou'd not find out a more convenient
place, for an hours Converfation than at
the Play-Houfe, therefore defired him to
meet her there betimes in the Pit, before
any Company came, that fhe might have
the more freedom of telling him the fecrets
of her Soul. She defcribed her Cloaths
which were Rich and Gentile, and yet was
as great a fnare to him, as to any young
fluttring Beau in Town. This Letter I fent
by a trufty Meffenger, that I was fure he receiv'd it, and did believe he wou'd not fail
a fair Lady at the place of Rendezvous.

In the afternoon I dreft up *Iris* in the
fame Clothes I had defcrib'd : This young
Girl had a great deal of Wit, and therefore
I thought her a fit Perfon to banter the
Knight. *Valeria* and my felf had dreft our
felves like Women that had no defign of
making of Conquefts; this contrivance of
ours we imparted to a Gentleman that was
related to me, in whofe difcretion I much
confided. We all went in a Coach to the
Play, but *Iris* and Mr. *Z* ——went out firft,
for

for he was to Conduct her in, and to fit behind her, as one that had no knowledge of her, he order'd the Coach to drive to the door contrary to that *Valeria* and I came in at; when we were in the Pit, there was only our own Company : But in fix minutes after, we fee Sir *Formal Triffle* enters, it was not difficult for him to imagine who was his fair Captive, and to her he directed his fteps, and fets himfelf by her. *Valeria* and my felf were at fome convenient diftance from 'em, fo that we could not diftinctly hear him, but by his Geftures and Vehemence we foon imagin'd his heart was caught; for he was deeply ingag'd in a very earneft Difcourfe with her, and as fhe fince related it to me, Sir *Formal* expreffed himfelf very Paffionately to her, and importun'd very earneftly to fee her face, which fhe not granting, he preft her more earneftly, and beg'd fhe wou'd meet him at fome other place, where he might with more freedom tell her how much he was in Love with her ; for of all the Women I ever convers'd with (which are of the beft Quality) I never was pleas'd with any one's Wit, fo much as yours, dear Madam.

Iris return'd his Praifes with great Applaufes of his Merits, which had wrought this wonderful effect in her Heart, and nothing but the difficulty of going out alone,(for fhe was under the Eye and Gardianfhip of an old Uncle) cou'd prevent her giving her felf

the

the Honour of his Converſatioñ another
time. The old Amoret, was tranſported
with theſe Charming words, and at her O-
bligingneſs, that in three nights ſhe wou'd
meet at the place agreed upon, tho ſhe ran
the hazard of her Uncles Diſpleaſure, but
requeſted of him to leave her as ſoon as
the Play began ; the joy he felt in his Soul,
for this kind promiſe of the unknown Lady, was viſible in his face, for he departed full of the thoughts of his being Belov'd,
and conſequently ſhou'd be better treated
than he was by me.

But whilſt *Iris* was ingag'd with Sir *Formal*, *Valeria* and my ſelf met with very good
Entertainment, for tho' we thought our Ordinary Dreſs wou'd have ſecur'd us from a-
ny diverſion of that ſort, yet it was not
our good fortune to eſcape ſo ; to my lot
there fell a ſpruce Officer, who for an A-
muſement, exercis'd his Wit in talking to
one that little underſtood it, he ſaid a
thouſand obliging things, to perſwade me
he was Charm'd with me, and believ'd I was
not a Perſon ſo mean as I appear'd by my
dreſs ; for he was certain that under my
Maſque there was much Youth and Beauty. I
muſt confeſs that this ſort of banter was
not diſpleaſing to me, tho' I had not vanity
enough to believe I merited the praiſes he
gave me : Yet I was delighted with what
he ſaid, for he ſpoke his words with ſo
good a Grace, and there appear'd ſo much
good

good humour in his Countenance, that I thought it was no Crime to encourage the Converſation of one who ſeem'd ſo deſerving. He aſk'd me ſeveral Queſtions about indifferent things, which I had the good fortune to anſwer pertinently enough, and this confirm'd him (he ſaid) in the high opinion he had of my Ingenuity. But ſince he had form'd an Idea of me in my Maſque that I was ſenſible did not belong to me, I thought it prudent not to convince him of his error, and tho he uſed abundance of pritty Arguments, to let him ſee ſome part of my face, yet all his Rhetorick was in vain; at length ſeeing he could not perſwade me to gratifie his requeſt, when the Play was almoſt done, Madam, crys he, you'll at leaſt condeſcend to grant me one civil petition, and that is to ſuffer me to write to you. This requeſt I thought more unreaſonable than the other, for then I apprehended. he muſt come to a further knowledge of me; I believe he partly gueſs'd at my thoughts, and without giving me leave to explain my ſelf, he told me his Letters ſhould be left at any ſhop, or place I thought fit, directed to any one I pleas'd, and by what name I thought good, and he wou'd give me a direction to write to him, and by this means we might hold a Correſpondence, which would be extream delightful on his ſide.

I do

I do Ingenioufly confefs to you *Indamora*
that this Propofition pleas'd me Infinitely, for I was fo much Charm'd with his
Converfation, that I form'd in my mind no
little pleafure, from fo agreeable a Commerce : At laft I refolv'd to grant his humble fute, upon Condition he would not follow me out of the Play-houfe, nor ever
make any enquiry who I was, if I did cor-
refpond with him ; he promis'd an Implicit obedience, and at my requeft to be gone
as foon as the Play was done.

But 'tis time to fay fomething of the
Adventure that *Valeria* had, whofe Fortune
was not fo good as mine ; for the Spark
that apply'd himfelf to her was of a different humour from Colonel *Hernando*. His
Wit was abufive, and full of detraction, and
the Common fcurrilous banter of Pawning
Cloaths for Tobacco and Brandy ; which it
feems is a Science that fome are great Pro-
ficients in, fhe not being us'd to that fort of
Difcourfe, was much offended at him, and
her anger fo improv'd his Fancy, that he
run on at a moft extravagant rate, and
ceas'd not tormenting her till the Play began, and then he left her, (as he faid) to
fhift for her felf.

As foon as the Play was ended, and the
Crowd pretty well difpers'd, we went out,
and Mr. Z——— who was our Champion,
took care of us and *Iris*, who had perfwaded the Knight to leave her as foon as
the

the Actors appear'd on the Stage: When
we came home she gave us a full Relation of
the Conquest her Eyes had made, and how
many Amorous things this Libidinous Knight
had said to her of his impatience of seeing
her; which she had promised to grant in
three nights, and that he had given a very
advantageous Character of himself, for it
seems nothing would put him out of his
old method. We had a great deal of laughing about him; and to carry on the Jest farther concluded *Iris* should send him a *Billit-
Doux* to this purpose.

That being inform'd (since she last saw
him) that he Courted a Lady of a confiderable Fortune, whose Youth and Beauty
far exceeded hers, she could not flatter her
self so much as to think he would Relin-
quish his Pretensions for her sake, and she
not being of a humour to be content with
part of his heart, chose rather to continue
in that unhappy state she was in, than be
made more miserable by knowing she had
so fair a Rival; that to prevent a greater
ill she wou'd endeavour to withdraw her
affections from him, believing it not possible for him to be guilty of an Infidelity to
the Lady he lov'd; and she wou'd conceal
from him the little Beauty that she has, lest
he should quite repent him of the kindness
he had for her in her Masque; and therefore begg'd his Pardon for the Disappointment. In the Postscript she told him, that

if

if he pleas'd to write, how he might direct
to her. This Letter I sent by the Penny-Post,
the morning she was to meet him. But the
day after this Adventure at the Play, Sir
Formal made his Visit to me, and *Valeria*
was there at the same time, for we were
both full of Expectation of having an Account of his Intrigue with the Lady in
the Masque ; and he fail'd not of recount-
ing to us, how much a young Lady of
Quality was in Love with him, and that
she had writ to him, to meet her at a Friends
House, (which he could not refuse,) and
that she exprest to him the most tender
and passionate things in the World, but for
your sake, fair *Lindamira* (said he) I have
dash'd all her hopes, by telling her of the
Pre-Ingagement of my affection to a Lady,
I shou'd suddenly marry. Tho' I knew e-
very Syllable of this to be false, yet I had
not patience to hear him when he talk'd of
Marriage, and I should rather have chose
to have been shut up in some horrible Vault
with Ghosts and Hobgoblins, Screech-Owls,
and Bats, than to have been the Bride of
so nautious, and so disagreeable a Man : At
last I interrupted him, telling him that I
thought I had never given him any ground
to hope I wou'd ever be his Bride, or at
least it was not my design to favour the
deceit, and if the young Lady cou'd Diffemble Love so well, as to perfwade him into a believe so contrary to Reason, he wou'd
do

do well to fnap at her Heart, whilſt ſhe was
in ſo good a humour to let him take it.
And as there is no Reaſon, why ſome love
Blew, others Red, Green, or Yellow, ſo
'twas not to be wondred that ſhe ſhou'd liké
what was my Averſion. But Sir *Formal* cou'd
not bear the reproach of the Ladies want of
Judgment, but ſaid 'twas no contemptible
thing to be Sir *Formal Triffles* Lady. Then
they that are fond of the title (ſaid I) you
ought to Honour with it; but ſince I had con-
verſt with Colonel *Harnando*, he ſeem'd more
infupportable to me than ever; and to paſs
away the time, I call'd to *Iris* to bring us
ſome Coffee, for the Clock had ſtruck but
four times ſince he came in, when it was
brought to me, I could not but in Civility
offer him ſome, which he readily accepted,
and being Paralitick, and the Diſh very full,
and the Coffee ſcalding hot, he ſpilt it all upon
his Shins, which made 'em ſmart Exceſſively:
we could not help Laughing at the unlucky
accident, and ill nature prevail'd ſo far, that
we knew not when to give over; which much
inrag'd the Knight, and put him out of Humour: But at laſt I told him a remedy to hold
his Shins to the Fire, for one Fire wou'd
drive out another, and it wou'd be the beſt
Expedient he cou'd uſe, to perſwade himſelf
to Love this Young Lady of Quality to drive
me out of his thoughts, for which I ſhould be
eternally oblig'd to him. But the Anguiſh
he was in, put him in a fret, and in a great

D   Pet

Pet he left us, before the fix Hours were expir'd. His abfence always gave me great relief, for he ftill took care, fo to mortifie me, with his long Inconfiftant Speeches, that they were Days of Jubilee with me, when he did not come; as foon as he was gone, *Valeria* asked me if this was not the Evening that I was to receive a Letter from Colonel *Harnando*; which was then out of my thoughts, and I fent a Meffenger away immediately to the place affign'd for the receiving of it; and with fome impatiency waited the return of the Meffenger, believing the Colonel would have forfeited his word, but I found him, to be one, that was very punctual to his Promife, which the quick return of him I fent, confirm'd me in, when he prefented me with this following Letter.

Colonel *Harnando,* to *Lindamira.*

Madam,

I am fo far convinc'd, that nothing can equal my Fair unknown, that 'tis impoffible for me to entertain any other notions of you than what are highly Advantageous, to your Honour and Reputation. Be kind my Charming Fair, and deliver me out of this
Perplexity,

Perplexity, that I may know on whom I have beftow'd my Heart, and fix'd my Thoughts entirely : were you but half fo impatient to know your Captive, as I am to know my fair Conqueror; you wou'd out of a fentiment of Generofity difcover to me, what I fo ardently defire. You tell me. Madam, that my Letter fhall be anfwered, which gives me fome faint hopes, that you will conceal your felf no longer from the knowledge of,

Madam,

Your moft faithful Admirer

Harnando.

I read this Letter over feveral times, and tho I was much pleafed with the frolick, yet I could not harbour fo mean an opinion of the Colonels Wit, to believe he cou'd have any affection for one, that he had only feen in a Mafque; and as I won'd give him no occafion to reproach me, with being worfe then my word, I concluded upon fending him this Anfwer, which *Valeria* approv'd to be enough to the purpofe.

Lindamira

Lindamira to Colonel *Harnando.*

SIR,

I think my felf extream Happy, in the good Opinion you have of me, and I fhould be infinitely to blame, fhou'd I convince you of the Error you are in, which is fo much to my Advantage, that tho' I have Youth, (which I hope will extenuate my folly) yet the little Beauty I have, (fhou'd you fee it) wou'd oblige you to make Vows, againft your paffing your Judgment on a Mafque for the future. You have by this Artifice of writing, prevail'd with me to difcover my Ignorance, to a Perfon who is fo good a Judge of Wit ; and am liable to your Cenfure, which pray let be as favourable as poffible ; and grant this Petition to your Friend and Servant

In Cognito.

I fent this Anfwer by the Penny-Poft, what effects it produc'd you fhall know in my next.

I am, my Dear Indamora,

Your fincere Friend and Servant

Lindamira.

LET-

LETTER V.

BEFORE I proceed any further concerning the Colonel, my deareſt *Indamora*, I muſt make a Digreſſion, and give an account of the Reſentments of the Knight, who left me that Night much diſſatisfied with the treatment he receiv'd : and tho' the Accident was not intentionally on my ſide, yet he was highly diſpleas'd that I laugh'd, when I ought to have pittied his misfortune ; and being in great wrath with me, he return'd a very kind Anſwer to the Maſqu'd Lady, which gave me much diverſion, as without difficulty you will imagine.

According to his Cuſtom he came to viſit me, I was more Complaiſant than ordinary, on purpoſe to bring about the Diſcourſe of the Lady of Quality. He told me, notwithſtanding the ill uſuage he had receiv'd from me, that nothing cou'd ſhake his Conſtancy ; and tho' he had receiv'd a Letter from the Lady, yet he would not give her another meeting (as ſhe deſir'd) till he knew of a certainty, whether or no I would vouchſafe him the bleſſing of being his Co-Partner in all his worldly Goods. I anſwered him without any Heſitation, that to be his Wife was to be of all Women the moſt accurſt ; and

if

if he pleas'd he might let the Lady know, that I laid no claim to his Heart.

Sir *Formal* receiv'd with Indignation this Anfwer, for he had very high thoughts of his own Merits, and told me that his Birth, Perfon and Eftate, might challenge a kinder treatment than what he receiv'd from me : to this purpofe he chattered a long time, but I return'd him no Anfwer; and to my Relief there came fome Ladies to have me to *Hide-Park*, where I thought the Air extream refrefhing, for his Company and his Tobacco together had almoft tired me.

But when I return'd at Night I found a Letter from the Colonel, which was obliging, paffionate and kind; he us'd many arguments to perfwade me into a belief, that he was real in his Pretenfions, and that I had a great Afcendant over his Heart, and was yet more impatient to fee me than ever.

Tho' I was Charm'd with his Wit, yet I receiv'd all he faid as things that proceeded more from his *Exuberant* Brain than his Heart; and that thefe Letters or the fame Expreffions, had been faid to twenty Women before me, however I fent him an Anfwer that gave him as little Information who I was, as my firft did, and expreft as little defire to know him, but he might well enough fee, I was not difplea'd at the Correfpondence, which encourag'd him to continue, till fuch time as an accident broak it off.

the

During the time of this Diverfion, I refolv'd the next time that Sir *Formal* came, to
make him fenfible that I knew him to be a
Vain, Pragmatical conceited Coxcomb; and
that I wou'd Confute him by his own Letters,
that he had not related one word of truth,
concerning his new Miftrifs; and in order
thereto, I gave directions to *Iris* what fhe
fhou'd do when he came, for I made no
fcruple to affront one, who had quite tired
me out with his Impertinencies.

When he came (which was not long firft)
I fent to *Valeria* to be Witnefs of his Looks
and Actions. After he had been with me an
Hour, *Iris* came haftily to me, and brought
me a Letter, faying that a Porter ftay'd for
an Anfwer, and out of a pretence of Civility,
I asked Sir *Formals* leave to read it before
him; which he affented to. When I open'd
it, I found another inclofed, and directed for
Madam *Price*, which I feem'd much to wonder
at; when I had read my own, I read that,
and giving it to *Valeria*, fee there *Valeria*
(faid I) how conftant Sir *Formal* is to me;
this is he, that nothing could fhake his Conftancy! The Knight feem'd much amaz'd,
but I believe he guefs'd he was betrayed, and
ask'd me coldly, why I reproach'd him with
Inconftancy? I do not alledge it as a Crime
to you Sir *Formal*, (faid I) for nothing can
pleafe me better, than to find you what I
ever wifh'd you, that is full of falfhood
and difingenuity, but to prevent your excufe
D 4   in

in this matter I will read to *Valeria* the two
Letters.

Madam,

I Once thought my felf happy in the entire
Affections of Sir *Formal Triffle* , who
folemnly fwore to me, that he lov'd none
but me ; and when I was upon the point of
refigning up my Heart to him, I heard he is
a pretender to your felf ; Be fo fincere Madam
as to let me know the truth, which if it be as
Fame reports I will never fee him more. I
can only reproach my felf with the too eafie
belief of the Vows and Affeverations that drew
me into this Snare,

      I am,

          Madam your Servant.

   Whilft I read this Letter, *Valeria* obferv'd
the uneafinefs he was in, and wou'd have prevented my reading the other, which were in
thefe terms.

                       Dear

Dear Soul,

YOU injuſtly tax me with want of Love, which is ſo great that I am in Admiration of my ſelf, to find the Magick there is in that Paſſion ; which has receiv'd an additional Recruit, by your Jealouſie of Madam R — to whom I have no pretentions in the leaſt ; but as ſhe is Young and Fair, I love to trifle away a few Hours with her, but all my Happineſs Centers in you, my lovely Angel. Let nothing hinder me from enjoying your Company which is ſo Ardently wiſh'd by Madam,

Your moſt Obſequious, moſt

Humble Servant, F. T.

I think I never ſaw a Man look ſo like an Aſs as Sir *Formal* did, for he had not preſence of Mind to evade the thing, by pretending his Hand was Counterfeited ; or that it was a trick put upon him to try his ſincerity, but his looks betray'd him ; and being Conſcious of his Fault he made but ſlender Excuſes : and that Eloquence, he had ſo often boaſted ſtood him in little ſtead ; ſo that all he could ſay for himſelf, when I repreſented to him how unfaithfully he had related his Intriegue with the Lady, and that no body cou'd confide in any thing he ſaid, was that he always
ſpoke

fpoke Inigmatically, that it was his conftant method, and if it was not grateful to my Humour, he fhould not put himfelf out of his way, to pleafe the little pretenders of this Age.

I feem'd to refent the affront put upon me, that he came to fee me only to triffle away a few hours, which he excus'd fo foolifhly, that I plainly perceiv'd, that if he was put out of his Road, he was the moft empty fhallow Monfter in the Univerfe.

After a long Parly on both fides, Sir *Formal* took leave of me, faying it had been better for him, had he never feen my Face : I was not curious to pry into this Miftery, but bad him heartily Farewel ; wifhing him good fuccefs with the Ladies of Quality. The Charming Mufical found of his Adieu, fill'd my Heart full of Joy ; but he only bannifh'd himfelf for fix Weeks : during which Ceffation, I fhall acquaint you with things more remarkable, and more worthy of your knowledge.

You may remember my Dear *Indamora*, that in my firft Letter I mention'd one Mr. S — who was an Admirer of *Valeria*, whom you fhall know by the name of *Silvanus* ; this Gentleman had a good Eftate Equivalent to her Fortune, he had many excellent Qualities, that ferv'd to recommend him to her Affections, their Loves were Reciprocal, and in all Human appearance, they might live happy after Marriage, for their Humours were

agreeable,

agreeable, and fo was the'r Age: after fix
Months Courtfhip, *Silvanus* prevail'd with
Valeria, to be Married, and tho' fhe efteem'd
him very much (and indeed he was a Perfon
that merited all things) yet 'twas with much
difficulty fhe confented to his Propofals, for
her Liberty fhe prefer'd at a high rate; but at
laft the Wedding Day was appointed, and I
had the Honour to be one of her Bride-Maids;
this Marriage happn'd, during the bleffed
truce, I had from the importunity of Sir
Formal, there was nothing remarkable at the
Wedding, which was confummated with
much fatisfaction to all her Friends.

About a Week after, *Silvanus* wou'd have
Valeria to the new Play, and me to accompany
her thither, we both of us had the advantage of fine Cloaths, and good Dreffing to
fet us off; but my Dear *Valeria* had many advantages over me, for fhe was very lovely
and full of Charms, and the Addition of fine
Jewels, made her out fhine, Perfons of the
greateft Quality. *Silvanus* plac'd us in the
Kings Box, and went himfelf into the Pit,
but before the Play was begun, I difcover'd
amongft the Croud, Colonel *Harnando*, the
fight of him gave me fuch a difturbance, that
I wifh'd my felf out of the Houfe a thoufand
times, for *Valeria* being fo glorioufly dreft,
that fhe attracted the Eyes of all the Beaus
in the Pit. I fetting next to her could not
efcape being look'd upon, and being Confcious of my own weaknefs, was afraid I
fhould

ſhould betray my ſelf by my looks, to be the
Perſon that Correſponded with him, he fix'd
his Eyes much upon me, which both pleas'd
me, and gave me great Inquietudes ; for ſo
Capricious is Love, that I was uneaſie if he
look'd on me, fearing he might diſlike me,
and then again I wiſh'd he might be pleas'd
with me; but a ſudden thought came into
my mind, that all Women in general were
pleaſing to him ; ſo that if he look'd that way
or turn'd his Eyes another, I was diſſatisfied
with him; that all he could do, wou'd not
pleaſe me. But I had this private ſatisfaction
of ſeeing him, that took up all my thoughts,
and of being ſeen by him, and yet he to be
Ignorant that I was there in view of him. He
ſeem'd that Day more lovely than the firſt
time I ſaw him, but whether it was, that I
ſate more to the Advantage of ſeeing him, or
that the good opinion I had of him, made me
partial in my Judgment, I voted him to be
the handſomeſt in all the place, and I wiſh'd
as much to know who he was, as 'twas poſſible
for him to know me : but my Soul was full of
Prophetick fears, that I was not the only
Woman he lov'd. When I came home, I
enquir'd of *Silvanus* who the Colonel was,
whom I deſcrib'd by his Cloaths, he preſently
inform'd me that he was a Man of Quality,
that he was lately married to a Rich Widow,
and that they did not live very happily together : that he was a great Profeſſor of Gallantry, and a very Amorous Man. This
news

news ſtruck my Heart like a Thunder-bolt,
for then I knew I had more than a common
Eſteem for him, 'twas that time my *Indamora*,
that I ſtood in need of all my Reaſon, Prudence and Diſcretion, to hide from *Silvanus*,
the Agitations of my Soul; I reproach'd my
ſelf often for my Indiſcretion, in believing
what he ſaid to me, which was in words ſo
tender, that they wrought a greater effect
upon my Heart than they ought. When I
was alone with *Valeria*, I complain'd of my
hard fate, that I ſhould Love a Man not worthy of my Affections, becauſe of his Pre-ingagement, and I could not without offence to
my own Honour and Reputation, continue
my Correſpondence with him: ſo I took a
full Reſolution, to Write to him but once
more, to repreſent to him, his Crime and his
Folly, which I did the next Night ; what follow'd after I will acquaint you in my next.
I am my Deareſt *Indamora*, Your

Moſt Faithful Humble

Servant Lindamira.

LETTER VI.

I Muſt Ingenuouſly Confeſs to you, my Dear *Indamora*, that I was ſenſibly afflicted at the Diſcovery I made of the Colonels Infidelity, of whom I had conceiv'd ve y high thoughts. I could not in all this time, perſwade my ſelf to diſcover to him who I was, yet I was concern'd that he ſhould thi..k that Women kind were ſo eaſie of belief. But what can I ſay to Extenuate my fault ? I was Young and unexperienc'd in the Arts of Love, and abandon'd my Thoughts too much, in the Contemplation of his Merits? For *Harnando*, had all the Advantages of a fine Education, and his Perſon was Charming, and that which pleas d me moſt, I thought him neither Fop nor Beau. Several Letters had paſt between us, which prov'd ſo Pernicious to my Repoſe ; and I could not diſguiſe my ſentiments ſo well, but that he might plainly ſee, I was not iſenſible of his Affections. 'Tis needleſs to ſend you more than this one Letter, that I receiv'd the Day after I had ſeen him at the Play.

Harrando

Harnando to *Lindimaria.*

I Love too fondly not to be perplext with deep Difpairs, fince your Obdurate Heart will never yield to let me know, who 'tis has Robb'd me of my Repofe. This is a misfortune not to be fupported, for my Dearest Love, my Soul is fo fondly fix'd on you, that I cannot bear a denial of what I fo much wifh. Your obliging concern for my Indifpofition, has fo link'd my Soul to yours that you can never doubt my kindnefs, Ill ufuage alone will make me fmother what I feel. My dearest Life, after what I have fo often profest, you will deny me a fight of that Face, I believe fo Divinely Fair ; let me Conjure you to heal the Wounds you have given, and repent of your unkindnefs, and Command my Life.

Adieu.

This Letter wrought a Contrary effect to all the former, for whereas thofe ufed to fill my Heart full of Joy, at the reading of this I was fiez'd with a violent Grief, and Shame, and Confufion was feen, difufed all over my Face, I look'd upon my felf as a Criminal, believing I might poflibly have alienated his Affections from his Lady, who was a deferving

Perfon,

Perfou, I found I lov'd him, and reprefented
to my felf the danger in loving one, already
married, tho' all might be cloak'd under the
name of Friendhip ; and fearing my opinion
fhould alter, and knowing the Imbecility of
my Nature, as well as the Pow'r he had gain'd
over my Inclination, I fent him that Night
this Letter.

Lindamira to Colonel Harnando.

IS it poffible, that after fo many Vows of
an Eternal Fidelity, you can be guilty
both of Deceit and Perjury? tho' alas you
deceiv'd me ; that adds not to your Glory,
and thefe mean Atchievements will not Il-
luftrate your Trophies ; and falfe Vows and
Oaths will add much to your Reputation!
I was Ignorant of the Stratagems of Love,
and Judg'd of your fincerity by my own, which
was incapable of a deceit or trick. What
fatisfaction cou'd you propofe, in a reciprocal Affection with me that had already plight-
ed your Faith in the prefence of Man and
Heaven? 'Tis in vain to deny that once I
efteem'd you, but you have taught me fo
much Repentance, by mifplacing my Affec-
ions,

ions, that I may fay I owe more to your
Crime, than to my own Reafon, for the cure
of a Paffion that might have proved fo Pernicious to my Reputation. But thanks to
Heaven I am unknown to you, and fhall for
ever let you remain in Ignorance; fend me
no more Letters, for I have folemnly fworn,
never to anfwer them.

Adieu.

You may perhaps wonder, my Dear Friend
at my Fantaftical Humour, in permiting *Harnando* to Love me, and yet I conceal'd from
his Knowledge who I was, but I was fo nicely
fcrupolous, that I apprehended if once he
knew me, it would leffen his efteem ; and the
manner of our acquaintance, wou'd make him
Harbour mean thoughts of me ; and tho' it
was the only frolick I was ever guilty of in
that nature, yet I thought he would imagine
it was my ufual Paft-time.
So Ambitious was I of his good opinion,
and tho' I fometimes half confented in my
own thoughts to meet him, at fome Friends
Houfe; yet I was unalterable in my denials;
and 'twas happy for me, for he had fo ingage-
ing, and obliging a way of expreffing himfelf,
that I fhould have abandon'd my Heart to the
Power of my Deftiny, and not found it fo
eafie a matter, to have cur'd my felf of a
Paffion, which on my fide was grounded on
E   Vertue.

Vertue. I foon gain'd that Victory over my felf, that I may fay he imploy'd my thoughts, but was a ftranger to my Heart.

I receiv'd feveral Letters from him, wherein he expoftulated with me, that Souls being free born, they ought not to be inflav'd by foolifh Cuftoms, and if I had ever permited him to have feen me, he would have acquainted me with his whole Life and Fortune, but I return'd him no more Anfwers, and being quite tir'd out with writing, he left of correfponding, and I believe ingag'd himfelf in a new Amour.

You have by the influence of your Commands, drawn from me a fecret, that none but my Dear *Valeria* knew, of whofe difcretion I was fo much affur'd, that to *Silvanus*, I was confident fhe never fpoke of it : But my Dear *Indamora*, one misfortune feldom comes alone, for I was now to lofe my dear Companion, who at her Husbands requeft, was preparing for the Country, his Relations having earneftly invited him, to Congratulate with him his Happinefs with *Valeria.* I efteem'd him, as he was worthy in himfelf, but more as he was the Husband of my deareft Friend.

The news of her departure extreamly afflicted me, for I had no Friend in whom I cou'd confide, or that was capable of giving me Advife like to her felf : but before fhe went I was tormented with the returns of a Love fit from Sir *Formal*, who was Born to be a vexation to me, and that which added to

my

my grief, was, that 'twas never known, he
had been fo conftant to any one as to my felf,
and 'twas believ'd he had a real Paffion for
me, notwithftanding the ill ufuage he receiv'd
from me; but after the Marriage of *Valeria*,
I was more abroad than ever I had been, for
fhe telling me, we were not like to injoy one
another long, fhe oblig'd me to be with her
continually, and by this means I was often deliver'd from the fulfome Love of one I hated,
my Mother who was always very Indulgent
to me, and perceiving I grew Melancholly,
told me, that if I had a mind I fhou'd go to
my Grandmothers for two or three Months,
who had a pleafant and delightful Seat in the
Countrey; fhe faid to me, now that your
Friend is going out of Town, it will no longer
feem a place of Pleafure to you; and alfo
knowing it was the beft way to get rid of Sir
Formal (which nothing elfe wou'd do) I was
well enough pleas'd with the propofition;
but when my Mother faid fhe could not go
with me, I very unwillingly confented to the
Journey, for I was never fo eafie, and fo
pleas'd as when I was under my Mothers care.

But when the time came that *Valeria* and
I muft part, and I found how heard it was to
bear the Abfence of a Friend, I almoft repented me I had ever lov'd her; and then I
fhould never have known the mifery of being
from a Perfon, that is ones Souls delight.
But fhe was lefs wretched than I was, becaufe
fhe went with a Husband, that was infinitely

fond

fond of her ; but why ſhould I dwell on a
ſubject that made me ſo Melancholly, and
not entertain you with my Adventures, that
perhaps may be more diverting to you. One
Evening I went with *Valeria* and *Silvanus* to
walk in the Park, and in the Dark-walk we
encountred Colonel *Harnando* ; He ſaluted
Silvanus, and Congratulated his Happineſs ;
he was oblig'd to preſent *Valeria* to him, and
I being in the Company he alſo ſaluted me ;
this unexpected Adventure had like to have
produc'd but bad effects, for all on a ſudden I
was quite diſpirited, and I had like to have
fainted away, which *Valeria* perceiving, pull'd
me by the Sleve, and bid me go along with
her ; we left the two Sparks a talking, and
Silvanus told me afterwards, that *Harnando*,
asked my Name, and was very Scrutinous in
his enquiry of me, but he only gave him this
Anſwer, that I was a particular Friend of
Valeria's : I know not what excited him to
this Curioſity, whether it was through Sym-
pathy of our former Amours, or out of a natural Curioſity to know the name of a new
Face, but his enquiry very much perplex'd
me. We had not walk'd twice the length of
that walk, but hard by the Bird-Cage, we
met *Philander*, and he having forgot his Reſolution of Traviling, as he promis'd when he
parted laſt from me, accoſted me with his
uſual Gayety, and flutt'ring way ; He ingag'd
himſelf in a Diſcourſe with *Valeria* and my ſelf,
and ſo walk'd a long with us ; I ask'd him if
the

the Park had not been the furtheſt extent of
his Travels, for I cou'd not imagin, that in
ſo ſhort a time, ſince I ſaw him, that he had
croſs'd the Seas twice, he reply'd pleaſantly,
that being banniſh'd from my preſence, it had
the ſame effect on him, as if he had Travel'd
all the World over ; and in Obedience to my
ſevere Commands, he had endeavour d to forget me, tho' with much Difficulty and Re-
luctance he had attempted it ; but if i wou'd
pleaſe to give him leave to wait on me, I
ſhould find him the moſt Obſequious of my
Servants, after this manner did he entertain
us till we came out of the Park.

But the next Day Sir *Formal*, according to
his method, came to wait on me, and was
very importunate with my Mother to lay her
Commands on me, to Marry him ; but my
Mothers diſlike to him was as great as mine,
and ſhe flatly refuſ'd his Propoſitions, and
Civily deſir'd him to withdraw from her
Houſe ; but he would go on in his way, and
would not baulk his method for any ones
Pleaſure : therefore did I reſolve to go into
the Country to be rid of his Importunity, and
Valeria being gone, I may ſay, the Town all
on a ſudden became a Deſert. I prepar'd my
ſelf therefore for my Journey, and never
ſpoke a word of my Intentions to Sir *Formal*,
but Places were taken in the Stage-Coach for
his and my ſelf. I had no regret in leaving
the Town, but upon the account of my Mother, to whom in my Abſence I ever fear'd

E 3   ſome

ſome accident or other might happen ſhe being very ſickly. The grief was great on both ſides to part, but with much ado we did ; and went to our Coach, where we were told that at *Highgate* we ſhould take up two Paſſengers.

What happned to me in my Journey, my Dear *Indamora*, I will acquaint you in my next, tho' I believe I have formerly told you the Adventure ; but ſince you deſire a Hiſtory of my Life, I will not omit the leaſt Circumſtance that is of Moment ; and I hope ſome time or other, you will repay me with an Account of your own Life, which is a mixture of ſuch variety of Fortune, that it will oblige me to be acquainted with the particulars; which I can only know from your ſelf. And as I am a Paſſionate Lover of my *Indamora*, I may Challenge this favour, as due to the Friendſhip I have for her. Who am moſt entirely her

Friend and Servant

Lindamira.

The End of the Firſt Part of the Adventures of Lindimaria.

THE

THE
Second Part
OF THE
ADVENTURES
OF
LINDAMIRA.

LETTER VII.

THE parting from my Mother, my Dear *Indamora*, was a very great Affliction to me, and I had scarce dry'd up my Tears when I came to *Highgate*, where the Coachman was to take in two Paſſengers more, he ſtopt at the Houſe according to Order; and there came into the Coach two Gentlemen; one of 'em a very grave ſort of a Man, and pretty well advanc'd in Years: the other in

the

the prime of his Youth, of a Graceful winning Behaviour. He was of a middle fize, exactly well fhap'd, his Hair brown, a good Complection, fparkling Eyes, and the whole Compofure of his Face was Lovely: there was an Invincible Charm in every thing he faid or did, and his extraordinary good Breeding, added much to his natural Beauty.

I have my *Indamora* given you a full Defcription of his Perfon, but to compleat his Character, I muft not omit the Excellencies of his Mind: tho' at my firft acquaintance, you may fuppofe, I did not make a full difcovery of 'em. He was of an equal Temper, had a Paffionate and Tender Soul, he was incapable of the leaft Envy or Slander, nor would he be guilty of a bafe Action, to purchafe the greateft Fortune imaginable: tho' he was owner of many Vertues, he did not affect to difcover his Perfectfons, but to thofe he was very familiar with: In fhort, befides his Mafterfhip of the Ancient and Modern Languages, he had a Sound and Solid Judgment. I might afcribe many Vertues more to him, but I have faid enough of *Cleomidon* to make you know him.

The firft Days Journey I exchang'd but few words with him, for my Eyes were fo fwollen with crying, that I had not affurance enough to look him in the Face, nor was it poffible for me that Night, to have given a Defcription of his Perfon. The next Day he entertain'd me with very diverting, Ingenious

nious fort of Difcourfe, and feem'd to bare a fhare in the Concern, I exprefs to leave my Mother, telling me, it was neceffary fome times to part from our Friends, to endear us the more when we meet ; that Abfence helpt to quicken, and fharpen our Affections, and till we come to know the want of a Friend, we did not know how to value him. He was very entertaining and agreeable upon this occafion ; and fince I have oblig'd my felf to difcover my moft fecret fentiments to you, I thought him a Perfon that merited my Efteem : but having a ftrong fancy, or rather an unquiet fort of an apprehenfion that *Cleomidon* was married, I durft not give way to admire thofe Excellencies, I difcovered in him, for I had not forgot my unhappy affection for the Colonel, the next Night when we were juft arriv'd at our Inn we faw a Coach, with a Gentleman and his Wife enter the Yard. *Clomidon*, accidently feeing of 'em, went up to 'em, and faluted 'em; they prov'd to be his intimate Friends, who were going to *London* ; and there not being any likely-hood of meeting a long time, *Cleomidon* invited 'em to fup with him ; and befpoke a Supper, that fhew'd the nobleneſs of his Mind. He fent me word of his good Fortune, in meeting with his Friends, and defir'd me to give 'em leave to fup with me. This requeft I could not handfomly refufe, and therefore went to wait on the Lady in her Chamber, who being left alone, (for her Husband was in another Room

with

with *Cleomidon*) I found an occafion to mention him ; and this Lady, being a Perfon of a free and open temper, told me as much of him as fhe knew ; that he was a Barrifter of *Lincolns-Inn*, that his Father and Mother died when he was Young, that he had a free Unincumber'd, tho' fmall Eftate, that his Unkle (to whom he was going) had Educated him as his own, and defign'd to leave him all his Eftate, when he died, if he pleafed him in his Marriage, and that he had fent for him this Vacation, to fee a Young Lady of a confiderable Fortune. but of flender Education.

All this fhe frankly told me, without the leaft Queftion on my fide ; as I was glad to hear he was not a married Man, I cou'd not forbear to be concern'd at the news, that he was going to fee a Fortune, knowing what invincible Charms there is in Money, this uneafinefs I had in my Mind was unaccountable ; nor could I difcover why I did intrefs my felf fo much in his Affairs : but at Supper, I obferv'd him, more then I had done before which confirm'd me in the good opinion I had of him ; for his freedom and eafinefs with his Friends, and his obliging way of entertaining 'em, extremely affected me ; the next Day which was the laft of our Journey together, *Cleomidon* told me fighing, that it was an unfpeakable affliction to him to think that this was the laft Day he was like to be happy in my Company, and that tho' he had but a fmall acquaintance with me, yet he had difcover'd

fomething

fomething in my Humour, that to him was Charming. It would be needlefs to repeat the Compliments, that fell from him upon this Article, fome of which, were fo extravagantly perfu'd, that I had reafon to doubt if he fpoke the fincerity of his Heart, fince he was fo liberal of his Incenfe to a ftranger, and treated me all the while at the Expence of the reft of my Sex. So all this I look'd upon as Gallantry, and the Inclination moft young People have; when we came to our Inn at Night, he drew me a fide to a Window, that look'd into the Garden; and asked me if I had no mind to take a walk, for the Air was Calm and Serene, I refufed his offer, alledging I was tired with my long Journey. He then faid to me, the moft Paffionate, and moft obliging things in the World, affuring me he was Charm'd the firft Minute he beheld me; that he dated his Captivity from that Interview, that my Tears had wrought a ftrange compaffion in his Heart, which infenfibly gave way to Efteem, and Admiration, that he was already become the moft Paffionate, moft fincere Lover in the Univerfe: and tho' he dreaded my Anger, for this Prefumptious Declaration; yet he was willing to undergo the moft fevereft Punifhment I could Inflict, if I would give him leave to hope one Day he might be happy in my favour. I muft confefs my Aftonifhment was very great, to hear him fpeak this with fo ferious an Air, for what he had faid to me in the Coach, I afcrib'd to the

gayety

gayety of his Temper, but now was convinc'd he had fome Affection for me. I had too great an efteem to be offended at this *Eclaircifement*, I evaded as much as I cou'd, the anfwering his Complements; thinking it neceffary to obferve, thofe Punctilioes of our Sex; which at the firft difcovery of a Paffion, obliges us to keep our favour at a diftance. I difingag'd my felf as foon as poffible, and would not give him any farther opportunity of fpeaking to me in private that Night. At Supper he faid little to me, but let his Eyes fpeak for him, when news was brought my Grandmothers Coach was come, his Countenance alter'd, and he feem'd extreamly troubled, I could not but take notice of the change I obferv'd in his Face, and I found fome regret in my own Soul to part from him. But when the next morning came, he found an opportunity, of reprefenting to me the greatnefs of his Paffion, and faid fo many kind, and obliging things, that to doubt of his fincerity, was to fuppofe him of a bafe mean Spirit, and that he only faid thefe things for his amufement: but I had nobler thoughts of one, that appear'd fo worthy of my efteem. When I was to go away, he offer'd his Hand to lead me down the Stairs, and then told me, he never was fenfible of the Pow'r of Love till now; but then began to feel the Tyranny of it; and beg'd of me by all the kindeft fofteft, words he cou'd invent, to give him leave to wait on me at my Grandmothers Houfe, for
'twas

'twas a place he was no ſtranger to: I apprehended no little danger from his viſits, knowing the Temper of my Grandmother, who
was of a very reſerv'd Humour, and did not
affect much Company, And according to the
Genius of moſt Perſons of that Complection,
tho' ſhe was very Religious, yet very Cenſo-
rious; for which reaſon I uſed all the Arguments I could to divert him from coming. I
rendred him all the Acknowledgments that
was due to his Merits, and let him underſtand
I was not altogether inſenſible of his Favours;
but as I lay under thoſe Circumſtances, of being with a Relation of that Humour (for
whom I had a great reſpect) I beg'd of him to
think no more of me; but thoſe words drew
from his Mouth, a thouſand Proteſtations of
his Love, and that he wou'd Adore me,
Eternally, tho' I was ſo Cruel to deny him that
favour.

Then I began to think my Heart in Danger,
and I was forc'd to borrow from my reaſon all
the Arguments it could furniſh me with; and
already I perceiv'd an Affection that pleaded
on his behalf, which made me ſtrive with my
ſelf, tho' not without ſome Reluctancy, to repreſent to him how diſagreeable his viſits
would be to me. But here my *Indamora* I
play'd a downright Hypocrite, I ſpoke not
the thoughts of my Heart, for I deſir'd nothing
more than his Charming Converſation; however I durſt not conſent to what was ſo agreeable to my Inclinations; and I dreaded a ſecond

cond Ingagement, which I thought I ought not to make without the Approbation of my Mother.

On thefe terms we parted, and I believe the Affliction was as great on my fide, tho' I endeavour'd to conceal it with more care. I was received by my Grandmother with great Civility and kindnefs, as alfo by my Unkle and Aunt *B—;* who was there at that time; the next Day they fhewed me all the Houfe and Gardens, and told me they referv'd one place more to fhew me the next Day, which they did, and becaufe the Knowledge of my Adventures, fomewhat depends upon a Defcription of this place, I will give it you in as Concife a manner as I can. This Houfe was fcituated on the rife of a Hill, at a convenient diftance ran a River, which in the Summer time rendred the place very delightful; not far from it was a Wood, incompaffing fome few Acres of Ground, and in the midft of it a Path that led to a little Rivlet, near half a Mile long, and a row of high Elms on both fides, fo that in the midft of the Day, one might walk without the leaft inconveniency from the Weather. At the head of this Rivlet was a Well, that was pav'd about with broad Stone, and Benches round, fix'd there for the eafe of thofe, that out of Curiofity came there to drink of the Water, which had a great Reputation for its extraordinary fweetnefs. A few paces from this Well after fome turnings and windings, you come into a little
folitary

folitary Valley, at the end of which ftands a
fmall Cottage, which formerly had been a
place of Retirement for a Gentleman that paft
his Days in folitude, but now it became the
Habitation of fome few Peafants.

I was extreamly pleas'd with this Rural
Scene, and I propos'd to my felf to fpend
fome Hours there in an Evening, for I thought
it look'd fo Romantick and pritty, and equal'd
the beft Defcriptions I had ever read on, I
expreft my Inclination to it, by my unwilling-
nefs to leave it; which furpris'd my Unkle
and Aunt, who told me they did not imagin
that a *London* Lady could be fo diverted with
looking on Trees, and in hearing the Birds
Sing, but were extreamly pleas'd at it, in
hopes I would make a confiderable ftay in the
Country.

I began from that time to reflect on the Innocence of a Country Life, and prefer'd it
before the empty noife and buftle of the
Town. I according to this Refolution walk'd
out every Evening with only *Iris* with me,
to pafs fome moments in this Valley, where
it was no fmall Diverfion, to hear the awk-
ward ilcontriv'd Complements, that the
Clowns made on the little Beauty of their
Miftreffes, and their Piping, Squeeking, and
Dancing before 'em, and now and then out
of abundance of Love, I fhould fee, thofe two
handed Clod-Pates, carry home their Milk-
Pails for 'em. Thus I diverted my felf for a
Month, in which time I had heard no news
of

of *Cleomidon*, fo that I concluded he was either falfe, or had repented him of his Weaknefs, or that the great Fortune, of his Unkles Recommendation, had produced the ufual Effects in his Heart, as it does in the reft of Mankind, and made him Sacrifice all former Vows and Proteftations. Tho' in ftrict Juftice I ought not to have expected it from him, having laid Injunctions on him not to vifit me, yet fometimes I wifh'd he had not fhewn fo implicit an Obedience, and that he would have contriv'd fome way to let me know I was not indifferent to him: which fhortly after he did in a very odd and furprifing manner, but I muft degrefs a little before I can acquaint you with this Adventure; that I may make you the better underftand the Capricioufnefs of my Fortune; but as this Letter my *Indamora* is already too long, I fhall not here engage my felf in the Defcription of fome People that I muft give you, till I have an opportunity to finifh it. Adieu my Deareft *Indamora*.

I am yours Lindamira.

LET-

LETTER VIII.

My dearest Indamora,

I Have only two People whofe Characters I am to acquaint you with, that liv'd in the Houfe with my Grand-mother, one of 'em was her Chaplain, a jolly young Levite, very Amorous, and fufceptible of Love, his Converfation not impertinent, and they tell me he pafs'd amongft his Brother *Spintext's* for a man of very good Parts, and made no fmall figure at a Country Vifitation. The other was a grave Gentlewoman, my Grandmothers everlafting Confident, and tho' fhe had pafs'd the Glory of her youth, yet fhe thought her felf handfome enough to attract a Lover : her Complexion was indifferent good, her Skin fmooth, her Eyes brisk and lively, which fhew'd her to be of a quick apprehenfion ; her fhape, tho' not exact, yet agreeable enough. Her humour had been very Jocofe and Pleafant, but Love had alter'd her before I knew her, and fhe put on an affected ferioufnefs, and was naturally Jealous of all her Friends, and did entertain very extravagant notions of 'em, that were inconfiftent with Reafon. This Perfon, I know not for what defign, made great profeffions of Friendfhip to me, which I believe proceeded from noble Charity, for I was young

F   and

and unexperienc'd, and did not apprehend the Plots and Stratagems that are laid under ground to deceive the Innocent, and therefore offered me her advise, both in the management of my self and in my affairs. I received these marks of her Efteem with all due acknowledgments, and suffer'd my self to be guided by her advice, which she was very free of, and wou'd often repeat to me the sin of giving way to Paffion, adding that she her self had been very subject to it, before she had read *Seneca*, and that she owed all her Moderation to that worthy Stoick, that now she could forgive offences with ease, and despis'd the Arts of envious Tongues, and could bear Detraction and Calumny without concern. These Vertues I highly applauded in her, and thought her a Woman the most worthy of my Envy of any living, that had gain'd so great a Conqueft over her Paffions, and told her I wish'd I were capable of receiving those good Inftructions she had given me : This pleas'd her so well that she lent me the Author of all her Moderation, and suppofing I was not exempt from Paffions no more than the reft of our frail Sex, she told me she hop'd I would receive great advantage from it, and that she would have me read no other Book till I had finifh'd that.

About 5 days after she came to vifit me in my Chamber, to learn what progrefs I had made, and what effects it had wrought upon my mind (as if a change of Sentiment cou'd happen to
one

one in an inftant) but my *Indamora*, admire at
my ill Fate, for fhe found me reading of a Romance, which I was very intent upon, and
being deeply ingag'd in the unfortunate Adventures of a Difconfolate Lover, I minded
her not when she came in, but continued my
reading, and fhe perceiving what my ftudy
was, affum'd a fupercilous look, and a contracted brow, So *Lindamira*, (faid fhe) how
much you value my advice that prefers the
reading of an Idle Romance, before the Precepts of the Wife and Learned *Seneca* ? Take
my word, continued fhe, (raifing the tone of
her voice)nothing fo much corrupts the minds
of young People, as the reading of thefe foolifh Books that treat of fulfome Love, and
fils their heads full of Chimera's. I could not
help laughing at my Friend for the wrong notions fhe had taken of the Books that fo pleafantly had fpun out my time, and I very ignorantly began to defend the Wit of the Ingenious Author ; but this fage Lady, whofe
Wifdom was much greater than my fmall Experience, told me I fhould reap more Advantage in one day, in reading *Seneca*, *Livy*, *Plutarch* or *Tacitus*, than I could my whole Life
in fuch Fabulous Stories ; but then being perfwaded into an opinion of her high Vertues
and good humour, I did venture to intreat her
to hear out the feqnel of my ftory (for there
was notning that could offend her Chafte ears)
and did believe, notwithftanding her averfion to Love, she had good nature enough to

F 2   deplore

deplore the misfortunes of an unhappy Lover,
that was made so by the rigour of his Cruel
Miltrefs, and that the defpairs she had put
him into, made me to Compaffionate his In-
felicities ; and that I had not power to leave
off till I saw the refult of his Deftiny, whom I
fear'd wou'd be banish'd her fight for ever.
But inftead of intreffing her in thefe Adventures, she very sharply reprov'd me, reprefenting the ill Confequeuces of imploying my
time fo ill, and made fuch Invectives againft
Love, and fo protefted againft it that I thought
her a meer Stoick indeed, but our difputes
lafted fo long that it was time to go walk,
that I ask'd her if she would pleafe to breath
the fresh Air after our hot difpute, but she
was fo much out of humour for the contempt
I shew'd of her advice, that she refufed to go
with me, her denial pleas'd me very well, for
I took my Book with me, and finish'd what I
defign'd as I walked in the shady Grove. But
from this time I alter'd my opinion of her, I
neither believed her fo great a Saint, nor a
Philofopher as she pretended, and my Conjectures was not ill grounded as it appear'd a
few days after : But I will leave her a while
to fret; whilft I relate my Adventure with
Mr. *Spintext* the Chaplain ; who, unknown to
me, was become my humble Admirer. This
Levite had often entertained me with his Poetry, and *Sylvia*, *Phillis* and *Cloris* were often
times repeated, that I fuppos'd him a general Lover of the Sex, he would beg my opinion

nion of his Peoms, and as I was no Judge of
the Excellencies of his Performances, I commended thofe verfes the leaſt elevated, and
found the moſt fault, where his flights were
the moſt furprizing. But thefe errours in my
Judgment he eafily excus'd, as mountain faults
in Lovers Eyes, feems but Mole-hill, but ſtill
I did not fufpeſt I was the Theme of thefe
Compoſſions, till one morning that I was fitting in the Summer-Houfe in the Garden, for
the conveniency of my Painting (there being
a North light) I had only *his* with me, and
had not been there an hour but Mr. *Spintext*
enter'd, under pretence of viewing my draw-
ings (for I was then but a learner) but this
obliging *Levite* commended what merited not
his applaufes, and admir'd as ignorantly my
Paintings as I his Poetry.

From one difcourfe to another he fell upon that of Love, and after he had fetch'd two
or three deep fighs, (which was the Prologue
to what he had to fay) he told me I was infinitely efteem'd by all that knew me, but in
that numerous train of Admirers none had a
greater Veneration for me than himfelf, and
was very Ambitious to be admitted into the
Catalogue of my Humble Servants, adding,
with a figh, that I was the fole Objeſt of his
Thoughts, and the only Theme of his Poetry. I heard out his Harangue, without interrupting him, and exprefs'd my refentments
for his boldnefs, in terms that fufficiently let
him fee how fenfibly I was affronted, that my

Grand-

Grand-mothers Chaplain shou'd dare to talk
to me of Love ; faying that ; I thought my
felf in a Sphere too high to be entertain'd by
him with fuch difcourfe, that it became him
much better to mind his Flock, and, to
give 'em fpoon meat in due feafon, and that
the greateft folacifm a Divine could be guilty of was to make Love, and that People of
his Cloath should never condefcend fo low,
as to encourage a foolish paffion, but entertain themfelves with their Fathers and Coun-
cels.

I rallied him in this manner, and made him
fenfible of his folly, for a guilty dumbnefs
feiz'd him, he faid not one word to excufe or
juftifie himfelf for what he had done : Seeing him fo much out of Countenance, I was
almoft forry I faid fo much, but I was convinc'd in my own thoughts, it was the beft
way to reprefs his boldnefs in the beginning ;
however, believing he might apprehend fomething from my difpleafure, and that I might
acquaint my Grand-mother with what had
paft, I fatisfied him I had no defign to do
him a prejudice, provided he obferv'd a due
Decorum in his Actions for the future.

Now my *Indamora*, do but obferve what
Malignant Planets reign'd over me, for I had
no fooner given over my Reprimand to Mr.
Spintext, and had hardly compos'd my Countenance, but the Difciple of *Seneca* enter'd,
who you muft know was fecretly in Love with
this young *Levite* ; and she being older than
he,

he, was troubled with that pernicious Dif-
ease call'd Jealoufie, and for fome time had
fufpected he had an Inclination for me, for
she was Eagle-ey'd, and had a quieker apprehenfion than my felf. She obferv'd him when
he went into the Garden, and he ftaying longer than in her Wifdom she thought he ought,
she put Wings to her feet, and came flying
after, and was refolv'd to be an Occular Witnefs of his Deportment to me. When she firft
came in, I obferv'd a difturbance in her Eyes,
but could not Conjecture the caufe of it. I
told her, I was forry she did not come fooner,
for I had juft finish'd what I defign'd to do, and
that her Company would have made the time
pafs more agreeably away. But she anfwered
my Civility in a moft furprifing manner, and
in an angry tone told me I had fuch good Company with me, that if I had fpoke the truth
of my Heart, her Abfence would have been
moft pleafing to me, and that I knew as young
as I was how to diffemble my thoughts. What
is your meaning, Madam (faid I) for I am as
little guilty of Diffimulation as any one, and
this is a great piece of Injuftice to accufe me
wrongfully? You are fo infenfible (reply'd
she) and pretend fo much Ignorance, that
'twill be a difficult matter I warrant you, to
convince your Ladiship that you are belov'd
by Mr. *Spintext.* What if I be (faid I haftily) I hope Madam, it will give no Chagrin, if
he could be guilty of fo great a folly? This
anfwer did more inflame her anger, fo that

F 4   she

ſhe forget all her pretended **Patience** and
Diſcretion, and wholly abandoning her ſelf
to her fury, she multiply'd-her words ſo faſt
that ſhe would repeat the ſame thing over
ſeveral times. She told me I was young,
fooliſh, and conceited of my ſelf, and took a
pleaſure in hearing my ſelf flatter'd, and having Amorous Songs made of me, and that I
incourag'd Mr. *Spintext* in his pretentions of
Love to me. By this I perceiv'd she had not
heard our diſcourſe, and it was only the effects of her Jealouſie that made her to accuſe
me, and therefore wou'd not acknowledge
the truth, but in a bant'ring way, demanded of her, it I ſhould not return her *Seneca*'s
Morals, for I fear'd through the defect of her
memory she had forgot how great a ſin it was
to give way to paſſion, and that it was alſo
Injurious to beauty ; and that the fault was
greater in her, who had made ſuch ſolemn
profeſſions of Moderation and all that, than
in others who were ſo ſincere as to own the
frailties of their nature.

She was ſo tranſported by her anger, that
it choak'd her words, and she ſtampt and ſta-
red about the room, she hurried up and down
like a Frantick *Baccanel*, at laſt she was forc'd
to have recourſe to her tears which fell in ſuch
abundance from her Eyes, that she repreſented old *Hecuba* in the Play : And on a ſudden
the Sky was Calm and Serene, and she dry'd
up her tears with her dirty Handkerchief, and
giving a ſudden turn towards Mr. *Spintext*,
she

she darted fiery looks at him, and thundered in his ears such peals of her Indignation,
that she amaz'd him in such sort, that I never see one look so astonish'd as he did ; for
till that time he was ignorant of the violent
affection she had for him. But she so ill express'd her Passion, that she serv'd for an An-
tidote against it. But during this long Con-
versation, she acted the part so well of an
Indefatigable Talker, and a most unequall'd
Scold, that from that time I ever call'd her
Xantippe, who was wife to *Socrates* of patient
memory.

That Evening I related to *Olympia* (my
Grand-mothers Woman) this surprising Adventure, telling her how much I was mistaken in the humour of *Xantippe*, whom till then
I believ'd to be a Woman of great Discretion and Prudence, but in this emergency she
behaved her self like one that had neither
sense nor reason. *Olypia* reply'd that I was
not the only Person that had been mistaken
in her, for the Character she had given of
her self had deceiv'd many, and she was of
a humour not to bear a contradiction, but
always acted a Superiors part, to those she
honour'd with her favour. But from that
time I esteem'd her less than any one, and
look'd upon her as a dangerous acquaintance,
for in her Passion she was guilty of Detraction to the last degree, that I was ever after
only Civil to her, with thanks return'd her
Book again. You may judge, my *Indamora*,
she

she was not a Perſon in whom I durſt confide,
and after that I entertain'd my ſelf more
with *Olympia*, who was well Born, and vertu-
ouſly Educated, and had a Genius leſs moroſs
and more conformable to my own humour.

Thus have I given you a faithful account of
what paſt till that time without concealing
my moſt ſecret thoughts, which is the greateſt
proof I can give of my ſincere affection to
my *Indamora*, to whom, I am

A faithful humble Servant
LINDAMIRA.

LETTER IX.

IT will be time now, my *Indamora*, to acquaint you after what manner I was ſurpriz'd with the ſight of *Cleomidon*, who, during my ſtay at *Palarmo*, had not heard any
news of him. One Sunday being at Church, I
obſerv'd an aukward ſort of a Country Clown,
who unalterably kept his Eyes fixt on me, his
Dreſs was that of the meaneſt Peaſants, and
nothing drew my Eyes towards him, but his
continual ſtaring at me, When Sermon was
done, I met him in the Church Porch, who made
me ſeveral Reverend ſcrapes, with his Hat to
the ground, I could not help ſmiling at his officious care, to make me look at him, which
I did without the leaſt ſuſpicion, whom he
was. Before I was got into the Coach, he
whiſper'd to *Iris* (in giving her two Letters)
for

for Heavens fake, dear *Iris* faid he, give this to *Lindamira*. Her furprife was fo great that fhe let the Letters fall, but he gave 'em her again without the leaft obfervation by *Xantippe*, who was juft by her. As foon as we came home and that I was in my Chamber, fhe prefented them to me, telling me in what manner fhe receiv'd 'em. My aftonifhment was greater than can be imagin'd, I knew not what to do in this emergency, nor what to think of this Adventure, but at laft I took Courage to open the Letter, and found thefe words from the faithful *Cleomidon*.

CLEOMIDON to *LINDAMIRA*.

Never did Soul feel fuch anguifh as mine did that ill boding morning that rob'd me of your fight; all things feem'd to join to wrack me, already too much oppreft with grief; fo that I left untold a thoufand fond things my foul was full of. Madam, be juft to my Paffion, and reward it with a return fuitable to my fincerity of it, if my prayers or wifhes be the leaft prevailing, let me receive an anfwer, and deny not the happinefs of an hours Converfation to him that would facrifice his life in your fervice. Adieu.

I read this Letter over a hundred times, revolving in my thoughts what I fhould do, and 'twas a long time before I could come to any Refolution; but the refult was, that I
would

would return him an anſwer by *Iris*, to whom
he wrote alſo, to inform her where to en-
quire for him. It is impoſſible for you to conceive, unleſs you had ſeen as I did, that a
Man that was Gentile, of a Noble Preſence,
and who had ſo particular an obligingneſs
with him, could ſo alter himſelf by his dreſs,
for 'twas *Cleomidon* that was in this diſguiſe,
which he put on to faciliate his deſign, being
reſolv'd to ſee me, and durſt not appear in
his own ſhape, for fear of giving ſome ſuſpicion. I was in ſome Inquietudes about
him, for I had more than a common eſteem
for him, but I duſt not indulge my inclination, becauſe that at *Palármo* a Viſiter of that
Sex, would have been a very great Crime,
therefore I gave him no Incouragement to
make a ſecond attempt to ſee me, and only
wrote him theſe few words.

LINDAMIRA to CLEOIMDON.

IS it poſſible that abſence has not proved an
effectual Cure for your Paſſion? Since I
have already told you I will not beſtow my
Heart, without the Approbation of her that
has it entirely at her Devotion. I have commanded *Iris* to acquaint you with my reaſons
why I cannot gratifie your requeſt, which muſt
be to the hazard of my Honour and Reputation. If you have that eſteem for me, which
you profeſs you cannot take unkindly ſo rea-
ſonable a denial. Farewel.

When

When *Iris* demanded for *Cleomidon*, by the name he mention'd, and he came to her, she could not believe it was he, for not only his Countenance was alter'd, but the tone of his voice, which he had so well Counterfeited, that 'twas impossible to know him, but he soon deliver'd her out of the uncertaintys he was in, by speaking to her in his own natural voice(which was sweet,yet not effeminate) Dear *Iris*, said he, what news do you bring from *Lindamira*? Can she pardon me this device I have made use on to see her? For seriously continued he I have not had one hours repose since I saw her, and all the Divertisements and Caresses of my Friends and Relations have not been able to drive her Idea from my mind. *Iris* then gave him my Letter for which favour he exprest much acknowledgment; but when he had read it over, and saw I had deny'd his request, he seem'd like a man distracted. Is there no means *Iris* (said he) that I may possibly speak to *Lindamira*, and she run no hazard of her Reputation, which is dear to me next to her life? *Iris* represented to him that if my Grand-mother should ever know it, I should loose her favour for ever. But he Expostulated with her so long, and used so many inforcing Arguments to add her endeavour to bring him to a sight of me, that the poor *Iris* at last being overcome by his great Impressment, that she promis'd she would use her interest to perswade me to meet him in the
Valley

Valley at the end of the Wood, but fhe fo
much apprehended the Confequence of its being known, that fhe already dreaded the Encounter.

At her return fhe related all that had paft,
adding many things in favour of him, and
pleaded fo well in his behalf, and fo effectually
laid before me, his impatience of feeing me, that
I yielded to her requeft, and in the Evening,
according to our wonted cuftom, we went to
take our walk. But when I came into the
Valley and bethought my felf that I came to
meet a Gentlemen with whom I had but a
fmall acquaintance, I reproach'd my felf for
my weaknefs, that I fhould fuffer the perfwafions of *his* to work any effect upon my
mind, and I was juft upon making a retreat
and refolvl'd to turn back ; when at the fame
inftant I perceiv'd *Cleomidon* come from behind a great Oak Tree, that had fhelter'd him
from my fight, he perceiving my intentions
advanc'd towards me with much precipitati-
on, faying, Madam, do you fhun me ? What
cruel Deftiny is mine ? Is this all I am to hope
for Heavens fake hear me fpeak, my *Lindamira* ! I made a ftop at thefe words, nor had
I power to go, and by my filence he might
judge his fight was not unpleafing to me.
Tho' I ought to have condemn'd him for this
boldnefs, yet when I look'd on him, I difcover'd fo much Love and Paffion in his Eyes
I had not the heart to make him any reproaches. He faid to me the moft Paffionate
things

thins imaginable, and reprefented his own misfortunes, after fo feeling, fo fenfible a manner of being fo long depriv'd of the fight of me, that I thought there was no room left for doubt, but that his heart and his lips agreed, for fuch was the powerful Rhetorick of Love, that I believ'd *Cleomidon* could not be guilty of a falfhood. To remove my wonder for the extraordinary kindnefs he expreft, which I feem'd to doubt of; he told me it was not ftrange to fee that Love at its firft birth, fhould fometimes arrive at all its Perfection, which time and a greater knowledge do generally give it. For, purfu'd he, I love you to that degree that 'twas impoffible my Paffion fhould admit of an increafe.

Cleomidon afterwards related to me all that the Lady at the Inn had acquainted me with, but flightly ran over the defign his Uncle had to marry him to *Cleodora*, I was I confefs very fcrutinous in my enquiry into what perfections this Lady had, and what recommendable Qualities, fhe had to fubdue a heart, and as her Fortune was very confiderable, I did fear it might fhock his Conftancy, but to remove thofe doubts, he would often fay, that fince he had feen *Lindamira*, he could not be pleas'd with any other, and added fo many obliging expreffions in favour of me, that I had no fufpicion, but that he fpoke his real thoughts.

Our Converfation lafted above two hours, and I muft own to you without Shame and
Confu-

Confufion, that thofe Amiable Qualities I
difcover'd in him wrought a greater effect
on my heart than they ought ; that being confcious to my felf, I ought not to have ingag'd ·
my affections without my Mothers knowledge, I was extreamly troubled to find that
my heart was no longer at her difpofal. But
the Humour of *Cleomidon* was the moft Gallant, the moft agreeable, and moft diverting
of any Man in the world, he has naturally
an Eloquence, fo eafie and fluent, that few
Perfons can explain their Conceptions after
a more entertaing manner than himfelf. I
could not after I had thoroughly confidered
them, but acknowledge I was not infenfible
of his affection, he made me vows of his e-
ternal Fedility, that nothing fhould be able to
fhock his Conftancy. I anfwer'd him in the
moft obliging terms I cou'd, and gave him
leave to hope, that if my Mother fhould approve of his affection, he should not find me
ungrateful ; and I begg'd of him to be content with that efteem I had for him, and
had promis'd to anfwer his Letters, and tho
he lived but twenty miles from *Palarmo*, yet
our Letters were to pafs by *London*, for fear
of giving a fufpicion. After we had fettled
this Correfpondence, I told him it was time
for me to return home, it being Supper time,
and I faw by my Watch, I had already out-
ftay'd my time ; but the word depart extreamly troubled him, and he durft not in
prudence prefs me to ftay ; I left him I muft
acknow-

ledge with much Reluctancy, and him no lefs
concern'd for this feparation. But wheh I came
home, I found my Grandmother at Supper, from
whom I receiv'd a fevere Chaftifement, for in
my abfence *Xantippe* had aggravated my being
out fo late, as a very Criminal matter, whích
poffeft my Grandmother with fome unufal difquiets, and had fent a Servant in Queft of me.
I hearkned to all that was faid with much patience, and was glad I had efcaped without being difcover'd, that I was very filent and wholly
abandoned my thoughts, to *Cleomidon*, after fup-
per I retir'd into my Chamber, where I had the
liberty to recolleĉt in my thoughts this Evenings Adventure, and upon Examination of my
Heart, I found all the figns of a tender and fincere affeĉtion, and wifh'd to reign abfolute in
his without the cruel apprehenfions of a Rival;
Rich and Fair as was *Cleodora*.

This was the Condition of my Soul, when
I was fo happy to fee my dear *Indamora*, at that
delicious place *Lauretta*, where a few days after
this Adventure happned to me. I waited on my
Grandmother to fee *Lucretia*, and from that
time I may date my happinefs in your friendfhip, in whofe agreeable Converfation I paft a-
way 3 Weeks, and tho' at the firft interview I
had a great efteem for you, yet I did not acquaint you with the Affeĉtion I had for *Cleomidon*, leaft you fhould difapprove of my Conduĉt;
but you may perhaps remember fomething of
the Relation I have given of *Philander* and Sir
Formal, but you telling me you had forgot the
particulars of their Amours, I thought it not

unneceſſary to the compleating of my Adventures, to bring them in their proper places.

Your goodneſs has made you commed what merited not your Praiſes, and your Indulgence to my ill performance, encourages me ſtill to go on, that you may command from my Pen, whatever is worthy of your Knowledge ; but I owe much to your good humonr, and am without Complement, with all the ſincerity as may be,

My Deareſt Indamora,
Your true and faithful Lindamira.

LETTER X.

WHilſt I was at *Lauretta*, my Dear *Indamora*, I wrote to *Cleomidon*, and gave him an account how happy I was in a new Friend, I had gain'd ſince I came to that place ; I will not tell you what I ſaid of you, becauſe your Modeſty will not bare the juſt Praiſes of your Friends ; but in anſwer to that Letter, he ſaid he was charm'd with the Character of her, I mention'd, but look'd upon her as a Dangerous Friend, becauſe ſhe had robbed him of part of my Soul. Tho' I receiv'd this Anſwer whilſt I was at *Lauretta*, I ſaid not one ſilable of it to you, being of a humour not to be very free till I am jntimately acquainted, I left untold ſeveral things, that I wiſh'd ſince I had inform'd you of, and for the time I have been known to you ; you have gain'd a greater

Intereſt

Intereſt in my Heart than any one, accept my
Dear *Valeria*, for whom I had, and have ſtill a
great value and eſteem ; but ſhe being married,
and much taken up with her Domeſtick Affairs,
I ſeldom heard from her whilſt I was at *Palarmo*,
nor durſt I acquaint her with any thing concerning *Cleomidon*, fearing leaſt my Letters might
come to the view of *Silvanus*.   When I went
from *Lauretta* you beſt can tell, with what un-
willingneſs I parted from ſo agreeable a ſociety,
and what was my grief to leave ſo Charming a
Friend ; for at my return to *Palarmo*, I was to
Converſe with a Jealouſie, Froward, and Impertinent Woman, without any further per-
ſute of her Character, you may gueſs her to be
Xantippe ; for ever ſince ſhe treated me ſo li-
berally with her *Billings-gate* in the Summer-
Houſe, ſhe began to hate me, and Clandeſtinly
did me all the ill offices ſhe could to my Grandmother, tho' to my face ſhe was Civil, but
jealous of my Pow'r, which ſhe thought greater
than her own : but her humour made me not
uneaſie, for my thoughts were wholly taken
up, upon a ſubject more worthy of my Love
and Friendſhip, and I often receiv'd news from
Cleomidon, who ſtill continued his Affection,
and fail'd not to give me all the aſſurances of
an unalterable Love ; that I read over his Letters with Delight, and anſwer'd 'em with Pleaſure : ſo that the time paſt away as agreeably
as 'twas poſſible in the Abſence of the Perſon
lov'd.

But now I muſt ſay ſomething of Mr. *Spintext*,
who was a Man that had many good Qualities,

G 2

I mean that fell under my notice and obfervation ; his only fault was owning his Love for
me, for which it feem'd he was extreamly
troubled, and told *Iris* of it, wifhing he could
have an opportunity to beg my pardon and acknowledge his fault ; he own'd indeed that he
could not repent that he lov'd me, but that he
had difpleas'd me, in acquainting me with it ;
but for the future he would be as filent as the
Night, if he could but once but eafe his Mind
of the pain and anguifh he did labour under.
But tho' *Iris* told me this, I was unwilling to
gratifie his requeft upon the account of *Xan-
tippa*'s jealous Humour, whom I knew was very
watchful both of him and me, and as I had long
fince forgot his Crime, I thought it not neceffary to let him fpeak to me.

About a Month after my return to *Palarmo*,
I receiv'd the furprifing news that *Cleomidon*
lay conceal'd in the littleCottage that is in the
Valley, he fent me a Billet, wherein he con-
jur'd me not to refufe him the fight of me once
more, deploring his unhappinefs, that he had
not the freedom of waiting on me at my Grandmothers Houfe, that he might publickly own
the Paffion he had for me, and was grieved
that he was put to the neceffity of defireing me
to meet him, when it was his part to have
come all the way, but thefe Niceties are eafily
facrificed to Love ; and I found Arguments
enough to Paliate his fault ; and wifhing to fee
him (tho' at the hazard of my Grandmothers
difpleafure) I fent him word I would meet him
at the Well, which place being more publick,

I

I thought lefs dangerous, in cafe any one fhould perceive me talking to him. With *Iris* I went, and when I came to the place of Affignation, I faw *Cleomidon* lie faft afleep upon one of the Benches of the Well ; he fince told me he had ftaid fo long waiting for me, that his Spirits were tired with Expectation, that he laid him down in hopes to fleep, to delude the tedious Hours. But I had then the fatisfaction of looking on him with more attention, than ever I had done yet : and the more I view'd him, the more I was confirm'd in the good opinion I had of him ; but fearing he might awake and find me in this contemplating pofture ; I walk'd away, and bid *Iris* awake him, for I had no time to lofe. She no fooner obey'd me, but he ftarting up and feeing only her by him, he expreft in his Eyes all the marks of difpair, but *Iris* took Compaffion on him, and told him I was hard by, which reftor'd him to his former tranquility of Mind, and feeing me coming towards him, he ran to me, and with open Arms receiv'd me, faying the moft kindeft, tendereft words that his Paffion could furnifh him with. I faintly reproach'd him, for his returning again, alledging what hazard I ran for his fake ; but he wanted not Expreffions to excufe himfelf, for Love made him fo Eloquent, and acknowledging, that I could not be angry at him. 'Tis endlefs to repeat what vows of Fidelity he made me, that nothing fhould fhock his conftancy ; I on my fide gave him all the Innocent marks of an Affection, that I thought might be juftifiable to the World. He told

G 3   me

me he defign'd to be in *London* in three Weeks,
and did hope he might perfwade me to haften
my return thither; but then I had not thoughts
of going fo foon, as it afterwards fell out.

After this manner we paft our time, and the
hours glided pleafantly away, when at a diftance I difcover'd Mr. *Spintext*, who directed
his fteps that way; I interrupted *Cleomidon*, telling him whom I faw, and that I feared my
Grandmother had fent him after me, it being
near Supper time. But this Adventure did fo
fowre his Joys, and juftled all thofe thoughts
out of his Mind, that he defign'd to have acquainted me with, which too late I knew afterwards; but the approach of this unwelcome
Divine, made us refolve to feparate, and I affured *Cleomidon* I would follow him into the
Valley as foon as I had learn'd what his Errand
was, but I then little apprehended he came upon
his own; at his approach to me, I read in his
Eyes, fome concern, and was affraid to know
the truth, being only apprehenfive upon *Cleomidon's* account: but he foon deliver'd me out
of that perplexity, and drove me into another:
for this was the fatal time my *Indamora,* that
he took to make his Recantation, and to beg my
pardon for his Temerity; affuring me he was fo
fenfible of the offence he had given me, in fuffering his thoughts to roam beyond a Sphere
too great for him; but as his judgment was
not in fault, he hop'd I would have fome Indulgence for his Crime. He expreft himfelf in
a very Pathetical ftrain, and made very Inge-
nous acknowledgments of his faults; that had

my

my refentments lafted till that time, I muft have
pardon'd him; and did affure him I wou'd provided he obferv'd that Decorum that became
him ; as I ended thefe words I rofe up with an
intention to be gone, not giving him leave to
prolong the Difcourfe ; when at a diftance, I
difcover'd a Creature make towards me, who
rather flew, than went on feet, but fo far off I
could not well diftinguifh what it was ; that I
concluded it was fome Hobgobling, or fome
wing'd Monfter of the Night, for there appear'd nothing of Human in the fhape or form
of it. I ftop'd a while to behold what this Pro-
teus might be, for it appear'd in feveral fhapes,
but as it nearer did approach my Eye, I faw it
was a Woman ; but to compleat my ill fortune
it was the terrible Xantippe! whom Rage and
Jealoufie had led thither; and with all the fury
of a Woman in Difpair, came to reproach Mr.
Spintext with his Ingratitude to her, and me
with my Intriegues with him. But as I thought
it not confiftent with Prudence to retreat (believing that fhe knew me) I took a refolution
to ftand the brunt of her Anger; tho' Mr.
Spintext would have perfwaded me to have
fhun'd the Storms that threatned me. No
fooner did this Furiofo approach me (tho' quite
out of breath) but fhe darted Fire from her Eyes,
which prepar'd me to hear her Thunder ; and
as her Voice was fhril and loud enough upon
occafion, it was fo now, more than ord nary ;
for being poffeft with an unaccountable Jealoufie, fhe gave a lofe to all her thoughts, and
quite forgot her boafted Moderation. Such

ftreams

ſtreams of words flow'd from her Tongue, that 'twas amazing where ſhe found Expreſſions ſo ſutable to her Paſſion ; but the Rage of *Juno* was not greater, when *Paris* gave the Apple from her, than was *Xantippe*, to ſee her dearly belovedDivine, ſo near to me. And after ſhe had recover'd breath, ſhe told me, ſhe thought her ſelf bound in gratitude to my Grandmother, to take ſome care of me, for ſhe perceiv'd my walks was not deſign'd ſo much for my Health, as to give Mr. *Spintext* an opportunity to Court me : at laſt (ſaid I Madam) you are in as plea-ſant a humour to Day, as when I ſaw you laſt in the Summer-Houſe, I wiſh you were always thus diverting, and I would contribute what lay in my pow'r to give you ſubject for your mirth. But ſurely never Woman was ſo inrag'd and ſo diveſted of all Reaſon ; for ſhe acted the part of a Frantick Creature, and began to role her Eyes about, and roſe up haſtily, and came towards me (I ſuppoſe) with a deſign to play at pull-Quoif with me ; but her Carear was ſtop'd by Mr. *Spintext* interpoſing between, who then thought it high time, to give her a gentle Correction, for her immoderate Anger; which he did in a very mild way, and at laſt did reduce her to ſome Reaſon, for ſhe made him no reply, but watred the Moſſy Bank whereon ſhe ſat, with her pretious Tears.

As ſoon as I thought the moiſter of her Eyes was exhail'd, and that to her Paſſion ſhe had giv'n vent enough; Come let's be gone Madam (ſaid I) for what will my Grandmother ſay that we are out ſo late ? And what excuſe can you make ?

make ? but this fage Lady only anfwered me with an ominous look, and leading the way fhe follow'd me. I fail'd not to entertain Mr. *Spintext* as I went along, which I fuppofe fhe never cou'd forgive. But all this while the poor *Cleomidon* fuffer'd difquiets that cannot be expreft; Itherefore whifpred to *Iris* to go to him, and give him an account of this unlucky accident, adding that the next Day I would furely write to him.

When I came home I found my Grandmother much out of humour that I was out fo late, and to Excufe, and paliate my fault, I faid that *Xantippe* was with me : but fhe like an Indifcreet and Malicious Creature, retorted that by accident fhe met with me and Mr. *Spintext*, and thinking it not convenient for me to be alone with him, fhe ftaid out the longer to keep me Company ; and that I had fent *Iris* to go home another way.

I was never more perplext than at that time, not knowing what defence to make, for the truth I durft not own, and my Countenance betray'd fome guilt, which my Grandmother obferv'd, and was confirm'd in a belief that I had made an appointment with Mr. *Spintext* ; and therefore in a very angry tone, forbad me ever walking there again, unlefs *Xantippe* wou'd do me the favour to bare me Company. I reply'd fhe fhould be obey'd, that I never more would frequent a place, that had caus'd her fo much difpleafure.

Soon after I retir'd, and *Iris* not being return'd, I had a thoufand fears fhe fhould be difcover'd ;

cover'd ; but I was foon after releas'd from all
my Cares, for her fight fill'd my Heart with a
Joy unfpeakable. She recounted to me, the
vexfition this dif ppointment had caus'd in
the Soul of *Cleomidon*, who depended much
upon the promife I had made him, of writing
to him the next Morning, which I fail'd not to
do, with the affurance of my Eternal Fidelity
to him.

Iris, who carried this Letter, found *Cleomidon* a walking in the Valley in expectation of
her ; as foon as he had read over my Letter
(which feem'd to pleafe him) he fate him down
under an Oak Tree, and return'd me an Anfwer, that gave me all the reafon in the World
to believe, that his Fidelity was unfhaken and
nothing could be more tender, and kind, than
what he wrote to me. He preft me much to
haften my Journey to *London*, and that I would
ever preferve him intirely in my Heart.

After this Adventure, I fhould not have
taken any pleafure in thofe fhady walks, tho'
I had not been forbidden by my Grandmother,
and fhould have bannifh'd my felf : for fince this
accident *Palarmo* feem'd very dull to me, but as
reading and my painting was my greateft diverfions, I converft very little with any one,
and with *Xantippe* the leaft, for this Philofophical
Lady had given me a very bad opinion of all
pretenders to Philofophy, that I made thofe
Books the leaft of my ftuddy, and took an
opinion they were the leaft ufeful of any I could
read. But it was my Ignorance, and her Im-
moderation, that made me difpife the moft
profitable

profitable Authors. But I will not longer entertain you with my fentiments upon that
matter; but will finifh this, with the affurance
of my ever being,

My Dear Indamora's

Moft affectionate faithful, Lindamira.

LETTER XI.

KNowing that *Cleomidon* defign'd for *London* in a fhort time, I refolv'd my Dear
Indamora, to write to my Mother to fend for
me away, which accordingly I did, and in ten
Days receiv'd an anfwer, that I fhould prepare
my felf for my Journey, but was firft to expect
another Letter; and being depriv'd of my
ufual Diverfion, I began to ftuddy mifchief.

And as I was but too fenfible that *Xantippe*
had leffened me in the Efteem of my Grandmother (who through her means had entertain'd
fome unjuft fufpicions on me) I refolv'd to quit
fcores with her, and requite all her Civility at
once. For as I've told your, *Xantippe* had a moft
violent Affection for Mr. *Spintext*, and he no
Efteem for her, fo I reprefented to my felf no
fmall fatisfaction, to fee this Furious Lady depriv'd of all her hopes: (tho' they were ill
grounded) and therefore I fpoke to a Gentleman who had fome influence on the Mind of
this young Levit, to Buz in his head that *Olimpia* wou'd make him a very good Wife, who
was Pritty, very Difcreet, and much efteem'd
on by my Grandmother, that 'twas probable
for her fake, he might get preferment, being
fhe

she had a good Living at her difposal. This I faid to his Friend who had Senfe enough to know how to amplifie matters, and fhew 'em in the moft Advantagious Situation; and he being young and and fufceptable of Love, I fancy'd my Plot might take. On the other hand I knew, that *Olimpia* had no difefteem for Mr. *Spintext*, and therefore might be perfwaded to admit him as a Lover.

I no fooner mention'd this, but it was propos'd to this worthy Levit, who at the firft flighted his Friends Advife, but being prefs'd to conlider his own advantage, he at laft refolv'd to try his Fortune, in hopes to fucceed better than in his laft Amour : and at the fame time I prevail'd with *Olimpia* to receive his Addreffes favourably; and I having fome pow'r with her, Mr. *Spintext*, met with no great opofition in his Courtfhip, for they having known each other a good while, there was no need of frivilous Complements ; the firft opportunity I confirm'd him in the good choife he had made, and that I thought *Olimpia* a Perfon very worthy and deferving, and my Friendfhip to her, would make me the more Affidious in promo'ing hisIntreft to myGrandmother,which Ihoped to do effectually,when once they were married, which I wifh'd might be, before I went to *London*.

A few Days after, this Marriage was confumated, and with all the fecrecy Imaginable, without giving the leaft fufpition of any fuch defign, and tho' *Xantippe* was like *Argus* with his hundred Eyes, and rowl'd 'em up and down

in

In every place, yet was she blind to this Affair, which gave no little Joy, to our Bride and Bridegroom ; to whom was observ'd all the formalities at a Wedding. For there was Bride-Cake, Sack-Posset, and flinging of the Stocking, and none there, but the Bridegroom's Friend, my self, *Iris*, and one Maid.

You may perhaps wonder how this could be done without the knowledge of the Eagle-Ey'd *Xantippe*, and yet we were all to cunning for her; but as 'twas necessary my Grandmother should be acquainted with this Marriage, I took my opportunity in the absence of *Xantippe*, to let her know of it, and withal to beg both their Pardons, that they did not know of their Design ; tho' this news was surprising, to my Grandmother, and perhaps at another time would have resented it, yet I could discover a secret Joy in her Countenance, that her Chaplain had dispos'd of himself, for *Xantippe* had lane a Train of Designs, to destroy me in my Grandmothers good opinion : She then asked me where they were that she might wish 'em Joy; I went immediately to 'em, to let 'em know the favour that was design'd 'em, and to prepare 'em for this Enterview.

When they made their appearance, they both beg'd my Grandmothers pardon that they had not asked her Approbation and Consent ; but she very obligingly saluted the Bride, and turning to the Bridegroom, wish'd 'em both much Happiness together. In this intrim, *Xantippe* entr'd at another Door, and stood like one amaz'd, revolving in her Mind what

was

was the meaning of this falutation : for being
Ignorant of the Marriage fhe did not prefently
apprehend it. But when fhe did, fhe was like
one in *Bethlehem*, for fhe threw her Eyes about,
grin'd with her Teeth, ftamp'd with her
Feet, and in fhort fhew'd all the marks of a
Defpairing Creature ; but fhe was under fome
Reftrictions, being in my Grandmothers prefence, or I believe fhe would have pull'd their
Eyes out. This was fo amazing to my Grandmother, who was a ftranger to her Paffions,
that of a long time fhe could not fpeak, but at
laft turning towards her, do you know *Lindamira* faid fhe, the Reafon, that *Xantippe* looks
fo difturb'd ? Alas ! Madam (faid I) her diforder proceeds from Love, Difpair and Jealoufie ; for Madam, fhe was in Love with Mr.
Spintext, and would have been glad to have
been in *Olimpia's* place. I fpoke this I confefs
in a Malicious tone, and did Ridicule her
Grief fo much, that having loft all patience,
fhe fet no bounds to her Anger; and without
making any reply (for her pretious Tears had
ftopt her Speech) fhe flipt of her Shoe and
flung it defignedly at my Head, but miffing her
Aim, it light on the Chimney-Piece amongft
the Cheiny, which tumbled down great part
that was there, which made fo great a noife,
and a difturbance, that what with her Sobs
and difmal Sighs, this was a Scene of Diforder
and Diftraction.

But what were my Grandmothers thoughts
in this Emergency I can't well tell, but fhe
could not but fee fhe was deceiv'd in her opinion

of *Seneca*'s Difciple ? But after fome time *Xan-tippe* began to recolleƈt what she had done, and being ashame'd of her ridiculous behaviour, withdrew out of the Room with much Precipi-tation, and in her hafte tumbled down a Chair or two, and having but one Shoe on, she hob-led away in a very ungraceful manner, and went into her Clofet, lock'd her Door, where 'tis fuppos'd after she had vented her Sorrow, she confider'd that the World was full of difap-pointments, and there was no true happinefs to be found. For four Days she continued in this contemplating Humour, and converft with no-thing but *Seneca*; and during this happy truce, I fail'd not of my Defign of prevailing with my Grandmother, to beftow that Living she had in her Gift on Mr. *Spintext*. My requeft was granted without much difficulty, and I faw a profpeƈt of this Cupple's living Happily to-gether.

But when *Xantippe* made her appearance a-gain, (not being without the Senfe of shame) she look'd very much out of Countenance, and dejeƈted, that I almoft repented me, of what I had done ; but my Mirth coft me dear, for I then receiv'd a Letter from a Friend of my Mo-thers, that acquainted me, of her being taken very ill, and that I muft come away with all the fpeed imaginable. This News, ftruck me with fuch a fadnefs, and fo fenfible a grief, that I hardly knew what I faid or did, for I was ever very apprehenfive how great my lofs would be, in the Death of my Mother. This news caus'd a general difturbance in the Family, and my

Abfence

Abfence a Grief to all but *Xantippe.* I left *Palarmo,* without regret, for having loſt the greateſt part of my pleaſure, ſince I did not frequent the Grove, I had no other Grief, than that of leaving a very kind Relation, but was going to one more dearer to me.

From that fatal Journey I may Date all my Unhappineſs, for then began the greateſt change in my Affairs; and what afterwards befel me when i came to *London,* I ſhall reſerve for a more Convenient opportunity, and tho' ſome Years are paſt ſince, yet I cannot think on that great misfortune, without ſome Senſe of Trouble, I find my ſelf already too much affeſted with the thoughts of it; ſo will reſerve that Adventure, for a more proper opportunity; and muſt alfo beg my Dear *Indamora's* pardon for all faults, and being aſſur'd of your goodneſs I ſhall only aſſure you,

I am,

Your affeſtionate Friend

and Servant Lindamira.

The End of the Second Part of the Adventures of Lindamira.

THE

The Third Part of the Adventures of Lindamira.

The XIIth. LETTER.

NEver was Soul poffefs'd with fuch juft
Apprehenfions, as I was for the Sick-
nefs of my Mother : For when I came to
London, my deareft *Indamora*, I receiv'd the
unwelcom News of her being in a dangerous Condition : Her Joy of feeing me (fhe
faid) gave her new Life ; but 'twas but a
Vapour ; for fhe foon return'd to her fainting
Fits again, of which fhe had many in a day ;
but I receiv'd from her all the marks of a
tender Affection; and during her intervalls,
fhe fail'd not of giving me thofe neceffary
Inftructions for the Conduct of my felf ; adding alfo, That if I Married, fhe wifh'd I
might make Choice of one who had Principles of Honour and Generofity, and would
fcorn a bafe Action, but left me to my own
Liberty. I found that her Sentiments were
ftill the fame of mine, and did believe the
Humour of *Cleomidon* would anfwer the
Character fhe gave of one that might make
me Happy ; but I had not Courage to ac-

H   qnaint

quaint her with his Affection to me, but defer'd it till such time, that I might, without
inconveniency to her self, give an account of
the whole Affair.

In the mean time, I heard ev'ry day from
Cleomidon, but would not admit of a visit
from him, in the Condition my Mother was;
for I was never a Minute from her Bed-side;
but as Lovers are sometimes more impatient
than others, he could not absent himself any
longer from me; but that Day he came to
see me, it fell out unhappily for us both;
for scarce had he been with me a quarter of
an hour, but I was call'd away in all haste,
being alarm'd that my Mother was a Dying,
I almost lost my Sences at this Summons;
but calling up all my Courage, I ran to her to
assist her the best I could. She was then but
in a fit, and recover'd out of that in a short time
after; but they return'd upon her so fast, as
all that Night she hardly knew any one;
but the next Day, was much better, and
spoke to me of several things : Finding that
she was not long for this World, my dear
Child (said she) take that Care of your self,
as I have done for you, and be not over hasty
how you bestow your Affections : For as
your Fortune will be in your own hands, you
will not want Pretenders, and every one will
hope that you way be his Prize. Your unexperienc'd Mind (continued she) may bring
you into Inconveniencies, because you'll judge
of others by your self : But now, my Child,
you will be left without any other Defence
then

then your own Innocency; which preferve, and let Vertue be your Rule, and Prudence guide you. Be ever Deaf to Rumours that detract from the Honour of your Friends; and if you can, warn 'em of Dangers, and beware of Flattery, a Bait that ruins many.

I gave my dear Mother, a thoufand thanks for her good Inftructions;but my Grief was too great to fay to her half I defign'd : But that very Day I did refolve to acquaint her with *Cleomidon*, and to beg her Approbation ; but that Night—was the fatal Night that rob'd me of a dear Mother, and put a Period to her Life. I loft, at once, a tender Mother, and a wife Counfellor ; and, I may fay, without Flattery, that all her Friends had a lofs of her.

Thus was I left, my *Indamora*, in this deplorable Condition ; and being feiz'd with a violent Grief, I faw not the Face of any one till after her Funeral Rites were performed ; and tho' I received all the Confolation, as was poffible, from *Cleomidon*, by Letters, yet it wrought but little effect upon my Reafon : And my Mothers words ran much in my mind, *That I was left without Defence :* For, indeed, I was ; for I had no Relations near me, only an Aunt that liv'd beyond the *Tower*. and I could fee her but feldom; but her young Daughter, fhe, out of kindnefs, let be with me. The poor *Udotia* had but dull time with me; for the Melancholy I was in, brought me into the Yellow-Jaundice, that I was fcarce to be known. My

Illnefs

Illnefs very much afflicted *Cleomidon,* and he fhew'd himfelf very induftrious in procuring me the beft Advice, and with his perfwafions, and the Medicines I took, I recover'd my Health, and look'd as formerly I ufed to do.

I being well enough to go abroad again, *Cleomidon* thought he might, without any indecency, prefs me to a confent of Marriage : For as I was abfolute Miftrefs of my felf, and Fortune, there was no Oppofition on any fide if I would give confent : But a humour took me, that I thought in half a Year, after my Mothers Death, I ought not to Marry, and could give no other Reafons for my denyal. *Cleomidon* therefore comply'd with my Humour, hoping that then I would (as he faid) make him Happy. I faw him very often ; all my Friends knew of his Defign, and approv'd of my Choice ; that I may fay, I had all the fatisfaction I could defire. But as the Joys of Lovers are not lafting, fo did I meet with an Affliction, as I am certain, my *Indamora*, will raife your utmoft Compaffion.

One Day, as *Cleomidon* was with me, who entertain'd me with News of the Town, and, tho', what he faid, was pleafantly related, yet I difcover'd a Shagrin in his Mind, which he feem'd to take care to conceal from me ; but my prefaging Thoughts immediately Divin'd fomething there was of Confequence, that gave him a Difturbance ; and being affur'd I had given him a caufe of Jealoufie, or

Fear,

Fear, I importun'd him ftill the more, to
know the caufe of that Penfivenefs, that
often times hurried his Thoughts away, that
he did not fometimes anfwer me when I fpoke
to him, but he would wave the Difcourfe,
and faid, he did not deferve that obliging
Care; but then I was the more confirm'd in
my Sufpicions, and being in hopes I might
difpel his Grief, by bearing a part with him,
I forc'd the fecret from his Breaft; which
was, my *Indamora*, that *Cleodora* was in
Town; her very Name chill'd my Blood; I
knew not why; and in my fancy rowl'd a
thoufand extravagant, Ill-boding Thoughts;
but more was yet to come; for *Alcander*,
Cleomidon's Unckle, was in Town alfo, and
with him the moft fomous *Lyndaraxa*, *Cleodora*'s Aunte; and that their Bufinefs was,
to make up the Match with *Cleomidon* and
Cleodora. But when he related this, he
fhew'd fo much Concern and Trouble as cannot be imagin'd; and tho' *Cleodora* was to be
prefer'd before me in feveral refpects, yet the
obligining *Cleomidon* told me, That if I
would comply with his Wifhes, I fhould
find the difference he made between us. But
as I fear'd *Alcander* would not confent to his
Defires, fo I fear'd he would be fruftrated of
his Hopes for ever, if he difobey'd him in
his Marriage. But *Cleomidon* reply'd, That
he had rather forgoe all his Hopes there,
than loofe his intereft in me; that fince we
might both live happy with our prefent Fortunes, did beg of me, not to confider his in-
H 3   tereft

tereft for the future. I was at an non-plus
what to refolve upon, that tho' his generous
Humour made him to flight his intereft, yet
I ought to weigh well what I did, and not
be the caufe of fo great a difappointment :
'Tis true, I was affur'd of his Affection, and
knew very well, that only he could make
me happy ; but, if he did, 'twas poffible he
might loofe his Uncle's Favour for ever. I
had as ftrong a Combat in my Soul, as ever
was t'wixt Love and Honour, and I could
not come to any Refolution. That Night I
let him depart without any hope I would af-
fent to his Requeft : But the next Day he
came again, telling me he fhould be mifera-
bly unhappy, if I would not promife to be
his : (If faid I) you can gain your Unkle's
Confent , you fhall not fail of mine ; but if
he difapproves of your ill Choice, you muft
not difoblige him. Madam, faid he, to Lovers this is nonfence ; why fhould I pleafe
an Unkle before my-felf ? It is not his Opinion of my Happinefs can make it fo ? But
I'm the beft judge in this Cafe , what will
either make me happy, or miferable. Cleomidon this time, had like to have vanquifh'd
my obftinate Humour ; but being unwilling,
for my fake, he fhoul'd lofe fo confiderable an
Eftate, I urg'd him ftill to try to gain his
Unkles Approbation : But, Madam, faid he,
what if my Unkle will not Confent ?
what Deftiny muft I hope for ? to marry
Cleodora, faid I---Alas ! Madam, reply'd Cleomidon, you do not Love me then, that can thus
eafiy

eafily refign me to another ? Do not flatter
me any longer with vain Hope, but tell me
I'm become indifferent to you ; tho' if you
will not avert my Doom, there will be a
neceffity that I obey my Uncle; and when
too late, perhaps, you may repent of all
your Cruelty.

In Juftice to *Cleomidon*, I muft acknowledge,
that never greater Love was fhewn, nor never worfe rewarded : For he that could defpife twenty thoufand Pound, flight his Unkle's Favour,who had fo plentiful an Eftate to
leave him (provided he pleas'd him in his
Marriage) and yet to prefer me before *Cleodora*; and fo infenfible was I of my Happinefs, that he could not extort a Promife from
me to be his, and would have Married me
immediately, before his Unkle had urged
him farther. But ftill I continued in the
fame Sentiments, that unlefs *Alcander*
would agree to his Requeft, I ought not to
deprive him of all his Hopes : But he finding me inflexible, and not to be wrought upon he took his leave of me, reproaching me
me with Barbarity and Inhumanity. But
fure fome Magick did influence my Mind,
that made me fo Deaf to all his Intreaties,
that I could let him depart without one
word of Confolation ? But I have fince fufficiently repented of my Cruelty.

Cleomidon, that Night, went ftrait to his
Lodging,where he found an unwelcome Gueft,
his Unkle, who had waited for him three
Hours : That day *Alcander*, by fome unluc-

ky

ky Accident, had heard of our Amours, and upbraided *Cleomidon* with it as a great marke of his Folly, but defired to know the truth of that Report.

But *Clemidon*, who had a generous Soul, fcorn'd to deny the truth; and did frankly own to him, That no other Woman in the World could make me happy ; and that, if I had pleas'd, he had been Married to me fome Months fince: For before he had ever known *Cleodcra*, he had given me his Heart. This free Declaration put *Alcander* in fo great a Rage, to fee his Defigns oppos'd, that he told him, in a moft imperious tone, That this was a bafe Recompence for all his care in his Education, to think of beftowing him felf on any Woman without his approbaticn. Sir, faid *Cleomidon*, I ask your Pardon, but our Hearts are not always in our own Power, and by furprize fometimes are loft : There is a Deftiny that we cannot refift, and muft fometime, or other, yield to Loves Empire, But the Old Gentleman, who was infenfible of fo foft a Paffion, and who ador'd noth-ing but Riches, was not mov'd, but more exafperated at fo dull an Excufe , faying, That Intereft ought to govern the Affections, and that a wife Man would look to the fu-ture, and not to the prefent : And, faid *Al-cander*, I do expeft, that Filial Love and Obedience from you, that you comply with my Commands.

But

But all the Reafons that *Clemidon* could alledge, in excufe of his Ingagement to me, faying of me the moft advantageous Things that his Paffion could furnifh him with, was of no effect : For, reply'd *Alcander*, has your *Lindamira* Twenty Thoufand Pound ? Can fhe make you fo happy as *Cleodora*, who has a fine Houfe to bring you to in the Country, furrounded with a good Eftate ? And can you hope, that your Difobedience will be rewarded with my Eftate, I defign'd to have left you when I Died? which fince you can difpife to gratify your Love, I can beftow it on your Brother, who, perhaps, will have more regard to my Commands. But nothing that *Cleomidon* could fay, would mollify the Obdurate Heart of *Alcander* ; for he finding that he had no inclination to Obey him, he flung out of the Room in a Paffion, threatning him with his eternal Difpleafure.

In fuch a ftrait never was any left, nor could any one give higher proofs of an unalterable Affection then did *Cleomidon*, who found my humour fo Refractory, that I caus'd him more difquiets , than all his Unkle's threats : But the fequel of this Adventure, you fhall know in my next. Adieu, my *Indamora*.

I am your

Faithful Servant,

Lindamira.

The

The XIIIth. L E T T E R.

THat Night *Cleomidon* took but little reſt,
my dear *Indamora*, who ſuffér'd inquietudes that cannot be expreſt ; and the
next Day recounted to me all that had paſs'd
between *Alcander*, and himſelf. That now
Lindamira, ſaid he, if you refuſe to make
me Happy, I muſt accuſe you of too much
ill-Nature and Inhumanity ; but inſtead of
working that effect on my Heart, as it ought,
I ſuffer'd my ſelf to be vanquiſh'd by my
Generoſity , and told that faithful Lover ,
that I would rather chooſe to be miſerable
all the Days of my Life, than he ſhould looſe
the reward of his Obedience : That I would
live unmarried for his ſake, and retire to
ſome ſolitary Place, where I ſhould never
hear the Name of *Cleomidon* ; that I would
not oppoſe his Felicity with *Cleodora* : For,
ſaid I, how do I know how your Sentiments
may change hereafter, when I have loſt that
little Beauty I have ; and that you once con-
ſider, that for my ſake, you diſoblig'd a kind
Unkle ?

Cleomidon took thoſe words mortally ill :
For, ſaid he, they found not kind from the
Lips of *Lindamira* : And, Madam, continued he, what have you obſerv'd in my Humour,

mour, that can infpire you with fo mean an Opinion of me? Have not I given you all poffible proof of a faithful and unalterable Affection? And have not I Sacrificed a confiderable Fortune ; and, what I value more, a moft kind and obligeing Unkle to you? Tell me, Madam, what further Demonftrations you can require of my Sincerity? Tho' I had all imaginable reafon to be fatisfied in the Humour and Affection of *Cleomidon*, yet, as our ill Deftinies would have it, his great Merits were not Crown'd with thatRecompence he defir'd. I refus'd abfolutely to Marry him, and perfwaded him to comply with his Unkle. This he refented fo ill from me, that thinking I had a fecret Averfion for him, and that the thoughts of a near Alliance difgufted me ; He Sighing, faid, well,Madam. I will Marry *Cleodora*, becaufe I fee it pleafes you ; and if I can as well difguife my Averfion to her, as you have your Affection to me, I may, in time, forget *Lindamira*, that has fo ill rewarded the moft conftant and faithful of Lovers.

This Reproach extreamly afflicted me ; for I valu'd *Cleomidon* beyond all things in the World ; and tho' I ought to have been more juft to his Merits, yet I could not perfwade my felf, he fhould mix his Fortune with mine. This dire Refolve, was an unexpreffible Affliction to him ; and being poffefs'd I had an Antipathy to him, he rofe up to be gone, telling me he would obey me, and, as a Demonftration of his Love, that

I

I fhould fee he would make all things eafy
to him, when it might contribute to my fatisfaction. Thefe words were like a Dagger
to my Heart, that he fhould have fuch
wrong Notions of that Friendfhip I had for
him; I therefore endeavour'd to convince
him, that greater proof could not be given
of a fincere Affection, than to Sacrifice my
own Quiet and Happinefs to his Intereft, and
that in perfwading him to comply with his
Unkle, was his advantage, not mine. Ah!
Madam, faith he coldly, you are fo much
Miftrefs of your Heart, and of your Affections, that I being unworthy of fo great a
Bleffing, as being your Husband, I muft not
pretend to vanquifh a Refolution, you have
made of rendring me for ever miferable. So
I will take from your fight, a Perfon, that is
become Deteftable and Odious to you.

He gave me not time to reply, but made a
Bow, and went out of the Room, fetching
fuch Sighs, as would have made a Heart of
Stone to relent. Then I began to fee my Error, and blame my felf for my Infenfibility;
I fent a Servant immediately after him, but
for my ill Fortune, could not fet Eyes on
him; for he went the quite contrary way.
I gave vent to my Tears, but they brought
me fmall relief; for my ill-boding Heart
told me, I repented too late; nor could I
refolve to fee him in the Arms of my Rival,
which fhew'd that he was not indifferent to
me. I was then more fenfible how unworthily
I had requited fo fincere an Affection, which
merited

merited a better State, than what he fo ardently defir'd. The next Morning I wrote
to him, but the Meffenger brought back
my own Letter, which put me in a great
Conflernation, what the reafon fhould be;
but he told me, that *Cleomidon* was gone out
an Hour before he went, that his Man knew
not where, who faid, that his Mafter feem'd
extreamly Afflicted, and had not flept all that
Night. This News gave me the moft cruel
and fharpeft Pain I ever felt; for I was
confcious to my felf, I was the caufe of that
Difturbance in his Mind. I fent again that
Afternoon to his Lodging, but he was not
return'd; but in the Evening, the Meffenger,
I fent, met with him, who gave the Letter
to *Cleomidon*, which he read, and Sigh'd extreamly, and Tears were feen to fall from
his Eyes, which he endeavour'd to hide; but,
faid he, tell *Lindamira*, I have not time to
Anfwer her Letter; for this is my Nuptial
Night, but fhe fhall have a Letter from
me to Morrow.

Where fhall I find words, my *Indamora*,
to exprefs my Grief, my Surprize, and my
Repentance? My Paffion was without moderation; I was almoft drown'd in my Tears,
I was Deaf to all Reafon, to the perfwafions of thofe that were with me; nothing
but the Name of *Cleomidon* could I utter;
his Love was magnify'd in my fancy; my
Rival appear'd, to my Imagination, Fair, and
fond of him, who was infinitely more fortunate than I; for without knowing the

leaft

leaſt uneaſy Thought, ſhe poſſeſs'd the moſt
deſerving Man alive; and I had loſt him
through a fooliſh Caprice of my own: I
could blame none but my ſelf for my ill
Fate ; I had not this relief to think he had
deſerv'd my Reſentments by any negleſt of
his; but, on the contrary, he was Faithful
and Generous, to an infinite degree. Thus
did I torment my ſelf all that Night, without
letting Sleep to cloſe my Eyes; tho' ſometimes, I was willing to flatter my ſelf, this
was a trick to try my Conſtancy, and by that
he might find if my Affeſtion anſwered his.
But alas! it was too true, for from a Letter
from *Cleomidon*, I receiv'd a Confirmation
of the Meſſage he had ſent; which contain'd theſe few words.

Cleomidon to *Lindamira*.

*I Have obey'd you, Madam, and am Mar-
ried to* Cleodora; *but with that Reluſtancy,
that it had been a generous Charity, to have
depriv'd me of my Life; when by the rigour
of your Commands, I gave my hand to Cleodora : But my Heart is ſtill yours, uſe it as
ſeverly as you pleaſe; for you can make no
addition to my preſent misfortune; for I am, of
all Men, the moſt miſerable; and the only
Comfort I can find, is that I have oblig'd my
cruel* Lindamira, *whom, in my Heart, I muſt
adore, whilſt Life remains in*

your Diſconſolate
Cleomidon.

I

I read this Letter with such Inquietudes of Mind, that I knew not what I read; nor could I believe, at firſt, that it was the hand of *Cleomidon*; but by often peruſing it, to my unſpeakable Grief, I knew my Doom, and that the Heart of this faithful Friend, belong'd to another, tho' he told me it was ſtill mine. It was a long time before I could reſolve what Anſwer to return. I wrote him twenty ſeveral Letters, before I pitch'd upon one I thought proper to ſend him; for ſtill my Pen would write ſo kind, and ſo ſenſible of his Grief, that I thought I ſhould commit a great Indiſcretion if I did not alter my Stile; ſo, at laſt, I concluded upon this Anſwer.

Lindamira to *Cleomidon.*

I will not endeavour to excuſe the rigour you accuſe me of, ſince Cleomidon has put himſelf out of the power of being mine. May my Wiſhes be propitious; and that in Cleodora, you may find more Happineſs than you expected : Look upon her as your Wife, and forget Lindamira, who merited not the Happineſs of being yours: But, in ſpight of my hard Deſtiny, I muſt eſteem what I once thought worthy of my Love. Adieu.

To

To this Letter he return'd an Anfwer, too kind for the Husband of *Cleodora*, but not for the Lover of *Lindamira*; but as fuch, I was to look upon him, therefore I concluded, that I ought not to fend him any more, left it fhould keep up the Flame, I wifh'd might be extinguifh'd in his Heart ; I only then fent a Meffage by *Iris*, to defire him to write no more, for I would not anfwer any Letters from him. This he refented unkindly, which, he faid, was an aggravation of his Grief ; for he propos'd fome Redrefs, by receiving thefe innocent Teftimonies of my Affection ; but he would fubmit to whatever I thought fit.

At the return of *Iris*, I was inform'd of the particulars of this Precipitate Refolution he took, and Executed : For when he parted from me, in his way home, he encountred *Alcander*, who oblig'd him to go along with him, which was to *Cleodora*'s Lodging; when he was there, the cruel *Lyndaraxa* fo craftily plaid her part, as to prevail with *Alcandar*, to refolve upon the Marriage the next Day betwixt her Niece and *Cleomidon*, who was then fo extreamly difcontented at my denial; as being pre-poffefs'd with an Opinion, I had a fecret Averfion to him, that he confented to the Propofal, without the leaft thought of having any fettlements made at his Marriage, as *Alcandar* had always promis'd him ; but blindly he obey'd him the next Morning, for which rafh Deed, he faid, he never could enough repent of.

About

About a Month after, in the same Family, an other Wedding was Celebrated, which was that of *Alcander* with *Lyndaraxa*, who, by her cunning and insinuation, had so flatter'd the Old Gentleman, as to perswade him to marry her ; for she had deep designs in what she did : For tho' *Alcander* was of a Covetous Temper, yet he would have been just to his Word, had not *Lyndaraxa* influenced his mind so far, as to make him forget the Duty *Cleomidon* paid him.

At another time, this Disappointment in his Uncles Marriage, would have been a great Affliction to him ; but his Soul was so ruffled and disturbed, at what could not be remedied, that he seemed not the least disgusted at it ; but made what haste he could out of Town ; for in the Country he could better conceal his Discontents from his Friends, then when he was continually amonst them. I will leave him there for two Years in the enjoyment of his *Cleodora*, who had no reason to be dissatisfied with him ; for he treated her with great Civility and Respect. I heard by some Gentlemen of that Country, that he was grown extream melancholy, and did not much care for Company : He walked much alone, and Books were his greatest Entertainment.

A little before the departure of *Cleomidon*, you, my dear *Indamora*, came to Town with the amiable *Lucretia*, from whom I have received a thousand Obligations, which I dispair of requiting. It was through your perswasions, I was

I   induced

induced to take that Journey into *Suſſex* with
Lucretia, and your ſelf: The agreeableneſs
of the place ſo inchanted me, that 'twas with
much regret I quitted ſuch ExcellentConverſa-
tion ſo ſoon, but you know, my Aunt, *Udotia*'s Mother, ſent for us up to Town, to be
at the Wedding of *Doraliſa*, her Eldeſt Daughter, of whoſe Virtues, till that time, I had
not much knowledge. I muſt confeſs; I was
loath to go, for your ſeaſonable Counſels
helpt to ſupport me, under the greateſt preſ-
ſures I then ſuſtained: But I ſaw no Remedy
but Patience, and that difficult Virtue I endeavoured to practice; the remembrance of
Cleomidon was ever preſent in my Thoughts;
He appeared to me more lovely than ever;
my Eſteem of him was equal to his Virtue.
I applied my ſelf to read Philoſophy; but
the Precepts of the Wiſe did not influence
my mind at all; for I found it impoſſible to
forget him, that had lov'd me even to Ido-
latry, and as great Souls are moſt capable of
a laſting Paſſion, I did not endeavour to oppoſe that inclination in my Heart, but did
reſolve to Love him eternally. Company
was troubleſome to me; and I renounced all
ſorts of Divertiſements for the pleaſure of
being alone, and of thinking on him: But
you, my *Indamora*, would not ſuffer me to
indulge my ſelf in ſo great a Melancholy;
and you argued ſo well againſt the ill effects
of thinking much, and of giving way to a
fruitleſs Repentance, that, at laſt, you made
me ſenſible, that we ought to ſubmit to
our

our lot; and that none were truly miferable,
that were not wanting to themfeves.

I left you then in *Suffex*, and came to *London*; my Aunt received me with all the kindnefs imaginable. I was much charm'd with
Doralifa, my Coufin, who had been come
out of *France* half a Year before, Her Humour was very lively and taking, and her
Converfation the moft agreeable in the
World ; fhe was fomething negligent in her
Drefs, which, I thought, made her appear
more Beautiful. Her Eyes are full of fweetnefs ; her Face is excellently well made, her
Skin of an admirable whitenefs; when fhe
fpeaks, fhe delights all that hear her ; for
what fhe fays, is full of Wit; but above all,
there is fomething in her Voice that is full of
Sweetnefs and Harmony.

You will not wonder, my *Indamora*, I took
an Affection for a Relation, fo very deferving,
who bore a part with me in all my Afflictions : She made me partly forget my Sorrows,
by her pleafant Converfation, fhe would entertain me with the Splendor and Magnificence of the *French* King, of his Amours,
and of the Gallantry of that Nation ; their
Politenefs and Acutenefs in Converfation ;
and made me an ingenuous Confeffion of a
Conqueft fhe had made of one of the greateft
Gallants of the Court ; and believing this
Digreffion will not be difpleafing to you)
fince nothing of moment happened to
me of a confiderable time) I will entertain
you with the Adventures of my Coufin, which
will

will ferve to pafs away your idle intervals in
the Country, which will be more diverting
than my own, wherein has been fo long a
fenfe of Melancholy, that in my next you
fhall have an account of her Amours, as faith-
fully as my memory can relate them,

But having finifhed that Part you fo much
defired to know, and by what ill Fate I became fo unhappy ; I have, my *Indamora*, given you an impartial account, both of my
Thoughts and Actions. I beg you will
have fome indulgence for me ; and tho' you
may juftly tax me with many Faults, yet I
know your kindnefs is fo generous, as not to
upbraid me with them, but, like a Friend, will
not defpife the fmall Prefent I have made
you, which, pray accept with the fame goodnefs, as you have ever done, whatever fell
from the Pen of, my deareft *Indamora*,

Your moft true

and faithful Servant,

Lindamira.

The Adventures of Doralifa, *and the pleafant Young Ovid.*

The XIVth. LETTER.

WHEN *Doralifa* went into *France,*fhe was in her feventeenth Year: She accompanied a Lady of confiderable Quality, and of great Reputation, to whofe Care fhe was committed by her Parents. She had not been long in *Paris,* but fhe was vifited by all the *Englifh* of any Fafhion; who were very Affiduous in fhewing her all the Diverfions, that mighty City afforded. Her Youth and Beauty foon made her be taken notice of: The *French* Ladies took much pleafure in her Company: And the bad *French,* fhe at firft fpoke, was exceeding pretty; but what by her Natural Sagacity, what by the influence of the beft Converfarie in few Months fhe become Miftrefs of Polite Language. As 'tis Natural to Love one better than another, fo *Doralifa* found in her Heart, a particular Efteem for a certain Lady, call'd *Corinna,* a very lovely Perfon, with whom fhe contracted a moft intimate Acquaintance. In her Company fhe

I 3 paft

paſt the greateſt part of her time; and *Co-rinna* being obliged to go to *Fountain-Bleau* for three Months, prevailed with *Doraliſa* to accompany her to this place; for, ſaid ſhe, it is the moſt delightful of any in *France*; it took its Name Originally from the fine Springs, that were accidentally diſcovered by one of the late Kings of *France*, who was charmed at the ſweetneſs of the Situation, that he built a ſtately Palace there; which, for the Magnificence of its Building, and fine Paintings, comes not much ſhort of any of the other Royal Structures. In the Park, which joyns to the fineſt of the Gardens, is a Fountain, which is called, *The Star*, by reaſon of ſeven Walks of high Elms, that proceed from it, which lead to ſeveral parts of the Park. This Place, continued *Corinna*, is ſo Romantick, that it raiſes the Curioſity of moſt Travelers to come from *Paris*, and fur-ther, to be witneſſes of what Fame has made ſo extravagantly pleaſant to them; they all agree, that it exceeds the beſt Deſcription was ever made of it: Therefore *Doraliſa*, ſaid *Corinna*, you muſt be witneſs of what has given ſo much ſatisfaction to all that have ſeen it: But that which adds to the Beauty of the Place, is the large Forreſt near the Town, which is ſo Rural, and withal, ſo Pleaſant, that ſome perſons pre-fer it to the Gardens, that are Cultivated, by all the Art imaginable. *Doraliſa* reply'd, That the happineſs of her Converſation was inducement enough to wait on her where-ever

ever fhe went; but fhe had received fo perfect an Idea of *Fountain-Bleau*, by the ingenious defcription fhe had given of it, that
fhe Figured to her felf, all that was delightful in that Place: But, faid *Corinna*, fmile-
ing, You will oblige me more than you imagine, by the enjoyment of your Company :
For that is the place where I firft took Breath,
and having fucked in that Air, I naturally affect it more than any place in *France*; therefore refolve upon this Journey, and let me
know if any place in *England* exceeds what
I fhall fhew you there. *Doralifa* could not
withftand her amiable Friend's Requeft, and
in few Days they took this pleafant Journey,
which was in the Month of *May*. The next
Day after their arrival, thefe two charming
Ladies went to view thefe Celebrated Gardens, the Grottoes, and the Fountains; and
Doralifa was extreamly delighted with the
Water-works, and admired the variety of
them: And within the Grotto, the Waters
fell from one Bafin to another, which made fo
melancholly a found, and yet fo pleafing, that
fhe thought her felf within an inchanted
Ifland; nor had fhe power to ftir, had not
Corinna forced her from thence, to take a
walk up to the Star-Fountain, which pleafed her beyond what fhe had feen yet; not
for the Beauty of the Fountain, but for thofe
feven fhady Walks of high Elmes that lead
from it, to feveral parts of the Park. Upon
the fide of this Fountain, thefe Ladies fate
them down to reft themfelves, and to ad-

I 4   mire

mire the excellent defign of all that they had
feen. I muft acknowledge, faid *Doralifa*,
that this furpaffes what I ever faw in *England*, and I think my time fo well recom-
penced for the pains I have taken in walking fo long, that I muft do juftice to *Fountain-
Bleau*, and I tell you, I think it the moft delightful and moft charming Place in the World.
But you have not feen all, faid *Corinna*, that
deferves your admiration, and that is the Palace of our great Monarch, which will merit
your Attention, in viewing the curious Paint-
tings in it.

At thefe words they rofe up, and went
into the firft Court, that leads to the front
of the Palace, where they beheld the Noble Defigns of the Architecture; but when
they entered this Magnificent Building, they
faw enough to admire. They paft into the
Galleries, where hung the Pictures of the
late Kings and Queens of *France*; as alfo,
the Portrait of the prefent King, the Dauphin, and Dauphinefs, and thofe of the moft
Celebrated Beauties of the Court, which
afforded to *Doralifa* a great deal of Delight,
who had a natural Genius to Painting, and
had fo much Skill to judge of how great
value they were, and being more knowing,
than moft Ladies are, could diftinguifh
Originals from Copies; that her Eyes were
never fatisfied, the more fhe looked, the more
fhe admired: But the obfcurity of the night
coming on, forced her to forfake a place,
that had fo charmed her Senfes. *Doralifa*
gave

gave her Friend a thoufand thanks for the Pleafures of that Evenings walk; and thefe two charming Beauties concluded upon pafling moft of their Evenings there; but were prevented by the fudden arrival of the Court of *France*, which was then extreamly Magnificent and Splendid, fo that *Doralifa*, unexpectedly, faw all that was rare in *France*, and the moft Celebrated Beauties of that time. We will fuppofe the Inhabitants of *Fountain-Bleau*, full of Joy for the arrival of their Monarch, and, in the midft of their Acclamations, I'll take leave of my dear *Indamora*, and am

Her moft faithful

Friend and Servant.

Lindamira.

The

The XVth. LETTER.

THE King, who seldom Honoured *Fountain-Bleau* with his Royal Presence, filled
his PeoplesHearts so full of Joy for his arrival,
that, they thought, they could never enough
express their satisfaction: And being informed the King, the next day, was gone to take
a walk in the Park, the Inhabitants flocked
thither in great numbers; and to shew their
Respect to their King, they all dressed themselves in their best Apparel, and made as
fine an appearance as they could. Amongst
this number was *Corinna*, and *Doralisa*, when
coming into the Park, they discovered, at a
distance, the King, and his Attendants a
walking, and being led on by their Curiosity,
they advanced towards the Fountain, where
they stood to expect the King, who, in another of the walks, was coming that way,
where they all waited for his arrival. When
His Majesty was arrived at the Fountain, he
was pleased to make a stop to shew himself to his People, who made their Obedience
to him, and he seemed much pleased to behold the multitude of People that was flocked thither to see him. Amongst the Crowd,
were a great many young Ladies, who had
placed themselves next to the Fountain, to
have

have a better view of the King, who was
pleafed to take a particular notice of them;
for, 'tis well known, he is no Enemy to the
Fair Sex, and having obferved them all, he,
at laft, fixed his Eyes on *Doralifa*, and preceiv-
ing fhe was not a Native of the Place (for her
Complexion far exceeded any there) it excited a Curiofity in him to know who fhe
was, and turning to one of the Lords of his
Retinue, demanded who *Doralifa* was, and
of what Country? But he not being able to
fatisfie His Majefty, made enquiry of fome
that ftood by; and all the information he
could get, that fhe was called, *La belle An-
gloife*: The King feemed much pleafed with
the innocence of her looks, and her modeft
Countenance, and faid to thofe that were
near him, *That if the Ladies of* England *were
all fo handfome as* Doralifa, *their conquefts
would exceed thofe of their Monarch over his
Enemies.* But the King fixed his Eyes fo
much on her, that all that perceived him,
looked on her, to admire what took up his
attention fo much; which, *Doralifa* perceiving, it made her Blufh, and fhe modeftly
withdrew from the Company.

Corinna faid a thoufand pleafant things,
to her upon this Adventure, telling her, her
Beauty would get her Enemies, as well as
Friends; for fhe could affure her there was a
Lady at the Court, that would be very
jealous of her, did fhe know what notice the
King took of her, which would be a Secret,
to her no longer, then till the news could be
brought

brought to her; to which *Doralifa* replied, *That her Charms were not capable of raifing Jealoufie, efpecially in the Breafts of the* French *Ladies, who, generally, had two much Wit to affift themfelves with what might never happen.* But tell me, faid *Doralifa,* when I fhall fee the fair *Bellamira,* in whofe praife you have fpoke fo much, that I am become impatient for a fight of that amiable Perfon ? We will go to morrow, replied *Corinna,* and I fhall oblige *Bellamira* in bringing her fo fair a Vifitant, and you will find her very Careffing and Obliging,

The next day thefe too agreeable Friends went to pay their Service to *Bellamira,* who received them with equal Refpect ; and *Corinna* prefented *Doralifa* to her, as a Perfon worthy of her Friendfhip ; for, faid fhe, Madam, this *Englifh* Lady is one whom I infinitely efteem, and whofe agreeable Qualities have fo indear'd me to her, that I could not refolve upon this Journey till I had prevailed with *Doralifa* to accompany me in it, which, I'm certain, fhe cannot repent of, fince I've procured her the fight of the Charming *Bellamira,* and your Friendfhip I alfo defire, as a Recompence of the favour fhe has done me. To which *Bellamira* reply'd, *That fhe fhould readily obey her ; for fhe found an inclination in her Soul to Love that Charming Lady ; but fince fhe was her Friend, fhe had an Obligation upon her to Love what fhe thought worthy.* Doralifa was fo charmed with the Obligingnefs of thefe two Ladies,

that

that fhe wanted words to exprefs her Gratitude, and Senfe of their Favours. And after thefe Compliments were paft, *Bellamira*
demanded of *Doralifa*, if fhe had feen the
Palace, and the appartment of the King and
Dauphin. *Doralifa* reply'd. *That fhe had
been over a great part of the Palace; but there
yet remained a larger part of this ftately
Building fhe had not yet feen.* If you pleafe
then, faid *Bellamira*, let me have the Honour to fhew you what remains, and I will
alfo procure you the fight of the King's
Clofet, wherein are Rarities of an ineftimable value. *Doralifa* readily accepted of
this offer, and fuffered her felf to be conducted by *Bellamira*. This fair Troop then
went firft to fee the King's Clofet, which
gave them caufe enough for their admiration; from thence they paft through feveral
Appartments, and came into the Stone-Gal-
lery, which leads to the Garden of Orange-
Trees: *Bellamira* defired them to obferve
how the Marble Stones of the Gallery were
difcoloured with Blood, in feveral places,
which the Art of Man could not wafh out;
for the Blood that is unjuftly fpilt, faid fhe,
will remain to perpetuate the memory of
the Murderer: Thefe words raifed a Curiofity in *Doralifa* to know the caufe of
it, which *Bellamira* acquainted her, was
done by the command of theQueen of *Sweed-
land*,to oneof her own Domefticks,whom fhe
thought worthy of her juft Refentments, and
caufed him there to be Shot to Death, whilft
fhe

fhe ftood by to fee him Executed: But
the particulars of it is in Print, which
makes me run it over fo briefly, and therefore. I believe, not unknown to your felf.

From thence they went into the Garden of
Orange-Trees, where once happened a Scene
of Mirth, which Bellamira promifed to acquaint them with : As foon as Doralifa had
furveyed the Garden, and beheld in what
order it was kejst, and her Sence of Smel-
ling fo gratified, with \he Odoriferous Scents
of Orange-Flowers and Jeffamin, that fhe
turned about to her two Companions, and
told them, fhe thought this fo delicious a
Place, that fhe could refemble it to nothing
fo much as to Cupid's Garden,he prepared to
entertain his fair Pfyche in : Others have been
of your Mind, reply'd Bellamira; but, if
you pleafe, you fhall fee thofe excellent
Pieces of the greateft Statuaries of their
Time, which fhe fhewed to thefe Ladies ;
but made them obferve a Marble Pedeftal ;
whereon was no Statue; but had on it once,
one of the faireft in the World : By what,
accident is it not there now, faid Doralifa?
You muft know, faid Bellamira, that one
Summer, when the Court was here, two of
the Ladies of the Queens Bed-Chamber,
took up an humour of walking here every
Evening, which they fpent in the admiration of thofe moft famous Artifts, that had
made thefe Statues you fee. They pretended to have much Judgment and Skill in true
Shape, and Proportion , and thought they
had

as much knowledge as the Artifts themfelves; this being their conftant Diverfion
in an Evening; there was a Young Cavalier of
the Court who defigned to play thefe Ladies a
Trick, which he thus Executed : One Night
he placed himfelf on the Pedeftal you fee,
in the pofture of a Mercury, with his Right
Hand extended out, and his Left Leg raifed
up, as if he was upon fome great Expedition to the Gods : Thus was he placed when
thefe Ladies paft by, and perceiving a
new Statue Erected, they made a ftop to
behold, what, to their Eyes appeared more
rare than any of the others. One of the
Ladies, who was named *Paulina*, made great
Acclamations of wonder, that any thing of
Art could imitate Nature fo well, and fo
much to the Life, faying, That never was a
truer proportion feen, and Limbs fo exactly
fine, and a Body fo exquifitely well made !
Ah! Mademeoifelle, faid *Lucina*, look on this
Face, and there you'll fee caufe for the admiration; fee how much Life there is in
thofe Eyes, what a noble mien he has,
How much Spirit appears through the lines
of that Face, which, to me, feems the moft
Charming of any thing Living I ever faw ! In
fine, faid *Paulina*, I never faw any thing fo
admirable, fo delicate, and fo much to the
Life, as this Mercury.

As they were thus employ'd in the Contemplation of their Mercury, the Spark being tired with ftanding fo long in one Pofture he gently lets fall his Leg to reft himfelf.

felf, which the Ladies perceiving, they
thought it had been a Spirit, and being extreamly furprized at this Adventure, they
ran away, and fcreech'd fo loud, that the
Court was in an uproare, and imagin'd fome
Perfon had been murdered. The Spark, who
apprehended the Confequences of their fcree-
ches, and loud Cries, leaps from the Pe-
diftal, and ran after them, to convince them
he was no Spirit, which they perceiving, redoubled their Cries and their Speed, and
came running into the Gallery like two Furies, but were not able to fpeak a word their
aftonifhment was fo great. In the mean time
fome Gentlemen had the Curiofity to go
into the Garden, to find out the caufe of this
out-cry, which they foon difcovered, by
meeting the Chevalier *de B* —— behind an
Orange-Tree, who was fo afhamed and con-
founded at this unlucky Accident, that, of a
long time, he was not able to fpeak to make
his Defence for this Frolick ; but his generous
Friends took pity on him, and caufed a Cloak
to be brought to cover him, and fo conducted
him a back way to his own Appartment,
where, after he had recovered the Vexation,
this Adventure had put him into, he gave
a moft pleafant Relation of the praifes the
Ladies had given him, and what Excellencies
they had difcovered in his Shape and Proportion, which he recounted fo agreeable, that
he afforded to his Friends, a great deal of
Diverfion, which they had to his Coft ; and,
after this Accident, nothing was talked of
but

but the Beau-Mercury. But this unhappy
difcovery' of the Chevalier *de* B —— caufed him much difgrace; for the Ladies were
fo malicious as to complain of him, that
had given them fo much fatisfaction, and
obtained of the King, that he might be
Banifhed from the Court, highly Exaggera-
ting the boldnefs of the Action, as being
committed in His Majefty's Garden Therefore Young *Mercury* tacitely withdrew;
and, in his abfence, his Friends interceeded
fo happily for him, that they procured
his pardon of the King; and after two
Months Exile, he returned Triumphant over
the Caufers of his Difgrace. The Ladies
were fo concerned at his good Fortune, that
they withdrew from the Court, for they
could not endure the fight of him : But they
repented of it afterwards; for fome New
Adventure happened foon after, which always drives the latter out of Remembrance :
For in Courts, where Love and Gallantry
are fo much practifed, as in the Court of
France, there never wants for News.

Bellamira having finifhed her Narration,
her two Charming Friends returned her
thanks for the Entertainment fhe gave them,
and went away very much fatisfied with
what they had heard and feen, and, at parting, made an agreement to be at *Bellamira's*
Appartment the next Evening, who had
promis'd to procure a Friend, that fhould

K   introduce

introduce them into the King's Prefence,
when he was at Supper ; for which Favour
Bellamira received a thoufand Thanks, and
fo they parted, and betook themfelves to
their Beds, where I will leave them to enjoy their pleafing Dreams ; and muft hope
from my *Indamora*'s Goodnefs, a Pardon for
my Inabilities in defcribing the Ginius of
thefe *French* Ladies, for the little Converfation I have had with thofe of that Nation
(more than what was requifite for my learning of the Language) I hope will atone for my
Fault, and that you will accept of this im-
perfect Relation from

Your

Lindamira.

The XVIth. LETTER.

THE time of Affignation being come, *Doralifa* and *Corinna* went to the Appartment of *Bellamira* , who impatiently waited their Arrival, and imbracing them both; my Charming Friends, faid fhe, none but your felves can judge what Inquietudes I have fuffered in your Abfence; that if I am as far advanced in your Efteem, as you are both in mine, you may apprehend what 'tis to be feparated from thofe one Loves. Her too Friends replied, *That their Sentiments were the fame, and had come fooner then the appointed Hour, had not Company prevented them.* Soon after, came in the Marquis of L ——— who was allied to *Bellamira*, and from him expeded the Conduct of thefe Ladies to the Palace of the King. The Young Marquis teftified, both by his Words and Actions, how great an honour it was to him. After fome Difcorufe of indifferent things, they fell upon that of Love and Gallantry : The Marquis, who was the moft accomplifh'd Man in the Court, and was Natutally very Amorous, faid many pleafant things upon this Subject. His Nature was Brisk, Airy and Facetious : For his Fluent, Natural, eafy Wit, he was cal-

led

led the Young *Ovid*, and was known more
by that Name, that by his Title: He had
an admirable Genius to Poetry, and his
Compositions of that kind, were of so Happy, so Polite, so peculiar a Character, and
withal, so excellent a Judgment, that few
could equal him ; and *Bellamira*, who knowing his admirable Talent that way, intreated
him to repeat some of his Verses to her two
amiable Friends, which the Marquis modestly refused at first ; but seeing the Ladies
would be Obeyed, he repeated some Verses
in imitation of *Virgil*, which he performed with an admirable Grace ; and *Corinna*
(who never yet discovered her Genius that
way) gave him such Praises, that let the
whole Company see her Wit and Judgment ;
and finding she was very Conversant in all
forts of Poetry, he desired the Honour of
hearing some of hers, and used so much Im-
prestment, that *Corinna* could not refuse the
Marquis what he desired, and repeated to
him a Copy of Verses upon the Tyranny of
Love, and another upon Jealousie, wherein
she discovered much delicacy of Thought ;
the Stile was, Noble, Lofty, and Natural.

Thus did these two Wits entertain the
Company ; and *Doralisa* told *Corinna*, she
never knew she had a faculty that way ;
and asked her most obligingly , why she
never entertained her with some of her Poetry, for she was a great lover of it ? She
gave her this Reason, *That she durst never in-*
dulge

dulge the Humour of *Verſifying*, for *fear*
of the Cenſure that attends Poets, who are
ſuppoſed to attribute a Power to Mortals, that
belongs only to the Divinity, eſpecially
when they pay Incenſe to the fair Ones they
adore.

Ah! Madam, ſaid *Ovid*, how great a So-
læciſm would it be both in a Lover and a
Poet, if he did not look upon his Miſtreſs,
as the ſublimeſt Object of his Thoughts ;
and they that declaim againſt Love, or his
Power, are not worthy to know it ; and
there is even a Pleaſure in thoſe diſquiet-
ing Amours, that are ſo much complained
of ; and the Honour of being Captivated
by a Lady of Wit, and bearing the glorious
Title of her Servant , does ſufficiently
recompence the Diſquiets that her Rigour
ſometimes cauſes : Since one Smile, or a
kind Look reſtores the Lover to his former
Tranquillity of Mind. You ſpeak ſo feelingly, ſaid *Bellamira*, as if you had Experienced the Rigour of ſome Fair One : But 'tis
not to be doubted, but that ſhe has repented
of her two great Severity, ſince you can ſo
well deſcribe the Joyes that one Smile can
give. I cannot deny, Madam, ſaid *Ovid*,
but that I have known the Joys, the Rap-
tures, the Hopes and Fears, and all the
Paſſions that attend a Lover, by my own
Experience : And yet I do not wiſh to have
my Heart free from the Torments of Love ;
for Love has ſomething of Pleaſure in it :
'Tis the Soul of Life, it quickens the Ap-

prehenſion,

prehenfion , makes a Man Lively , Brisk and Airy, notwithftanding the uneafy intervals that wait on it ; and Charming *Corinna*, faid he, turning towards her, I am in Love with your Poetry , with *Doralifa's* Modefty; and with *Bellamira's* great Bounty, in fuffering fo long my Converfation, and being all Ladies of Wit and Beauty, I know not on which to fix my Heart ; but if you would give me leave to Love you all, I would be a conftant admirer, and confine my Love to the narrow limits of three. You give fuch a pleafant Defcription of the inconftancy of your Humour, replied *Bellamira*, that 'tis no Glory to be the Miftrefs of *Ovid*, tho' it muft be a fatisfaction to be Loved by a perfon of fo much Wit ; and if thefe Ladies can content themfelves with part of your Heart, I'll be content to divide with them ; For my part, faid *Corinna*, I fear I fhall be Jealous of my two fair Rivals, that they will go away with the greateft fhare of it ; And I had rather have no part at all- faid *Doralifa*, and Smiled, than fhare it with two fuch dangerous Rivals, which I can as ill bear in my Love as a Monarch on his Throne ; therefore I will excufe the Marquis from being in Love with me, or of making any Songs or Verfes on me, being a Theam not worthy of fo great a Wit. You wrong your Judgment, Madam, replied *Ovid*, For what Theam can be more fublime, than that of the Fair ? And fince I love to be fincere, I find an inclination in my
Soul

Soul moſt to be yours. 'Tis then in oppoſi-
tion to thoſe Ladies Vertues, ſaid *Doraliſa*,
or to the humour I have not to accept of a
Heart by halves : You ſhall then have all,
ſaid *Ovid* jocoſely, if theſe Ladies will render
back what they have in their Power, and ſo
ſhew what Power your Beauty can produce :
You ſhall Reign Soveraign in my Heart, till
ſuch time that you are tired with the Sover-
aignty, or I with your Arbitary Power.

Theſe Ladies made themſelves exceeding
Merry at the indifferent Humour of the Marquis, and railly'd him ſo wittily, that he
was almoſt at a non-plus how to defend
himſelf againſt their attacks ; but he told
them they were all ſo Charming, ſo Amiable,
and ſo Agreeable, that if he did not depart
from them, he ſhould not have one bit of his
Heart left to throw at the next fair One he
met ; but if they would accept of it amongſt
them, it ſhould be at their Service. They
all thanked him for the Nobleneſs of the
Preſent ; but he being ſo indifferent on whom
he beſtowed it, they thought he had beſt keep
the Jewel for his own wearing. At this the
Marquis roſe up and was going away with a
ſmall fragment of his Heart, when *Bellamira* reproached him with what he had pro-
miſed the Ladies, who had undertaken to
Conduct them into the King's Preſence : But
he excuſed his ill Memory, and beg'd their
Pardon, that he ſhould forget to pay them
that Service he came to render them. It being time to be gone ; he led this Fair Troop

to the King's Appartment, and placed *Doralifa* where fhe might have the beft fight of
this great Monarch. The King no fooner
caft his Eyes on her, but he remembred he
had feen her at the *Star Fountain* ; and fhe
being a ftranger at the place, His Majefty,
in a great Compliment, prefented her with
a Plate of the fineft Sweetmeats there, which
particular Favour· was received with a very
graceful Action from *Doralifa*, and her Beauty
was then more taken notice of than before,
and that Day proved a Day of great Conquefts, which procured her the Envy of fome
of the greateft Beauties of the Court.

As foon as Supper was ended, thefe Ladies
retired to *Corinna*'s Appartment, where they
fpent the reft of the Evening in relating what
they had feen, and the Honour the King did
Doralifa, was fubject enough for Difcourfe.
But, all on a fudden, the Marquis became
very Dull and Penfive ; and *Bellamira* demanding the caufe of fo great an Alteration,
he, with a terrible Sigh, replied, *That he
was become the moft Amorous Man in the World,
and did believe, not any Loved with fo violent a Paffion as himfelf* ; *for he was already
Jealous, Fearful and Miftruftful.* Thefe Ladies diverted themfelves at his Difcourfe, and
told him, his ferious Humour did not become him fo well as his indifferent one. But,
faid the Marquis, turning towards *Doralifa*,
*Do you believe, Madam, that a Man loaded
with Chains, can Walk, Speak, or Look with
that freedom as when his Shackles were off ?*
No,

No, my Charming Fair (continued he) *you have not only Fettered me, but involved me in such a Labirynth of Love, that I know not when I shall be able to unwind my self, and get my freedom again ; for I already find I would not shake off your Fetters, and had rather Die than cure my Mind ; And all the frightful Visions of Love, of Dispairs and Jealousies, cannot divert my Thoughts of being eternally yours.* The Marquis spoke this so seriously, that all the Company Laugh'd at him, and begged of him to put off his Disguise, and become the same pleasant *Ovid* he was a few Hours before, and not the dull Lover, which did not suite his pleasant Humour ; but he only answered them with Sighs, and became so altered, that they feared he was become a Lover indeed : And *Bellamira* finding he could not assume his former pleasant Humour, took leave of the Company, and the Marquis Conducted her to her Appartment ; but had agreed, before they parted, to meet the next Evening at the Star, from thence to take what Walks suited best with their Inciination. Thus did this fair Company separate, as Night always parts good Friends, and at their next meeting you shall here more of

Your real Friend,

and Servant

Lindamira.

The

The XVIIth. LETTER.

THE next Evening; the Marquis was the firſt that appeared at the Fountain, where he attended the arrival of this fair Troop ; but *Doraliſa* had ſo wholly taken up his Thoughts, that he negleƈted anſwering a ſmall Billet before he parted from his Lodging : He being there all alone, and in a place ſo proper to entertain his Thoughts, and vent his Sighs, did often repeat the Name of *Doraliſa*; Oh! my adorable Maid, ſaid he, my Charming Beauty, were I ſo bleſt to be beloved by thee, my heart would have a Joy too great to receive increaſe! But how can I hope to mollifie 'a Heart already (perhaps) prepoſſeſt with ſome violent Paſſion? Have I not ſhewn that indifference to her , that will give her an Opinion I am incapable of Love ? And ſhe will think ſo poorly of my Love, that I ſhall want a thouſand Oaths and Vows to confirm her in what I ſay : But why, I know not; My Soul is ſo perplexed with Jealouſies and Fears, that I already ſuffer a Martyrdom ? She ſeemes to me ſo wond'rous Fair, ſo full of Charms and Innocence, that in my Extravagance of Love, I ſhall grow troubleſome, and dread every Look ſhe gives another.

other. Thus was the Marquis entertaining
of himself, when he was surprized by *Bellamira*, who was the next arrived, and over-
hearing some broken speeches, and seeing a
disorder in his Looks, confirmed her in the
belief, that he was really become amorous
of *Doralisa*; and accosting him with a Smile,
well, Monsieur le Marquis, said she, I am
of Opinion, you are become the slave of
Doralisa, instead of the Lover of us all three.
What are your Sentiments changed already?
and have you forgot you throwed your Heart
at us all? And must *Doralisa* be the *Venus*
that must go away with the Prize? And must
the *French* Beauties yield to the *English*
one? No, no, continued *Bellamira*, we shall
begin a Quarrel with you, and call your
Judgment in question; these latter words
she spoke with so serious an Air, that the
Marquis seemed much concerned he had dis-
obliged so amiable a Friend as *Bellamira*;
for whom he had a great Esteem and Friendship, and was about to make his peace with
her, when she prevented him, in saying, *That
she only Raillied him; and that she must allow
his Judgment unquestionale, since he had prefer'd* Doralisa's *Beauty before hers, or* Corinna's. The Marquis seemed over-joyed to
find her Sentiments so obliging; and he
freely acknowledged to her, that he adored
that Charming Lady, and Petitioned her
Assistance in the accomplishment of his Happiness; which *Bellamira* promised to the
utmost of her Power: And soon after an
opportunity

opportunity offered it's felf; for the other
two were far advanced into the Walk
before they were perceived. Come, Mon-
fieur, faid *Bellamira*, let us go meet your adorable *Doralifa*, and let her know, from
your own Mouth, how great a Miracle is
wrought in her Favour beyond us all; that
fhe has made a Slave of the moft Gallant,
and moft Accomplifhed Man in our Court.

The Encounter of this Hero, with *Doralifa*, feemed extream pleafant to the other
two; for as formerly there appeared a Joy
in his Eyes, a Tranquillity in his Mind, he
became Chagrine and Melancholly, and his
ferious looks fate fo ill upon him, that *Doralifa* pleafantly reproached him for the
ftrange Metamorphofe of his Soul, and wifhed him to affume his former Gaiety; for,
faid fhe, you cannot be good Company with
that difmal Countenance, you have fo affected. Did you but know, faid *Bellamira*,
the agitations of his Soul, you would not
thus rallie your Slave; for the Marquis has
made me the Confident of his Paffion, and
you, fair *Doralifa*, have robbed us of our
Hopes. The Marquis added to thefe words
all that a violent Paffion could infpire him,
and fpoke fo ferioufly, and ufed fuch inforcing Arguments, that *Doralifa* was forced to yield to her Reafon, in this Opinion, that
he had a real Affection for her. She received the marks of his Efteem as an Honour
to her; and, in the moft obliging terms imaginable, returned her acknowledgement;
but

but our Lover told her, he would have her alter the word acknowledgement to one more ravifhing and more fublime. What is that, faid *Doralifa*, that can be more pleaſing? 'Tis Love, Madam, replied the Marquis, and that Mufical found would ravifh my Soul, to have it fpoke by fo fair a Mouth as *Doralifa*'s! They continued walking and Difcourfing thus, for an Hour; and the Marquis, who had a Wit the moft refined of any Man living, faid fo many Endearing and Paffionate Things to *Doralifa*, that fhe, at laft, yielded he fhould own his Paffion for her: For, faid he, Madam, I not only make you a Prefent of my Heart, but I will not conceal the leaft thing in it, for I think it a Treafon in Love, not to be pardoned, to hide from the Perfon Loved, what ever they know, or think. This Evening feemed to the Marquis the moft delightful of any in his Life ; and tho' he was become a Prifoner of Love, his Chains were not heavy to him ; for he enjoyed all the fatiffaction imaginable. He Loved a perfon infinitely Charming, was Fair and Vertuous ; fhe ufed him with Refpect ; and he had hopes, that fhe one Day might be his: For he had a Fortune to make her Happy ; but as yet, only beg'd leave to adore her. For two Months did he pafs his time in the agreeable Converfation of thefe Ladies; and received from *Doralifa*, a Confiormation of her Efteem and Friendfhip,

But

But, as the Joys of Lovers are not lasting,
so it proved to the poor Marquis, who, according to his usual Custom, attended the
King's Levè , and one Morning, as soon as
His Majesty was Dreſt, he retired into his
Closet, and Commanded the Marquis to follow him ; as soon as he appeared, the King,
in a very obliging manner, told him, That
he designed to make him Lieutenant General
of his Forces, and that he must prepare to
to depart in ten Dayes ; and added, That
he knew none, in his Court, that could ac-
quit themselves so well as himself ; for
both his Courage and Fidelity had been tried.
This News was like a Thunderbolt to his
Heart; but he diſſembled his Trouble as well
as poſſible he could, and gave His Majesty
thanks for the Honour he did him ; and tho'
it was with Reluctancy, he accepted this
Commiſſion, yet durſt he not refuſe it. The
Marquis made his Obeiſance to the King,
and went ſtrait to *Bellamira*, to Communicate, to that Charming Friend, his Griefs
and Vexations. He complained to her of the
ſeverity of his Deſtiny ; for, ſaid he, I never
knew how to Love till now, I have made a
mock of that blind ¦Deity, and defied his
Power : But now, I find, he has revenged
himſelfe of my Inſenſibility ; and I am forced to depart from her that has poſſeſt my
Heart, my Soul, and all my Thoughts. *Bellamira* heard his Complaints with much Sorrow , for ſhe had a real Eſteem for him.
What think you, Monſieur le Marquis, ſaid
ſhe,

fhe, have you not fome Enemies at Court,
that have thought of this Expedient to remove you from His Majefty ? No, no, *Bellamira*, faid he, no Enemies would feek my
Preferment ; but 'tis only to His Majefty,
that I am indebted for this Honour, who,
doubtlefs, admires the Fair *Doralifa*, and is
become my Rival : Thefe furmifes of yours,
faid *Bellamira*, are ill grounded, and he may
admire the Beauty of *Doralifa*, and not Love
her : But confefs the Truth, continued fhe,
and fmiled, have you not writ Verfes and
Panegyricks on the Beauty of the Fair *Honoria* ? and have you not entertained her after fo gallant a manner, as to perfwade her
you were in Love with her ? 'Tis true, faid
Ovid, I have profeft much Gallantry in all
my Actions, and was kind to her , as I was
to the reft of the fair Sex ; but, I am certain, I never Loved any but *Doralifa* ; but
what does this import to my Departure,
Charming *Bellamira* ? O ! very much , replied fhe, for this incenfed Beauty is become
jealous of *Doralifa* ; and, to my knowledge,
is grown very Melancholy fince you have
owned your Love to the fair One you adore,
that fhe is hardly knowable. She Converfes
with very few ; and her moft intimate
Friend is *Angellina*, who, you know, has
a great Power with the King : With her
fhe fometimes fpends whole Evenings, when
her Royal Lover is not there ; and, my O-
pinion is, that fhe defpairing of a Happinefs
you would beftow on *Doralifa*, has bethought
her

her felf of this Revenge, that her Rival may
be as miferable as her felf, if poſſible. That
cannot be, faid the Marquis, if *Doralifa* can
but Love like me ; tho' long Abfences are
hard to bear ; yet if a Miſtreſs Loves, and
is Sincere, Faithful and Conſtant, the hopes
of feeing her again, makes one endure a
thoufand other misfortunes, and does excite
Courage in a Man, that he may do a brave
Action, worthy of the Honour of being her
Slave : But, to bear this feparation, I ſtand
in need of all my Courage, Fortune and Patience : But, after a long and fruitleſs Complaint, the Marquis left *Bellamira*, and went
to feek his Confolation in the fweet Converſation of *Doralifa* and *Corinna*, to whom
he related this News, which extreamly furprized and grieved them both ; and till this
Accident, *Doralifa* did not think ſhe had
more then Eſteem and Friendſhip for the
Marquis ; which he perceiving, Ah ! my a-
dorable *Doralifa*, faid he, am I fo happy to
have you partake in my Sorrows ? Can a Beauty, ſo Divine,mix her Griefs with mine ? This
is Raviſhing beyond all my hopes, and yet
it is but Juſtice, my *Doralifa* ſhould fym-
pathize with me, that pay her fo awful
an Adoration. *Doralifa* then did no longer
fcruple to own the perplexity of her Soul,
and told the Marquis, that ſhe ſhould fuffer
no lefs than he, in rhis cruel Abfence : But
the Eſteem ſhe had for him, ſhe would preferve entirely, or till fuch time that he had
forgot her ; but thefe words drew from his
Mouth-

Mouth a thoufand Imprecations, and Vows
of eternal Fidelity.

But, during this fhort time, the Marquis
had at *Fountain-Bleau*, he dedicated all his
time to *Doralifa*, and neglected fome Bufinefs of Importance ; but fo much fhe did
imploy his Thoughts, that this fair One
reign'd fole Emprefs in his Heart. All the
Evenings were generally paft away in the
Park, or Gardens, in the Company of his
adored Miftrefs, and her agreeable Companions, where he would bid a thoufaud Adieus
to thofe confcious Scenes of his moft faithful
Love. To the Trees, Rocks and Fountains,
did he bid an eternal Farewel, that fometimes
one would think that Love had quite Diftracted him. The time of his feparation
drew near, and he had but two Nights more
to pafs at *Fountain-Bleau*. When, one E-
vening, as he was in Company of thefe
Charming Ladies, a Page prefented him with
a Letter, faying, he waited his Anfwer ;
the Marquis retreating too or three Steps,
opened the Letter, and found thefe words.

I *Am driven to the laft Extremity, that am
forced to tell the infenfible Marquis, I
Love him a thoufand times more than my own
Soul ; and 'twere a Blefling to me to be deprived of this wretched Life, that I could no longer
fee the happinefs of my Rival. How many
times have I feen you walking with her, and
whifpering to her all the kind things your
Paffion could infpire? Judge then how it*

L   *wrecks*

wracks my Soul to behold her felicity, whilst I,
poor miserable I, have no Redress, but to my
Tears. Return, return, ungrateful Man,
and render back that Heart that only belongs
to me ; for it was first given to me, and in
exchange, I gave you mine! Say that it was
my own precipitate Inclination that seduced me,
yet it was your good Humour that Charmed
me ; and what is the effects of this, but Sighs
and Tears, and tormenting Disquiets ; nay,
and the worst of Deaths a Jealousie, insup-
portable ! Adieu

Honoria.

This Letter gave the Marquis great Difturbance ; but he called up all his Courage,
and turning to the Page, told him, he would
wait on *Honoria.* After this difpatch, he
made up to the Ladies, who expected his
Return, and *Doralifa* exprefs'd great inquietudes, fearing it was a Challenge he had received (tho' fhe apprehended none upon her
own account) but he being fo general an admirer of the Sex, fhe knew not what to imagine, and asked him, moft obligingly, if it
was good News : No bad, faid the Marquis,
and fmil'd, for the fair ones are too good
Natured to hurt thofe that pay them that
Refpect, their Merits claim from us. What
do you mean by thefe words, faid *Bellamira,*
has *Honoria* fent you that Billet? Why do
you guefs *Honoria,* faid the Marquis ? For
thofe Reafons I have formerly told you, reply'd *Bellamira,* and therefore conceal no
longer

longer from us what is no fecret ; and being
over-come by their intreaty, he promis'd to
fhew the Letter, provided they would not
fpeak of it : For he thought it beneath a
Man of Honour to boaft of Favours from
the fair Sex. They all promifed him fecrefy,
and then produced this Letter, that fo much
afflicted him, not being in a capacity of re-
taliating the kindnefs *Honoria* exprefs'd for
him : He prefented the Letter to *Doralifa*,
faying, that he never imagin'd his indifferent
way of making Love to *Honoria*, would
have produced thefe Effects : For he did believe fhe had Wit enough to take all in Ra-
illiery he had faid : For tho' he thought her
Fair, Witty and Agreeable , he 'n'ere had
more then Efteem for her. But *Doralifa* reproach'd him with the Inconftancy of his
Humour, and told him, the next new Face
he faw would drive her out of his Remembrance, and that fhe muft expect the fame
fate of *Honoria*, to whom, fhe thought, he
ought to go and make his peace before his
Departure : But fhe fpoke this in fuch a tone,
that let the Marquis fee he was not indifferent to her ; which extorted from him
Vows of Fidelity, and that his never Dying Paffion fhould continue to the laft Period of his Life. However, this Adventure
gave him fo much Difturbance, that he ftood
in need of all his Courage to bear up his
great Heart againft the reproaches of a Lady-
of *Honoria*'s Humour ; but being commanded by *Doralifa* to wait on her, he left this

agreeable

agreeable Company in the Garden, to go to
one, whom he had a mortal Averfion for.
But the Melancholly that appeared in *Doralifa's* Eyes, teftified to her too Fair Companions, that the Marquis was the caufe of
it; and that the Hazzards of War, made her
to apprehend much danger for him : But
fhe received from thefe Ladies, all the Confolation fhe was capable of; and whilft they
entertained themfelves on this Subject, the
Difconfolate *Honoria*, had, before her Eyes,
nothing but Difpairs and Jealoufies; and
the cruel Thoughts of the infenfible *Ovid*,
filled her fond Soul with fo much Grief,
that fhe often called on that kind Tyrant
Death, to take her from her reftlefs Bed ;
or that her faithlefs Charmer would come
Pofting to her, and bring her the welcome
Tidings of his eternal Love. Whilft thus
her Thoughts were bufied with his Ingratitude , the unhappy Marquis enter'd her
Chamber, with diforder, both in his Looks
and Steps, approached this incenfed Beauty,
who was fo buried in her Grief, that fhe
heard him not, till he had approached her
Bed ; the fight of him awakened in her all
her juft Refentments (for fhe thought her
felf difhonour'd to be abandon'd for *Doralifa)* that Anger took place of her Love, and
fhe rofe up from off her Bed, and Darting
flafhes of Anger from her Eyes, are you
come, faid fhe, to reproach my Weaknefs,
for having two much Love for an infenfible
and ungrateful Man ? Or are you come to
tell

tell me you will Abandon *Doralifa* for me?
Madam, faid the Marquis, I come in Obedience to your Commands, not to reproach
the Fair, nor to tell you I can alter my Sentiments for *Doralifa*. She hardly gave him
leave to bring out thefe words, but re-affum-
ing a fierce Look, and a fhrill Voice, fhe
told him, *That his Infenfibility fhould be rewarded, and that he fhould find the effects of
her Indignation*. The Marquis was about
to juftifie his Conduct to her; and that it
was only Gallantry he had profeft: She
multiplied words fo faft upon him, that no
Cannon Shot, in the Befiegeing of a City,
could fall with more Impetuofity, then did
her Reproaches upon the Marquis: She
thundered in his Ears, and ftorm'd about the
Room like one Diftracted: That tho' the
Marquis wanted not for Courage, and was
as Valiant as any Man, yet did he not know
how to defend himfelf againft her Affaults
and Batteries: But being refolv'd not to Retreat till the Danger was over, he expected, with Patience, the refult of this Hurri-
can; and when *Honoria* had faid all the bitter things, her Anger could fuggeft, fhe let
fall a fhower of Tears, which would have
mollified the Heart of any other then the
Marquis, whofe Soul was entirely fixed on
the invincible Charms of *Doralifa*, whofe
treatment, to the Marquis, was always mild,
and full of fweetnefs; when he faw fhe was
in a Condition of hearkning to him, he
grieved his hard Fate, that he knew not

fooner

fooner thofe generous Sentiments fhe had Honoured him with, that now he was not in a Condition to Retaliate Love for Love.

Honoria, who was of a high Spirit, could hardly bear this Declaration; but, being fenfible, her Anger would not make a Lover break his Chains, fhe repented herfelf of her Folly; and being out of hopes of making him of the number of her Admirers, fhe told him, *It was her that had procured his Commiffion of the King: For fhe found fome Confolation in knowing that her Rival muft fuffer Inquietudes no lefs than her felf: For to be Abfent,* faid fhe, (with a malicious Smile) *from the Perfon Loved, will be as infupportable; as the flights from thofe one Loves.* The Marquis hearken'd to her Reproaches, her Complaints, and her Wifhes, for his ill Succefs in War, and that the God of Love would fometimes punifh him for his Ingratitude to her : She rofe up, and went into her Clofet, and lock'd the Door after her. The Marquis, who was not forry for her Abrupt Departure, bid her Adeu through the Door, and came immediateiy to his Beloved *Doralifa*, to whom he recounted all that was paft ; and, upon this Occafion, faid to *Doralifa*, the moft moving, the moft paffionate Things, that his Love could infpire him with ; and the Malice of *Honoria*, in procuring his Preferment, he lamented in fuch terms, that *Doralifa* might fee he had for her a moft tender Affection. The Marquis offered to Marry *Doralifa*, in hopes

it

it might defer his Departure, or that he
might remit his Employment to his Brother;
but *Doralifa*, who was very Difcreet, only
teftified her acknowledgements for the Honour he would do her; but that fhe was under the Command of a Father and Mother,
and could not difpofe of herfelf, without
their Approbation; but fhe would always preferve, in her Heart, a moft real Affection for
him. It growing late, the Marquis took
leave of *Doralifa*, and left her in no lefs
Grief than himfelf for his Departure. That
Night he gave all Orders neceffary for his
Equipage, and betook himfelf to his Bed,
where his reftlefs Thoughts would not let
him take much Reft; he there gave vent
to his Sighs, uttering the moft bitter Complaints, that a Soul, feiz'd with fo much
Love, could fay. He fometimes Curs'd the
Malice of *Honoria*, and fometimes wifh'd,
that *Doralifa* were unfaithful; and like one
Frantick, would fay a thoufand extravagant
Things, all that his Love and Rage could
fuggeft to his Fancy. Thus did he Rave and
Sigh, and turn himfelf a thoufand times;
and after all he muft refolve to leave his better part, his *Doralifa* behind!

The next Day, as foon as it was proper to
wait on his three amiable Friends, he went
to take his leave of them, who all lamented
this feparation; but *Doralifa*'s Tears exprefs'd how great her Concern was above
the others. The Marquis, who had a moft
Paffionate Soul, was deeply touch'd with

the

he marks of *Doralifa*'s Affection to him;
But, said this Fair Afflicted one, is it not
poffible for you to forget your *Doralifa* in
the midft of your Triumphs and Acclamations of Joy for your Victories? And will
not Abfence work that effect, that your
Reafon has not yet done? No, no, Madam,
faid the Marquis, fear nothing from a Man
who is become conftant for your fake, and
whofe greateft Glory is to wear your Chains.
They promis'd each other to Write, and
freely to impart their Thoughts: Upon thefe
Terms did thefe Lovers part; and the Abfence of the Marquis was a very great Affliction to them all: For whether he was
Merry, or whether he was fad, his Converfation was extream delightful. The next
Day the Marquis, with his Equipage departed from *Fountain-Bleau*, where *Doralifa* remained full of Difcontent for the Abfence
of her Lover: Her two Friends endeavoured to divert the Chagrin that appear'd in
her Countenance, and left nothing unfaid that
could give her any Confolation. They continued their humour of Walking, whilft
they remained at *Fountain-Bleau*: But *Corinna*, who thought that *Doralifa* would
be more diverted at *Paris*, propos'd going
the next Week; and *Bellamira* being fo obliging to accompany them in this Journey,
they refolv'd in few Days to be gone. By
the firft Poft *Doralifa* receiv'd a Letter from
the Marquis, who gave her all the hopes
imaginable of his Fidelity; they continued
their

their Correfpondence during the time fhe ftaid in *Paris*, which was fix Months : He told her in his laft, that he would follow her into *England*, and demand her of her Father and Mother in Marriage ; but whether her Anfwer mifcarried, or he chang'd his Sentiments, I know not ; but fhe never heard more from him. But her Father, who had provided her a Husband, who was a Gentleman of a good Eftate, and one who might make her happy : She, at laft, confented to her Parents Commands, after fhe had expected half a Year to hear News from her faithlefs *Ovid*, therefore fhe refolved to obey them. And it was to her Wedding, my dear *Indamora*, I went , when I left *Lucretia* and your felf in *Suffex*.

This is the account that *Doralifa* gave me of her Adventures ; if I have related them wrong, impute it to the defect of my Memory ; and to deal plainly with you , I am fo fenfible, I have acquitted my felf ill in this undertaking, that I could never hope for a Pardon, but from fo generous a Friend as your felf.

Her Amours have loft great part of their Beauty by the difadvantage they have received in being Pen'd in fo unaccurate an order; but at prefent I fhall trouble your Patience with no more Apologies ; but fhall abruptly take leave of my *Indamora*, and am

her faithful
Lindamira.

The

The Fourth Part of the Adventures of Lindamira.

The XVIIth. LETTER.

TO refume my Difcourfe, my deareft *In-damora*, I muft begin from the Marri-age of *Doralifa*, who ftaid with my Aunt about two Months, and then *Liffidas*, her Husband, took her a Houfe, near St. *James's*, which had belonging to it a little Garden that look'd into the Park, which made the Houfe extream agreeable and pleafant: The Affection *Doralifa* had for me, and the Com-paffion fhe took for that Melancholly Air, fhe obferv'd in my Looks (which I could not always hide) oblig'd her to this great Civi-lity of inviting me to be with her, in hopes it might divert my Thoughts from *Cleo-midon*. I readily accepted her kind offer, and having Liberty of complaining to her of my unhappinefs; I often took the free-dom to reflect on the feverity of my Deftiny ; and as all unhappy People do, thought no misfortune like my own : But, at laft, I took a Refolution to act the part of a Philo-

fopher

lofopher, to be content with my Condition,
and not repine at what I could not help;
and having brought my Mind to this Se-
date Temperament, I enjoy'd much fatisfaction in the Converfation of *Doralifa* and
Lyfidas, who was of a very facetious
Humour: What Diverfions the Town
afforded, I had my fhare in a very moderate
way; for *Lyffidas* had an inclination to be
more abroad than at home, and was not
pleas'd unlefs *Doralifa* and I were with him;
and as he had a great many vifits to make
to his Relations, who had been with him to
Congratulate his Happinefs, we went very
often abroad for a Month or two; but one
Vifit amongft the reft, I fhould have been
very glad, could I been excus'd from make-
ing it with *Doralifa*; but fhe not knowing
my Reafons, which I was loath to tell her,
I put it to the venture, and accompanied her
to the Houfe of *Coll. Harnando*: You muft
know his Lady was near related to *Lyffidas*, and *Doralifa* had fome particular Reafons upon the account of Alliance, as well
as inclination to vifit *Elvira*, who was a-
dorn'd with much Beauty; Her Wit was
quick and apprehenfive, her Humour always
equal and full of fweetnefs, that I found my
felf Charm'd in her Converfation, and could
not but admire at the Collonel for his vola-
til Humour; but fuch is the Humour of
moft Men, that they value not a Treafure
they are poffefs'd of. But had not *Elvira*
been a Perfon of much Difcretion, his Humour

mour of Gallantry to the Ladies, would
have made her very uneafy. But fhe told a
Friend (as I have heard fince) that to be out
of Humour was not the way to reduce a
Heart that would fometimes go aftray ; but
his own Experience of the ficklenefs of fome
Women, would fooneft bring him back, and
convince him that fhe had Sentiments more
tender, and more fincere, than thofe Ladies
he lov'd to fool his time away with ; but
as fhe had a moft true and real Affection for
him, fhe was Miftrefs enough of her Refentments, not to be carried to the fmalleft
Action againft her Duty. *Elvira*, very obligingly invited us to come often to her
Houfe, faying, fhe feldom went abroad (for
fhe was then with Child) and would take it
as a favour if we would bring our Works
along with us: To which civil Requeft, we
confented, and went to vifit *Elvira*, more
than any Relation that *Lyfidas* had : And my
Fears being over, that the Colonel fhould
know me, or have any fufpicion of me, I
went with great freedom to his Houfe ; but
he had not forgot, he had feen me with
Valeria and *Silvanus* in the Park, and would
often make enquiry after their Healths. He
was extreamObliging and Complaifant,which
I fear'd, might give offence to *Elvira* ; but
fhe was of a contrary Humour ; and being
very Difcreet, fhe feem'd pleas'd with whatever the Colonell did ; and that which was
moft ftrange, fhe grew infinitely fond of me,
and would be fending continually for me to
play

play at Cards with her if fhe had no Company ; fo that, at laft, either *Doralifa,* my felf, or both, were there three times in a Week, and were very merry at our Play.

But fometimes were interrupted by troublefome Vifiters ; as there is Company of all forts, there were feweft of the number of generous Perfons: and amongft the reft, one impertinent Lady, who, in her younger days, *bad* had Beauty enough to engage Hearts into an Affection ; thefe Conquefts rais'd her Vanity to that degree, that, fhe thought, fhe merited all the Praifes that Flattery could invent, and all her Difcourfe was of her felf, what was faid to her, and what were her witty Reparties again ; that being fo full of the Thoughts of her Quondam Lovers, fhe would begin a Relation of them all at once, and fo confound one thing wi.h another, that there was no Coherence in all her Difcourfe ; yet would fhe oblige us to hearken to her, and take it very ill if great attention was not given : And fometimes when we were very earneft at our Play, fhe would come in and interrupt us She was not fo Complaifant as to play a Game with us, but proeffted againft it, and reprefented to us, how ill we paft our time, faying, *That the Converfation of ingenious Perfons was more profuable to us.* But *Elvira* reply'd, *That we only paft a few Hours this way, becaufe we had no News to entertain our felves with, and to talk of our Neighbours, and their management of their Affairs was not fuitable to*

our

our Genius. To this the venerable old Lady
reply'd, *That she would divert us with the
History of her Life if we would leave our
Cards*; which was immediately done , but
if it were to gain a Million of Gold, it is
impoſſible for me to remember the leaſt Fragments of her Diſcourſe, where nine words
of ſenſe hung together.But to conclude before
I begin, ſhe was Lov'd, Slighted, Hated,
Lov'd, Deſpis'd, and Lov'd again, and all in
a quarter of an hour.

And, I ſuppoſe, this is the very Lady you
have heard on : So Celebrated for the prodigious Conqueſts her Eyes had made, who
would entertain all People with theſe Stories ; but they muſt have better Memories
then I have, who can relate any one of them
again : But to make up the misfortune of
her Impertinence, amongſt other Viſiters, was
a Young Lady of an admirable Wit, and
pleaſing Converſation, who was very Cour-
teous and Obliging. She happened to be that
Day with *Elvira*, when this Lady came to
viſit her, ſo did partake in the relation of
her Amours : But certainly never did any one
divert themſelves ſo much as *Clarinta* did
with the Old Lady ; ſhe would ask her ſo
many particulars of the Sparks her Lovers,
and put her upon the Deſcription of their
Perſons, and their Humours, and her own
Barbarity to them ſhe much Condemned ; but
the Old Lady to juſtifie her Conduct, would
let fall words that let us ſee, that her Lovers were treated very kindly , and her fond-
nefs,

nefs, we believ'd, was the occafion of her loofing them fo faft, which *Clarinta* took great notice of, and Rallied the Old Lady very much, that , I believe, this venerable piece wifh'd fhe had not been fo Prodigal of her words, but her geftures did more Exprefs her Thoughts, then her Rhetorick : But, to our relief, came in the Collonel, to whom *Clarinta* faid, *She wifh'd he had come fooner, to have heard a moft delightful Relation of that Ladies Amours.* The Collonel, who was naturally Complaifant, and full of Gallantry, entreated the Lady to relate all that had been faid before, who was proud to Obey him, and tranfported to find him inclin'd to hearken unto her , which made her not omit the leaft Circumftance to imbellifh her Story. And the Collonel, who had that Illuminated Wit, that is capable of all things, and would fometimes be pleafantly Malicious, on this occafion, faid fo many Satyrical things, and made fo many Remarks, that the whole Company was diverted with him, and the Lady well pleas'd at the mirth her Folly created.

I have infifted too long upon this Subject, my dear *Indamora*, being it defers the recital of what relates to *Cleomidon*, for whom you have fo much Concern, that I will give you the fatisfaction, you defire, as foon as poffible; but I muft finifh this Days Adventure before I can proceed. In a fhort time the Lady went away, and *Elvira*, *Clarinta*, *Doralifa*, and my felf, went to take a walk in the

the Park, when unexpectedly we Incountered
Sir *Formal Triffle* with a Young Wench in
a Mafque ; thefe Ladies had not ever been
acquainted with his Character, or had known
he had ever been my Lover ; that, if they
pleas'd, I would give them a relation of his
Courtfhip, which was both comical and uncommon, if they were not already tyred out
with an account of Love Matters ; but they
Complimented me fo far to tell me, they
fhould be exxeamly well diverted with any
thing I would relate to them, which I did
as I have already done to you. The Novelty
of this Sir *Formal* pleas'd them beyond meafure, which made *Clarinta* have a great defire
to advance towards him, which fhe did with
Doralifa,whilft*Elvira* and I ftay'd behind fome
paces to obferve them. In the mean time,
Sir *Formal* got rid of his Mafqued Lady ;
and my two Friends plac'd themfelves on
the Bench in the dark Walk, where they
expected the return of Sir *Formal*, who foon
after walk'd his Spaniard's pace towards
them. He obferving them both to be handfome, he plac'd himfelf by them, and, in
a minute, began a Difcourfe ; and *Clarinta*,
who had an infinuating Wit, foon gain'd his
Efteem, and put him upon the relation of
his Amours, faying, fome time after, fhe
heard he had been ill treated by a Young
Gentlewoman, call'd *Lindamira*, at whofe
Name the old Knight blufh'd for Anger,
that it fhould be reported he had been unkindly ufed ; and to mention his true Character,

racter, told *Clarinta*, That he had forsaken her, because she had not a Fortune Equivalent to his ; and that he might have married her, if he had pleas'd. But my two Friends were so inraged at his Vanity, that they told him, *They knew* Lindamira *too well, to question her Judgment* , or to think she would marry a *Man of his Age,* and of his Infirmities (for, you may remember, he was Paralitick): At these words, they rose up ; for they durst not stand the brunt of his Anger, and left him to chew the Cud.

This Adveuture contributed much to that Evenings Diverſion ; and *Elvira* told the Collonel, when ſhe came home, That Sir *Formal* had been a pretender to me, and asked him, how he approved of ſuch a match for me : But his Eyes, as well as his words, told me, That I deserved a better Fate.

And allSupper-time were very merry about him ; and the Collonel ſaid a thouſand plea- ſant things of his Formality and Rhetorick ; for he had often been in his Company, and was no ſtranger to his vain Humour of com- mending himſelf ; and was as well able to judge as any one, how little he deſerved his own praiſes.

At laſt, *Doralifa,* and I, took leave of our good Company ; What hapned at my re- turn home, you ſhall know in my next, which will as much ſurprize you, as it did me. I am,

My Deareſt *Indamora,*
Your Friend and Servant,
Lindamira.

M   The

The XVIIIth. LETTER.

I Shall now acquaint you, my Deareſt *Indamora*, how pleaſantly I was ſurpriz'd
that Night I went from *Elvira*, when, on my
Toilette, as I was, undreſſing me, I caſt my
Eye on a Letter, whoſe Characters I knew
to be that of *Cleomidon* ; I took it up, and
turn'd it forty ways before I had power to
open it ; and *Iris*, who obſerv'd the different
agitations of my mind, asked me if I had
not Courage to open a Letter from *Cleomidon* ? No, *Iris*, ſaid I, for I cannot imagine
why he ſhould write to me, ſince hitherto
he has ſo Religiouſly obſerved my Commands.
It may import ſome good News, replied *Iris* ;
and I beſeech you, Madam, read what *Cleomidon* has ſent you : At her importunity, at
laſt, I opened it, and the Contents of this
Letter, ſtruck me with great Aſtoniſhment ;
for he acquainted me, that *Cleodora* was no
longer amongſt the Living, and that being at
liberty to diſpoſe of himſelf, he hoped I
would admit him to lay his Life and Fortune
at my Feet ; making it his earneſt requeſt,
that no capricious Fancies, or needleſs Formalities, might retard, or hinder his Happineſs, if I ſtill preſerv'd an Eſteem for him.
And, laſtly, That as ſoon as he could ſettle
his

his Affairs, he would come to Town.
leave you to judge, my *Indawora*, if my
Grief was great for *Cleodora*; but yet I was
in no tranfport of Joy ; for I knew he was
in fome trouble for her Death.

I writ to *Cleomidon*, and fcrupled not to
own, that neither Time, nor Abfence, had de-
fac'd the impreffion he had made, and had
entirely preferved my Affections for him :
The hopes of feeing him foon, made me lefs
copious in my Expreffions of that Efteem I
had for him. In a fhort time, I received an
Anfwer to that, which teftified his impatience of feeing me ; that as foon as a Month
was expired, he would wait on me. I then
began to think my felf in a ftate of Happinefs, fince I was beloved by the moft Vertuous, and moft Conftant of Lovers ; and that
Cleomidon was in a capacity of owning it to
all the World.

But before the arrival of my generous *Cleomidon*, I muft not omit to give you the
Character of the young *Octavius*, a Nephew
of *Lyfidas*, who made frequent vifits to his
Houfe.

His Perfon was well made, Gentile and
Handfome ; but there ever appeared a di-
fturbednefs in his Eyes, which was the effects
of an unbridled Jealoufie ; and, in a few
Days, was grown all Melancholly and Sul-
len : But 'tis the Nature of Jealoufie, to
force an interpretation of all things to their
own difadvantage ; *Octavius* was fallen de-
fperately in Love with a young Lady of a
M 2   good

good Fortune, who had for him a great E-
fteem, and always ufed him with greatRefpect;
and thofe innocent Favours fhe fhewed him,
would have made another Lover (that was
not of his Humour) thought himfelf very
happy. But, on the contrary, *Octavius* became jealous of *Belifa*, becaufe fhe was favourable to him ; and being prepoffeffed, that
all Men were treated like himfelf, he grew
miftruftful and pettifh, and imployed himfelf in obferving all the Actions of *Belifa*,
who was a Perfon very Charming and Agreeable ; tho' not a Celebrated Beauty, yet one
who had an Obligingnefs in her Countenance, that all that fee her, were pleafed
with her.

Octavius often coming to *Lyfidas*, I obferved this Change in him, and was curious
to know the caufe of it ; for I know he
was Efteemed very much by *Belifa*, that I
could not imagine the occafion of this Chagrine. He told me, that never Man fuffered
fo much for Love, as he did ; for his Jealoufie was fo great, that he found no Confolation in what was paft, nor in the prefent,
nor in what was to come.

I would not Flatter him fo much, to tell
him he deferved the Pity of any Rational
Creature ; for I would fooner marry a Man
that Hated me, than one that Loved me with
Jealoufie ; for no Torment was like the Jea-
loufie of an imperious Husband ; for that
Paffion wou'd feduce theirReafon, trouble their
Senfes, and make them find more than they

fee k

feek for. But *Octavius* would maintain, that Love and Jealoufie were infeparable. Our Opinio ns were Fire and Water, and could not. alter each others Sentiments upon the matter.

. I reprefented to him, the Injuftice he did *Belifa*, being jealous without a caufe, efpe-cially fince he found it fo Tyrannical a Paf-fion, and that it ran him into fo many mif-fortunes; but the jealous *Octavius* faid, he would ftill Love *Belifa*, and ftill be jealous. His obftinate Humour would fometimes vex me, and fometimes divert me; but all the Precepts and Examples I could offer, wrought no effect on him; till one day he came to make me a vifit, and was faying, he was ftill the moft unhappieft of Lovers; for when he was out of *Belifa*'s fight, he fancied fhe was befet with Rivals, and that fhe was kind to all, and that her refervednefs, was only an affected Humour; that fhe fuffered his Court-fhip only in Obedience to her Father's Com-mands; then the next minute would he run out extravagantly againft thofe Miftreffes, that fhewed any kindnefs to their Lovers, making fevere reflections on their Vertue and Conduct. I heard him with a great deal of Impatience, and interrupting his Harangue; I Rallied him extreamly for the injuftice he did *Belifa*, and for indulging fuch unaccount-able Fancies.

He then was pleafed to be very angry with me, but I let him vent his Paffion, and then afked him, Why a Man might not as well

quarrel

quarrel with a Glais, that fhews him an ill
Face, as with a Friend, that gave him the
true reprefentation of his Soul ? *Octavius*
made no reply of a long time, but kept his
Eyes fixed on me, when on a fudden he broke
the filence, and rifing up, *Well* (faid he) *my
generous Friend, you have awakened fomething in my Soul, and the Eyes of my underftanding begins to be cleared: Proceed then,*
(continued he) *and ufe your utmoft skill, to
cure me of this outrageous Paffion, Jealoufie
that defies Prudence and Reafon. I own it
is a weaknefs; but, if it be poffible, let me
conjure you, to rid me of this ftrange Ma-
lidy.*

I was glad to find he had a fenfe of his
extravagant Paffion; and having fome Efteem
for him, as he was a Relation to *Lyfidas*, I
reply'd, *That I would endeavour to approve
my felf his Friend ; that I would do nothing
by halves ; for fince it was a continual Spring
of Induftry, that I would ufe my utmoft skill,
to extinguifh his unreafonable furmifes,where-
with I found him fo cruelly tormented ; and,
perhaps, I might difcern better than he, what
was moft to his advantage.*

Octavius thanked her fa thoufand times,
and promifed me, he would add his own Endeavours to my Care, to be cured of his
Madnefs : And I doubt not, but he ufed his
utmoft Effort: But this Difeafe had taken
fo deed a Root in his Heart, that his Rea-
... was of little ufe, when the Frenzy Fit
. was

was on him ; for he would create Afflictions,
on purpofe to make himfelf unfortunate.

About a Week after this Difcourfe hap,
pened, he was to wait on *Lyfidas* ; and, when
I had an opportunity, I demanded of him,
if it was poffible to Love without Jealoufie?
Alas! Madam, replied this unhappy Lover, I
am not yet cured of my Weaknefs ; for this
unaccountable Humour has that afcendant
over me, that were the beft Phyficians of
all parts of the World Affembled together,
they would in vain endeavour to diflodge this
Difeafe, which occafions fo much mifchief,
and which is irreparable, becaufe, inftead of
feeking Remedies, falfe Praifes are generally
invented to flatter it.

You fpeak fo feelingly of your Diftemper,
faid I to *Octavius,* that I hope you will attribute your Cure, more to your own Reafon,
than to any Arguments I can ufe : But ftill,
let Reafon ftand fentinel at your Heart; for
this Jealoufie will certainly find entrance
there, if watch be not well guarded : 'Tis
the moft fatal of all the Paffions ; 'tis a
Complication of all the Evils in the World;
'tis the Fury of Furies.

But did you Love as I did, replied *Octavi-
ous,* you would not be fo great an enemy to
Jealoufie ; however, I will endeavour to
chafe from my Heart, a Paffion fo pernicious to my Repofe : Your Converfation has
fo far convinced me, that I muft allow, that
thofe Lovers are moft Happy, and moft Rational, that can Love without Jealoufie, or only

fo little to keep up the Flame: And for two months I had the glorious Title of Phyfician, for curing a Difeafe, that was thought above all Rules of Medicine: But the Fit returned with greater impetuofity, than before.

As *Octavius* was one day at Cards with *Belifa*, fhe accidentally let fall her Cards two or three times, and a young Spark, that fate next her, was very obfequious in taking them up ; and, out of a piece of Gallantry, would kifs the Cards, as, he gave them to her, as fhe received them fhe fmiled, and faid, *That fhe was afhamed of the trouble fhe gave him.* To which he replied, *That he fhould ever after Love the Cards, that had given him an occafion to render her a fmall piece of Service.* Tho' only thefe common Compliments paft between them, yet *Octavius* could not bear it, but Relapfed into his former capricious Fancies. His Reafon was of no ufe to him, fo blindly he Abandoned himfelf to his Paffion, which was then the moft Predominant in his Soul ; and the uneafinefs he was in, was fo vifible to all the Company, that *Belifa* left off Cards, and retired herfelf into her Clofet, where fhe made Vows to herfelf, never to fee him more ; for now fhe had loft all hopes of ever being happy with him ; wherefore fhe made it her Requeft to her Father, to forbid him his Houfe, who, in Complaifance to his Daughter, did as fhe defired, which fo enraged *Octavius*, that he was like a Man Diftracted (for he
Loved

Loved *Belifa* Paffionately) and being a-
fhamed of his Folly, would never fee me
more; but he fent me word by *Lyfidas*,
*That tho' his Difeafe ftill continued to plague
him, he thanked me for the Care and Application I had ufed, to cure him.* Upon this
Bufinefs he went out of Town, and fought
his Relief amongft a favage, unbred fort
of two Legged Brutes, in *Wales*, where he
Lived a very folitary Life.

I have infifted upon the particulars of
Octavius, my dear *Indamora*, to let you
fee, that Jealoufie is a Difeafe feldom to
be overcome; therefore acquaint your
Friend *Clorinda* with this Story, and the
influence you have over her, may prevent
her marriage with the jealous *Melicrates*;
for let the Wife be never fo Vertuous,
the jealous-Pated Husband is ever full of
Difquiets, for fear his Horns fhould not
fit eafy on his Head; when, at the fame,
time, he is laying Snares to trepan his
Neighbour's pretty Wife : But the Golden
Rule, of doing as you would be done unto,
is banifhed from amongft us.

Before I finifh my Letter, I muft add,
That I received a Confirmation of *Cleomidon's* intentions, of being in Town, as he
defigned; but that his Uncle and Aunt
Reproached him with too foon forgetting
his *Cleodora*; and were both much offended

at

ªt him : But, that fhould not deter his
ⁱntentions ; for his only happinefs was in
my Company. This affurance of his kindnefs, ftill more augmented my good Fortune; and I thought it long till I could behold my faithful *Cleomidon :* In my next
you fhall participate of my Joys ; but, at
prefent, l can add no more, than to affure
you, I am

My *Indamora's*

Sincere Friend,

and Servant,

Lindamira.

————————————————————

The

The XIXth. LETTER.

THAT Day, my deareft *Indamora*, that
I expeĉted *Cleomidon* in Town, pre-
ceeded the happy Night, wherein *Elvira* gave
fo much joy to the Collonel, in bringing him
a fine Boy into the World : To deal fincerely
with you, I was very unwilling to accompany *Doralifa* to *Elvira's*, fearing, in my
Abfence, *Cleomidon* might come to Town, as I
expeĉted. I fuffered fome Inquietudes upon
his account; for he came not, till three days
after the time he allotted, which poffeffed
me with an ĝunufual Fear ; and my Heart
foreboded fome ill Fortune to him; and, indeed, my Conjeĉtures were not ill-grounded ;
for the laft days Journey, he was over-turned
in his Coach, and falling, unfortunately,
broke his right Arm, which detained him
three days on the Road ; but was fo happy
to meet with a good Chirurgeon, who fet
it fo well, that in three Days he left the Inn,
where he was advifed to continue for fome
longer time ; but, as he told me, his defire
of feeing me, after fo long an Abfence, made
him fo impatient, that he refolved to comply with his Inclinations, and not with the
Advice of his Chirurgeon.

That

That Night he came to Town, he sent his Servant to acquaint me with his Arrival, and of the unlucky accident that detained him on the Road, and to beg excuse, for not writing or waiting on me : His indisposition easily sealed his Pardon ; and I was extreamly Afflicted at his misfortune. The next day, *Doralisa* and I went to see him; we found him laid on his Bed, fast a Sleep (for he had no Slept all the Night past) but he soon awoke, and seeing us by his Bed-fide, seemed much amazed. He expressed to us the most obliging acknowledgements , that a grateful Heart could imagine : And 'tis impossible to express the transports of Joy he shewed, as he said, for the favour we did him : He so over-valued the least marks of my Esteem, that I could not reproach my self from being too sensible of his Affection. Our Joys were both so great, and so tumultuous, that, of a long time, I did not think to ask him, what Life he led, since our fatal separation.

Then know, my dearest *Lindamira* , said *Cleomidon*, that a Month after I Married, I went into the Country with *Cleodora*; but we were obliged to live with the cruel *Lyndaraxa*, who, you have heard, did wheedle my Uncle to marry him. This couple were of as different Humours, as their Interest; and tho *Alcandar* adored his Money, and loved it entirely, yet his design was to make me happy with *Cleodora*, and to settle him a Joynture, answerable to her Fortune. But

Lyndaraxa

Lyndaraxa, whofe Sentiments were different
from thofe of *Altan tar's*, diverted the Execution of his intentions, on purpofe to bring
about her own hellifh Plots. She was E-
fteemed by fome, to be a Woman of Wit
and great Senfe ; but, alas ! fhe fo ill imployed her Wit, that her Genius was only
to circumvent her Husband, in whatever he
defigned. And I will do her this Juftice, as
to fay her Perfon was agreeable, and her Wit
very taking, when fhe was in the humour to
be good Company. She feemed inclined to
Melancholly, and to be very Studious, and
applied herfelf much to Reading. This gave
her the Reputation to be a Woman of a found
Judgment, and, having a happy Memory,
would relate what fhe had read, fo perfectly,
that her Auditors had a great pleafure in
heark'ning to her : But the fequel of my
Difcourfe will beft demonftrate how ill fhe
imployed her Tallent ; and that her Wit and
Memory, was of no other ufe, than to abufe
thofe, who had too good an Opinion of her :
And, amongft others, I had as high thoughts
of her Vertues, as any one, till, by accident,
I made a happy difcovery of her Perfidy and
Treachery.

Cleomidon had continued ┃ his Difcourfe,
had not his Phyfician come in, who put a
ftop to the fequel of this Adventure, which
had fo raifed my Expectation ; but fearing a
longer vifit might be injurious to his Health,
we

we took our leave for that Night ; but *Cleomidon* failed not to acknowledge this favour, and told us, that the next day he would wait on us, and finish what he had yet to acquaint us with.

From thence we went to fee my aimiable Friend *Elvira*, who was then in a happy way of recovery, and much delighted and pleaſed, that ſhe had an Heir to inherit ſo good an Eſtate. We paſs'd that Evening with her : and ſhe eaſily read in my Countenance, the ſatisfaction I received in having ſeen *Cleomidon*. As ſhe was no ſtranger to this Adventure, I did not ſcruple to acquaint her of his being in Town. Upon this Relation, ſhe ſaid a thouſand obliging things to me, that teſtified how great a part ſhe bore with me ; and expreſſed a great Curioſity to know in what *Lyndaraxa* had forfeited the good Opinion the World had of her : For, ſaid *Elvira*, I knew one of her Character, who deceived all that knew her ; and, being conſcious of her own evil intentions, was jealous, that all her Friends took her for a Hypocrite ; but, at the ſame time, made great proteſtations of Sincerity, and, by a mild affected way, deluded thoſe, who thought themſelves entirely acquainted with her Humour.

'Tis ſo frequent, replied *Doraliſa*, to meet with Perſons who profeſs much Goodneſs, and practice little, that I am not aſtoniſhed at it ; but her, whom *Elvira* has mentioned

mentioned, is for certain my Lady ———
Hold, faid *Elvira*, for I would not rake
the Afhes of the Dead, and fo will bury in
filence thofe unhappy Qualities of a Lady of
her Reputation.

We took leave that Night of *Elvira*,
and the next day I received a vifit from *Cleomidon* ; but the fequel of his Story I refer
to my next Letter.

I am,

My Deareft *Indamora*,

Your entirely affect. Servant.

Lindamira.

The

The XXth. LETTER.

IN this manner, my deareſt *Indamora, Cleomidon* continued his Narrative.

Know then, *Lindamira*, ſaid he, that it
was whiſpered about, that *Lyndaraxa* was
with Child ; and when her Friends Congratulated with her, ſhe ſeemed to deny it, in
ſuch a manner, that more coñfirmed them
in that belief ; but, in a ſhort time after, it
was viſible to all the World, and my Uncle
was extreamly pleaſed at it : And tho' the
conſideration of my Intereſt would have al-
laied my Joy, yet I bare a part with my Uncle in the ſatisfaction he had. But one day,
as I was ſitting in a back Parlor, that a door
opened into the Garden, I was Reading very
Studiouſly, and did not, of a long time, take
notice of any one thing under the Window ;
but hearing my ſelf named, awoke me from
the Conſideration of what I was a Reading ;
and raiſing up my Head, I ſaw *Lyndaraxa,*
and a Gentleman with her, who were both
in very earneſt Diſcourſe. But, as I told
you, having heard my ſelf mentioned, it raiſ-
ed a Curioſity in me, to hearken to them, and
purſued *Lyndaraxa,*before you gave me time-
ly notice, when I muſt begin to make Faces,
and complain of Pain ; for I can introduce a
Child

Child unſeen (either Son or Daughter) it
will diſappoint *Cleomidon* of his hopes. The
other aſſured her, that ſhe might depend upon her management, and that ſhe had contrived ſo cunning a way to introduce the
Child, that there would never be any ſur-
miſes, that it was an Impoſture. I believe
they had continued their Diſcourſe, had not
my Uncle paſs'd through the Parlor into the
Garden, and ſeeing me at the Window, asked me to walk with him.

'Tis not to be imagined, how I was aſtoniſhed at the ungenerous Temper of *Lyndaraxa* ; for I did not believe her capable of ſo
great a Treachery ; but, as I thought it ab-
ſolutely neceſſary to acquaint my Uncle with
it, I failed not, that day, as we were walking. The old Gentleman bluſhed for Anger,
and was ſo aſhamed to be ſo put upon, that
he expreſſed the higheſt Reſentments, that
ſuch an Affront could excite him to.

That Evening, he taxed *Lyndaraxa* with the
Diſcourſe ſhe had with *Sabina* in the Garden. She had not Impudence enough to deny it ; but finding her Plot was Circum-
vented, ſhe made an ingenuous Confeſſion,
and, on her knees, begg'd my Uncle's Pardon, in ſuch moving Words and Actions,
adding a ſincere Repentance, and Tears fell
ſo plentifully from her Eyes, that it ſo mollified *Alcandar*'s Heart, that he eaſily ſealed
her Pardon. From that day, ſhe pretended
herſelf not well ; and her great Belly being

N gone,

gone, it was eafily fufpected, why fhe kept
her Chamber.

But, from that time, *Lyndaraxa* bore me
a mortal hatred, and folemnly Swore to *Sa-
lina*, to be revenged of me, the firft opportunity fhe could find. And, on the contrary, my Uncle was more kind than ever,
as being confcious he had done me a piece of
injuftice, after the Promife he had made me,
to fettle his whole Eftate on me, if I Married
to his likeing; and, I doubt not, but he repented of his Bargain. At the end of the
fourteen Months, *Cleodora* was brought to
Bed of a fine Girl, and *Lyndaraxa* took an
occafion to be angry it was not a Son: This
was to fhew the capricioufnefs of her temper ; nor would fhe appear at the Chriften-
ing-day, nor be God-mother, as fhe did intend, had it been a Son : But her abfence
was the leaft of my troubles ; for her ill
ufage of *Cleodora* was an Affliction to me,
who often lamented the misfortune of being
Educated by one who took fo little care to
inftruct her in what was moft advantageous
to improve her mind ; but as her inclination
was good and vertuous, fhe had nothing of
the humour of *Lyndaraxa*, who finding that
Cleodora thought her felf happy, was refolved to deftroy her Tranquillity, by fug-
gefting to her mind, that I was in Love with
the fair *Hermione*, a young Gentlewoman,
that often did us the Honour, to come and
ftay a week together. Her humour being
Brisk and Airy, fhe very much diverted *Cleodora*,

dora, who naturally was melancholy : as I
was fenfible fhe came out of kindnefs to my
Wife, I often exprefs'd my thankfulnefs to
her; and knowing that *Cleodora* was very
well pleas'd with her Converfation, I took
thofe opportunities of being in my Clofet;
and, to confefs the truth, I fpent much time
in thinking on you, and writing to you: I
complain'd of the rigor of my Fate; I demanded your Advice, in a thoufand little Occurrences; I fent my Wifhes for your Happinefs, and for a fight of you, ten thoufand
more; but, after all, I durft not difobey
you; I burnt my Letters, then wrote again;
then facrific'd them to the flames; and in
this manner did I pafs my days.

But to return to *Hermione*, who was ignorant of the Plots and Stratagems that did fur-
round her, one day very innocently ask'd me,
before *Cleodora*, and *Lyndaraxa*, *Why they had
fo little of my Company?* for, faid this pleafant Lady, *I believe you agree with the Opinion of moft Men, That Women are not capable of giving a Rational Anfwer, having not
the advantage of Learning, and Reading thofe
Authors, that are fo improving to the Mind:*
But being willing to convince *Hermione* of
that Error, I faid to her a thoufand obliging
Things, in favour of the Fair-Sex, and endeavour'd to let her fee, I was not of a Humour to defpife thofe, from whom Learning
was not expected; and that I thought Women were capable of the deepeft Philofophy,
were it a neceffary Accomplifhment; but they

had

had fo many Advantages over us, that *Hermione* had no reafon to fufpect, that her Company was not extream pleafing and diverting; and that a Lady of her Wit and good Humour, ought not to have thofe unjuft Apprehenfions. For an Hour or two did we entertain our felves upon this fubject; and *Lyndaraxa* made her obfervations of what was faid; and from this innocent Entertainment, rais'd the foundation of a moft deteftable Defign. She took this occafion, to reprefent to *Cleodora,* how induftrious I was to convince *Hermione* of the refpect I paid to her Sex, and that fhe obferved, how Amoroufly I look'd on her, and that fhe receiv'd my Kindnefs with a great fatisfaction, and believ'd, there was a reciprocal Affection between us; that if a ftop was not put to it in the beginning, fhe would alienate my Affections from her; and *Cleodora* gave but too much attention to her; and being of a nature very Credulous, it took the effect that *Lyndaraxa* defir'd; and finding a change in the Humour of *Cleodora,* who was become more penfive and melancholy, I fear'd it proceeded from fome indifpofition of Body; but finding it was her Mind that was difturb'd, I prefs'd her extreamly, before fhe would difcover this Secret to me, but at lafts fhe frankly told me all that *Lyndaraxa* had fuggefted to her, and that fhe bid her obferve our Looks, our Words, and all our Actions; but I fo happily convinc'd *Cleodora* of the Error fhe was in, that fhe beg'd my pardon,
for

for having fuch unjuft thoughts of me; and
from that time, her Mind was reftor'd to its
former tranquillity, and fhe more than ever
efteem'd *Hermione*.

When *Lydaraxa* finding her Plot had not
taken fo well as fhe defir'd, fhe neverthelefs
endeavour'd to make us uneafie, but it was
not in her power; but fhe was not forgetful
of the Oath fhe had taken to *Sabina*, to be
reveng'd of me, which perhaps fhe might
have effected, had not Death depriv'd me of
Cleodora, who dy'd of the new Fever. Her
Death Afflicted me very much, for I had no
reafon to complain of any unkindnefs from
her ; and I knew fhe lov'd me paffionately ;
and that which aggravated my Grief,I thought
her Death was haftned by the wilful Humour
of my Aunt, who ply'd her fo faft with Medicines, that one Potion had not time to O-
perate, before they gave her another.

Soon after her Funeral-Rites were perform'd, and that I had fettled my Affairs, I
determin'd to come to *London*, but my Uncle
diffwaded me from it, and *Lyndaraxa* was
outrageous; and being poffefs'd I intended to
Marry again, fhe oppos'd my defign with all
the power fhe had ; but finding fhe could not
prevail, fhe faid, She *would take care of the
young* Hermelia, *my Child, and not let her
come under the Tuition of a Mother-in-law* :
As I had no Friend , to whom I could
fo well commit the care of this Infant, as
her felf, I let her take her own way ; and *Al-*

cander

cander has promis'd, No care fhall be want
ing.

Cleomidon thus ended his Narration, and I
found he had been no lefs Happy than my
felf; and I could not but Sympathize with
him.

And as the Afflíction of *Cleomidon* was no
ways leffen'd by a long Abfence, he entertain'd me with the fame paffion as ever he
had done; but as *Cleodora* had not been long
Dead, and his Arm not yet well, our Marriage was deferr'd for two Months: *If you
remember, my* Indamora, *you came to Congratulate with me, it being reported I was Marry'd, but you never yet knew the reafons that
hinder'd it.*

Cleomidon was no fooner well, and had left
off the Scarf wherein he carry'd his Arm, but
by the confent of all my Relations, and the
approbation of thofe Friends, that held the
greateft Rank in my efteem, as well as by
the obligations I had to be grateful, I confented to be Marry'd to him; the Day was
fet, and my Wedding-Cloaths made; and as
I was trying of 'em on, an Accident hapned,
that prov'd of ill-confequence to me, and
extreamly afflíted me, and that was, The
Death of *Elvira,* who unfortunately had taken Cold in her Lying-in, which caft her into
Fever, and in few days depriv'd her of Life.
I was fo much troubl'd for the Death of this
Lady, that *Cleomidon* had much a-do to comfort me; and *Lyfidas,* and *Doralifa* going
into Mourning, they oblig'd me to do the
fame;

fame: And as I had a great efteem for *Elvira*,
I really Mourn'd for her ; and for one Month
I refolv'd to defer my Marriage.

But Fortune was not yet tired with perfe-
cuting of me, and fhe had fomething in referve
to compleat my misfortunes : *Cleomidon* ftill
continu'd his affiduous Vifits to me ; and he
fail'd not a day, wherein he did not fee me.
How often would he expatiate on his former
Life, aggravating the leaft circumftance, that
might raife a compaffion in my Soul ; and
lamented his precipitate Refolution, in obey-
ing *Alcander* ; and did me that Juftice, as
to fay, *He never had reafon to complain of
any Bafenefs from me.* But I cannot think
on the change in his Affections, without fuffering o're again, thofe difquiets my Soul
was aggitated with ; and *Cleomidon*, to whom
I had given the Title, of *Faithful, Conftant*,
and *Generous*, forfeited that Name, and approv'd himfelf unworthy of my Affections.

This Character, my *Indamora*, I am certain will furprize you, as much as I was at
the news of his fudden departure out of
Town ; which gave me fo great Tremblings
of the Heart, that I was much diforder'd at
it ; and tho' his pretence feem'd plaufible
and juftifiable, yet my Prophetick Soul fuggefted to me fad Omens from his manner of
going ; and tho' it was his cuftome to fee me
every day, yet I took no notice, to be concern'd, that I had not feen him of a whole
day ; and the next day, I receiv'd a Letter
from him, with only thefe few Words in it.

Pardon

Pardon me, my dearest Lindamira, *for not waiting on you before I went out of Town; the suddenness of my departure you will excuse, when I tell you, my Uncle lies a Dying, and has sent an Express for me: The few moments I have to stay, are employ'd in assuring my* Lindamira, *I am,*

Her Faithful *Cleomidon.*

By the first Post, I will not fail to Write to you, and shall hope from your Goodness, an Answer.

This Letter both surpriz'd and troubl'd me; but not knowing what judgment to make, I waited impatiently for the first Post-day, wherein I expected a Letter from him; but I not only fail'd of my expectation that time, but several days besides. At last, I concluded, *Cleomidon* was Sick, if not Dead; but I wrote to him three or four times, but no Answer would he return: And that which aggravated my Affliction, was, That I heard by a Gentleman (whom *Lysidas*, unknown to me, had sent into the Country, where *Cleomidon* liv'd, to know what was become of him) that he was well in Health, but seem'd very melancholy, which was ascrib'd to the Death of *Cleodora*; that he had also seen the young *Hermilia*, that *Cleomidon* was very fond of her, and was often heard to say, He *never would*

would have any Wife, besides Hermilia. This news troubl'd me extreamly; for I plainly say, he openly contemn'd me; but I took a Resolution, not to complain, fearing it should increase his Pride, did he but know how great my Resentments were.

I endeavour'd all I could, to disguise that Grief, that did too sensibly touch my Heart; but all my endeavours were fruitless, for my Eyes too plainly shew'd my Discontent; and that which aggravated my Sorrow more, was, That all the World knew I was abandon'd by one, whom I defign'd to Marry; and several conjectures were made upon this occasion, every one to their Fancy. But tho' I was thus unkindly used, yet Love fill'd my Heart; and all my Anger could discover to me no other Fault *Cleomidon* had, but Inconstancy: But why he was so, after such proofs that he had given of an unalterable Fidelity, cast me into a Labrynth of Thought? But the more I did confider of it, the more I was perplex'd. As for Jealousie, I was sure he had no cause; or if he were so, he could not disguise it from me: And being thus disturb'd, and never hearing from him, I took a resolution to leave the Town a while, to try if the Fresh-Air could disperse those Clouds of Melancholy, that were too visible in my Face, and to remove that Tyrant Love, that monopoliz'd all my Thoughts. This design I did communicate to *Doralisa*, who unwillingly consented to my Removal, and deferr'd it for some time. But surely, my

Indamora,

Indamora, one Vexation never comes alone ;
for, much againſt my well, I made another
Conqueſt, when leaſt I did expeɕt my Eyes
ſhould do ſuch Feats ; and,I believe,you'll be
ſurpriz'd, when I acquaint you it was Colo·
nel *Harnando*, who wrote to me ſeveral moſt
paſſionate Letters ; and though I return'd all
back, but the firſt, (and ſome unopen'd) yet
this Heroe would not be repuls'd, but laid
cloſe ſiege to my Heart, and was reſolv'd upon the Conqueſt of it : But my Soul was in
no frame, to receive with pleaſure, the greateſt proof of Paſſion could be given ; for I
would not be deluded again : So reſolv'd
never to Love ; and ſince *Cleomidon* could
prove untrue, I thought the whole Sex was
capable of Change ; and being unwilling to
give any occaſion of diſcourſe, of my being
Courted by *Harnando*, I ſtole out of Town ;
and none but my two Couſins, and your ſelf,
knew of the place of my Retreat ; and tho'
it was not far from the Town, yet extream
Solitary, and agreeable to my Humour. The
Houſe was but ſmall, and a Garden and Or-
chard proportionable to it ; and at a little di-
ſtance from the Garden, was a Grove of
Cheſnuts and Walnut-Trees, where by accident, I diſcover'd a moſt ſurprizing Eccho.
This place was of great Entertainment to me,
for to amuſe and pleaſe my Fancy. I often
would call on the Name of *Cleomidon* ; 'twas
Muſick in my Ears, to hear his Name Re-
verberated ; and for that reaſon, would often entertain my ſelf, for hours together,
repeating

repeating fometimes thofe flattering Expreffions, that he fo freely gave. But furely
Love is a Madnefs; and they that are fo,
take a pleafure in being Mad; and at that
time, thinks that a Charm, which, when
their Reafon is return'd, they think a Mifery.

Thus, for a Month, did the time glide
away, in this fort of Entertainment; and
Reafon began to take place of that Dulnefs
that clogg'd my Brain, and I grew fenfible
I was to blame, to cherifh a Paffion for one,
whom I did believe did ne'er beftow a thought
on me. I therefore did endeavcur to caft
him from my Heart, and his Idea appear'd
to me, Ill-fhap'd, Deform'd, Decay'd, full
of Inconftancy and Treachery. But Time is
at laft our beft Friend, for he does more than
Reafon, or the beft Arguments in Philofophy. And being thus Re-inftated to my former Tranquillity of Mind, I could think upon *Cleomidon* without refentment, and a cold
Indifference took place of all my Love. And
being, my *Indamora*, thus happily Compos'd,
I'll bid you Adieu, before I change to another
Scene; for you may obferve, here's great variety in my Adventure. I am,

My deareft *Indamora*,

Your faithful humble Servant,

L I N D A M I R A,

The

The XXIth. LETTER.

I Had not enjoy'd my felf in this Solitude
two Months, my dearelt *Indamora*, before
I was Vifited by the Colonel, who, by fome
unlucky Adventure, had found out the place
of my Retreat ; but I was much furpriz'd to
fee him, as I was one day in the Grove, and
according to my ufual Entertainment, was
repeating the Name of the Faithlefs *Cleomidon.*

Ah! Madam, faid *Harnando*, (after the
firft Ceremonies were over) can you take pleafure in repeating the Name of a Perjur'd Lover, who cannot merit a Thought from you ?
I reply'd, That the remembrance of his Infidelity, was the belt defence I could find, a-
gainft a fecond Engagement ; and that the
Name of *Cleomidon* was not hateful to me,
tho' he was ungenerous. *Then is it poffible,
Madam,* reply'd the Colonel, *for you ftill to
love an inconftant, faithlefs Wretch, who va-
lues himfelf upon making you Unhappy?* He
fail'd not to extol my few Vertues, on purpofe to undervalue thofe of *Cleomidon.* He
entertain'd me much with his own Paffion,
and fhew'd a mighty eagernefs to have me
Marry him. His offers of Settlements were
very advantageous ; for he gave me the freedom

dom to make my own Terms, if I pleas'd;
tho' I had no reafon to doubt of the reality
of his Love, yet I could not forget, that Inconftancy is a Difeafe, as epidemical in that
Sex, as 'tis believ'd to be in ours ; but we
have not that ftrength of Parts, and Courage,
as is natural to theirs, to fupport us under
Afflictions ; and the Thoughts of being once
deferted, made me deaf to all the Arguments
the Collonel ufed to perfwade me to be his.
But all the repulfes I gave him, would not
make him retreat ; but the more oppofition
he found, the more vigorous he was to purfue his Defign, of gaining my Heart, which
was not a Conqueft worthy of his pains and
trouble. However, being blinded by his Paffion, he could fee no faults I had, but too
much Obftinacy, of which he often accus'd
me : But the frequent Vifits he made, I fear'd
would be prejudicial to my Reputation, which
made me think of leaving my Solitude, fooner than agreed with my Inclination.

I return'd to *London* in ten Weeks after I
had left it, and was frequently Vifited by the
Collonel, and few doubted but there would
be a Match between us ; as he was a very
Accomplifh'd Perfon, it was impoffible not
to be pleas'd with his Converfation : And
one day, as he was with me, a Servant
brought me a Letter, that came by the Poft ;
I knew the Hand to be that of *Cleomidon's,*
but had not fo much prefence of Mind, as
to difguife my Surprize ; for *Harnando* prefently fufpected the Truth, and his Countenance

nance changed,. and he look'd much difturb'd
at this Adventure. I ftill kept the Letter in
my Hand, looking on the Superfcription, as
if I doubted from whence it came, for the
Characters feem'd not fo clever, as thofe
which *Cleomidon* generally Writ ; but I knew
the Seal too well, to be in doubt. *Madam*,
faid the Collonel, (perceiving the diforderly
Motions of my Mind) *your Patience is without prefident : Methinks you are very dila-
tory in the perufal of what your faithful*
Cleomidon *has fent you ?* He fpoke this in a
Tone, that fufficiently exprefs'd his fence to
the contrary. I made him no reply, but
withdrew to a Window ; but none can reprefent the unartful pantings of a Faithful Heart,
unlefs they've Lov'd like me. I open'd this
Letter, with hopes, that *Cleomidon* was convinced of his Ingratitude, and had repented
of his Crime. But alas ! I found to my forrow, that his Thoughts were alianated from
me ; and I had hardly power to finifh the
Reading of this Letter, that was fo furprizing to me ; nor could I fcarce believe my own
Eyes, that *Cleomidon* fhould fend me word of
his own Marriage and in fo triumphant a
manner, as you will find by what follows.

Cleomidon *to* Lindamira.

Madam,

Your Marriage with Collonel Harnando, *will
juftifie mine, with the charming* Hermione, *to
whom*

*whom I have given my Heart entirely. I
have (tho' with some trouble) forgot your Infidelity, and your Falfhood has abfolutely extinguifh'd, in my Heart, that Love I had for
you. You have taken the moft becoming care
in the World, to let me know of your Happinefs; and tho' I could expatiate on your Ingratitude, I'll bury in filence my moft juft Refentments.*

Farewel Cleomidon.

'Tis impoffible to exprefs my firft Thoughs
and Apprehenfions of this Marriage; for this
fecond engagement was more terrible to me,
than the firft; for tho' he Married *Cleodora*,
it was thro' my perfwafions, which out of
a fentiment of Generofity I argued with him,
for his own advantage; but to think that
Hermine was poffefs'd of what I had fo
tender an Affection for, moft tore my Heart-
ftrings, and I could not bear with Patience
the Thoughts of his fecond Marriage; for
tho' I thought he was become indifferent to
me, yet in this emergency, I found he had taken
but too deep a root in my Heart: Nor could
I pardon his Inconftancy, tho' he was fure I
had been Married to *Harnando*: For whilft
Cleodora was Living, for his fake, I would
never engage my felf in any Converfation,
where Love was mention'd. But alas! my
Indamora, *Cleomidon* did not obferve thofe
Niceties; but, on the contrary, ufed me unkindly; would never Anfwer my Letters, nor
fend me word of his intentions, but left me,
under

under pretence, that his Uncle was a Dying, and had fent to him, when his Bufinefs was, to Court my Rival. A thoufand diftracted Thoughts tormented me, and I knew not what to judge, if this was a Banter, or a Reality. But all this while, the Collonel obferv'd the motion of my Eye, and the change of my Countenance, which made him conclude, that what I Read, difpleas'd me very much. *Confefs, Madam,* (faid he*) is not* Cleomidon *unfaithful? And can he pretend to Love like me ?* I only Anfwer'd him with my Tears, for my Grief had taken away the ufe of my Speech, and I was not able to fpeak one word. In the interim, *Doralifa* entred the Room, and demanded of me, the caufe of my Grief. I gave her the Letter, and went from her into my own Chamber, and flung my felf down upon the Bed, uttering the moft bitter Complaints, that my Sorrow could infpire me with. But during my Abfence, the Collonel took the liberty to Read my Letter, who was as much furpriz'd at the News, and manner of fending it, as I was my felf; and was much amaz'd, that it fhould be reported he was Married to me, fince all the Rhetorick he could ufe, would not prevail with me, to part with my dear Liberty. He told *Doralifa,* he was now in hopes, I would the fooner confirm the the Faithlefs *Cleomidon* in the Report, and difpofe of my felf, as he had done ; affuring her, That *'twas impoffible for Man to Love with a more fincere Affection than he did.* He
took

took his leave of her, and his Countenance
expreſs'd a ſecret Joy, that *Cleomidon* was
Married.

In this Extremity of Trouble, what ſhould
I have done, if *Doraliſa* by her Advice had
not mollify'd my Reſentments? To her I un-
loaded all my Sorrows, and in her Breaſt I
bury'd all my Griefs. This dear kind Friend
at laſt perſwaded me to dry up my Tears, telling me, That perhaps it might be a counterfeit Letter, unleſs the Conſtitution of his
Soul were alter'd ; and that if I pleas'd to be
convinc'd of the truth, ſhe would oblige
Martillo, Lyſidas his Friend, to go into the
Country, to know the certainty of it : But I
would not conſent to it, but ſaid, I would
endeavour to Deſpiſe him, that could uſe
me thus ungenerouſly ; and knowing his Hand
and Seal ſo well,I could not be deceived. And
then came floating into my Memory, the
Jealouſie that *Cleodora* had of *Hermione*, believing there was cauſe for it, and that
Cleomidon had deceiv'd me in the Relation of that Adventure : This thought rais'd
Storms of Anger in my Breaſt, and I could
not forgive his Falſhood.

Doraliſa and I, conſulted a long time,
what might give the occaſion of this Report, of my Marriage with *Hernando* ; or
what could oblige *Cleomidon* to ſuch a Silence, never to Anſwer any of my Letters ;
nor could he be Jealous of the Collonel, who
had not made his firſt Viſit to me, after the
Death of *Elvira*, of three Weeks or a Month

O   after

after the departure of *Cleomidon* ; so that
weighing all things, I was confirm'd, that
it was the Sickliness of his Temper ; and
that the Beauty of *Hermione*, had made him
forget all his Vows to me. This Perjur'd
Wretch I thought once to have Writ to, and
have justify'd my self ; but that Thought
was soon diverted, with this Confideration,
That he was Married, and it would signifie
nothing. I then used my utmost Efforts, to
banish him from my Thoughts, and would
not suffer *Doralisa* to mention his Name to
me.

Two days after, the Collonel came to Vifit me ; he was so Generous, not to Triumph
o'er my Misfortune, nor did he aggravate the
Inconftancy of *Cleomidon*, but only said, *That
the choice of our condition, was not always in
our power ; and that neither the counfels of our
Friends, nor that of our Reafon, could engage
our Minds, but that we were carry'd on by the
violence of a Paffion, that is irrefiftable.* After this manner did he entertain me, and
fuffer'd fome days to pafs, before he fpoke
any more of Love to me : But one day as
he was with me, I difcover'd a Dulnefs upon his Countenance, which I thought muft
proceed from fome great Caufe, and ask'd
him, How his little Son did? fearing he
might be ill: He reply'd, That his Son was
well, but —— and made a ftop ; and being curious to know the fignification of this
But —— I ask'd the Collonel, What ill
News he had heard, and what did fo difturb
his

his Mind ? He reply'd, That this Morning
he had receiv'd his Commiffion, and had
Orders to go for *Flanders* in fifteen Days.
He imparted this News to me with fo great
a Concern and Trouble, that I had reafon
to believe, I was partly the caufe of his Sorrow. He failed not to tell me as much,
making a thoufand proteftations of his Love
and Sincerity ; and faid, that he Lov'd me
from the firft time he ever converfs'd with me;
and that neither Time nor Abfence could de-
face the Impreffion I had made upon his Soul;
that unlefs I made him fome returns of Love,
he was, of all Men, the moft miferable:
And not being infenfible of my Obligations
to the Collonel, and that I knew he merited
a- nobler Fate than what he fo earneftly
fought after ; I failed not to affure him, of
the Efteem and Acknowledgement I had for
him. But the Condition of my Soul was
fuch, that I could not retaliate Love for
Love; but if he could content himfelf with
my Friendfhip, he fhould find it fincere and
lafting.

Thefe few civil words, drew from his
Mouth a thoufand affurances of his Fidelity ; and being in hopes that Friendfhip, in
time, might afcend to Love, he feem'd more
fatisfied than before ; And, to own the truth,
the thoughts of his Departure gave me
more trouble than I imagin'd it could ;
knowing the uncertainty of a Battle, the
Fatigue of a Compaign, and what hazards
he muft perpetually run, that I difcover'd

O 2   my mv concern both by my Looks and Actions, which gave him hopes, he was not so indifferent to me, as a few Days before, he fear'd he was. his visit was not long that Day, being oblig- ed to give his Orders about his Departure; and, as he was going, ' Tell me, Madam (said ' he) what Consolation may an absent Lover ' find, when separated from the Object of his ' Affections? May he hope he shall one Day ' be Happy, if he returns Victorious over his ' Enemies? These Thoughts (continued he) ' will charm the fleeting hours away; and ' the hopes, that *Lindamira*'s Love will be ' my Recompence, will so annimate my Cou- ' rage, and redouble my Force, that I promise ' my self the Victory before I go : But since I gave him no other hopes, than the continuation of my Friendship, he seem'd so dejected and cast down, that I really pitty'd him; and folding his Arms a-cross, ' Unhappy *Harnan-* ' *do*, said he, where shall my distracted thoughts ' find ease, if *Lindamira* forbids me to hope ? ' Alas! (said he) no Condition can equal mine; ' for I Love one passionately, that Loves an- ' other, that is perjur'd, unfaithful, and un- ' worthy of her.

I endeavour'd, what I could, to appeafe his Passion, and to represent to him, how much he offended me, for the little value he set upon my Friendship. He begg'd my Pardon, so much exaggarating the violence of his Love, that I could not be Angry at him.

When

When he was gone, I was fenfible, that his Departure would be a trouble to me; for thofe admirable Qualities both of Body and Mind, claim'd a Refpect and Efteem of all that knew him; and had I been inclin'd to a fecond Affection, I could not have refus'd *Harnando* the Requeft he made me to Marry him, with advantages beyond my Merits. But not being willing to be Fetter'd or Inflav'd by any, fince the beft of the whole Sex had deceived me, I kept to my Refolution, not to Marry any one. Adieu, my *Indamora*.

I am,

Your Affectionate Friend,

and Ser.ant,

Lindamira.

The

The XXIIth. LETTER.

THE Night before that Collonel *Har-nando* was to go for *Flanders*, my deareſt *Indamora*, he came to take his Farewel of me; but with a Countenance ſo dejected, that it grieved me extreamly to ſee him look ſo ſad; and believing there was ſome hidden Cauſe for it, I begg'd to know what 'twas that troubled him. He looking earneſtly on me, anſwered with a Sigh, *That ſome envious Plannet interpos'd between him, and all his hopes; that when he was Abſent, his Rival would be happy in the poſſeſſion of me.* Theſe Words he ſpoke in ſo diſmal a Tone, that it both ſurprized and troubled me; nor could I divine what he ment by his Rival; for he knew that *Cleomidon* was both Inconſtant and Married; wherefore I asked him, Why he was ſo ingenuous at tormenting of himſelf, ſince he had no Rival to fear: And that if *Hermione* were Dead, I would never Marry *Cleomidon*; and if I would change my Condition, it ſhould be in favour of himſelf, there being none I did eſteem ſo much as him.

But

But this Disconsolate Lover seem'd not satisfied with what I said, but ask'd me, if I would promise to Marry him (if Death did not make an eternal separation between us) at his return? 'For (added He) 'tis not to be ' exprefs'd, what my Fears suggeft to me; ' and my juft Apprenfions makes me fuffer as ' great Torments, as if ten thoufand Vulturs '' were tearing of my Heart. But Oh! my ' happy Rival, he will triumph in my Ab- ' fence, and Laugh at my Misfortune! Who is this terrible Rival (faid I) interrupting of him, that gives you fo great a Fear? Explain your Meaning, and I may rectifie your Miftake. 'You will but too foon know, Madam ' (faid He) whom I fear, and whom I dread; ' but pardon me, that I fay no more — He then rofe up to take his laft Adieu, begging of me not to forget him, to write to him, and to receive his Letters kindly. I promifed him what he defired, nor could I forbear fome Tears at our feparation, which I thought a juft Tribute due to his Merits. Thus did the poor Collonel take his leave of me, defiring I would fometimes fee his Son, which, might perhaps call into my Memory the unhappy Father.

The Abfence of fo worthy a Friend, gave me fome difturbance, and I could not think of his laft words, without Grief and Trouble; nor could I apprehend the meaning of thofe ambiguous words he fpoke. By the firft opportunity, I had an Account of his fafe Arrival: I anfwered his, and received

O 4   feveral

several others, which were writ with all
the Passion imagianble, and in a most Pa-
thetick Strain ; for none could express their
Thoughts more elegnatly than himself. ! Our
Correspondence continued punctually for
some Months, on both sides ; for the Collonel never failed to write to me, as often
as he had opportunity, or his Affairs would
permit. It was never my Humour to be in-
quisitive after News ; yet, for his sake, sometimes I would inform my self of the movements of both Armies, and Passes lost and
won. But this Curiosity gave me some di-
sturbance, as one Night I was at Supper, and
some Gentlemen Discoursing with *Lysidas* of
the Affairs of *Flanders*, lamenting the Death
of some of their Friends, I unhappily asked,
if they had heard any News of Collonel *Harnando?* One of them answered, That by
the last Post, he heard he was Wounded by
a Bullet, shot into his Neck, and that some
despair'd of his Recovery. This News was
the more surprizing, having had a Letter
from him but two Posts before; but the
disorder it cast in my Thoughts, was seen by
my Eyes; which *Lysidas* perceiving, endeavoured to divert my Fears, by saying, There
were many false Reports raised, on purpose
to afflict them who had any Friends in this
last Expedition.

As soon as Supper was ended, I retired,
with *Doralisa*, into my Chamber, where we
both lamented the unhappy Fate of the Collonel ; but being willing to hope, it was only

ly a flying Report, we endeavoured to comfort our selves; but the next day, had the News confirm'd to our great Sorrow. But two Posts after, I received a Letter from *Leander*, a Friend whom the Collonel had intrusted with the secrets of his Love, to give me an account of his Health, which was then in a very bad Condition; but, in a short time after, he made a shift to write to me himself, tho' he lay very ill of his Wound, desiring I would continue writing to him; and withal he rais'd my hopes, that his Life was in no hazard: But no sooner was my Mind re-settled for the danger the Collonel had been in, but a new and most surprizing Adventure befel me.

You may remember, I have formerly mention'd *Martillo* to you, *Lysidas*'s Friend, whose Business call'd him to *Byzantem*, a Town in the same County where *Cleomidon* Liv'd. It happened, at that time, there was a Horse-Race, where a piece of Plate of two hundred Pounds was to be Run for, which brought all the Gentlemen of the Country there-a-bouts, to be Spectators of this Sport; and amongst the rest, *Cleomidon*; *Martillo* seeing of him, (at whose House he had formerly Din'd) took the freedom to wish him Joy of his new Lady; at these words *Cleomidon* started, and desired him to explain himself, saying, he was never Marrid to any but *Cleodora*, who had been Dead near fifteen Months. *Is that possible*, replied Martillo, *and are not you married to the fair*
Hermoine?

Hermione ? 'Tis certainly fo, faid *Cleomidon*;
for *Hermione* has been Married thefe three
Months ; and there you may fee her Hufband (pointing to a Gentleman that ftood
near him:) But, Sir, you fo furprize me with
this News, that I muft befeech you to tell
me where you heard it : This place (replied
Martillo) is not at all proper to Difcourfe
of it ; for much depends upon the truth of
Hermione's not being Married to your felf :
And when the Race is over, faid this Friend,
I will meet you where you fhall appoint ;
for, perhaps, it may be in my power to do
you a fmall Service. *Cleomidon* complied
with *Martillo*; and as foon as the fport was
over, they met according to appointment.

The Confternation you have put me in
(faid *Cleomidon*) is not to be exprefs'd, nor
can I imagine, what could occafion fo falfe a
Report ; for fhe is a Lady I never pretended
to. No, Sir, faid *Martillo*, then why did
you write to a Lady you had formerly
Courted, that you were now Married to the
Charming *Hermonie ?* Alas ! Sir, (faid *Cleomidon*) what you tell me amazes me ; and
explain this Anigma, to deliver me out of
the pain I fuffer ; for my Heart forebodes
fome Treafon has been contrived againft me,
to deftroy my Happinefs ; and (if 'tis poffible) clear all my Doubts, and let me know
every Circumftance has been related, that
has confirmed this flying Report.

The firft News of your Marriage, faid
Martillo, I heard at a Coffee-Houfe you did
ufually

ufually frequent when you were in Town;
but it was confirm'd under your Hand and
Seal, in a Letter to *Lindamira* — Hold, (faid
Cleomidon) do you know *Lindamira*? And
did fhe receive a Letter from me, that mentioned my Marriage with *Hermione*? 'Tis
moft affuredly fo, (reply'd *Martillo*) and the
Letter I have feen and read over feveral times;
and, I believe, my Memory has retain'd it
all, or great part of it; and, at *Cleomidon's*
Requeft, repeated it to him.

But the furprize *Cleomidon* was in, at the
recital of this Letter, is not to be exprefs'd ; for a long time he kept filence, with
his Eyes fix'd on the Ground ; then lifting of
them up to Heaven, as to bear witnefs of
his Innocence: Oh moft unhappy *Cleomidon*,
faid he! Was ever conftant Lover fo much
abufed,or ever fo great a Villany contriv'd to
make me the moft wretched of Mankind !
How much am I become the loathed, de-
tefted Object of *Lindamira's* Thoughts, whofe
juft refentments nothing can appeafe ? For
could fhe believe me Married to *Hermonie*,
and yet preferve a Friendfhip for me ? Oh !
no, fhe has reveng'd herfelf on me, and
made *Harnando* happy.

How do you mean Happy, faid *Martillo*,
interrupting of him, fince the Collonel is
now in *Flanders* ? This Letter, reply'd *Cleomidon* (fhewing it to *Martillo*) has been the
caufe of my Mifery: And nothing but *Lindamira's* own Hand, could have perfwaded me,
fhe could have lov'd another.

Martillo

Martillo taking the Letter from him, read these words.

Lindamira *to* Cliomidon.

You will not wonder I have chang'd my Sentiments, when you know 'tis in favour of Collonel Harnando *, on whose kindness depends all my Happiness, which I esteem beyond the Western Mines. What has pass'd between us, let be buried in Oblivion, as shall the memory of* Cleomidon, *by*

Lindamira.

Martillo having read the Letter with Wonder and Amazement, returned it *Cleomidon,* telling him, That never so black a Treason was contriv'd to make two Persons so unhappy, whose Hands were so well counterfeited, that any one might be deceived : But yet he could not comprehend the meaning of his sudden departure out of Town, and why he never answer'd *Lindamira*'s Letters.

That which occasioned my Journey out of Town (reply'd *Cleomidon*) I imparted to *Lindamira* ; my Uncle then being extream ill, as my Friend wrote me word, urging many specious Reasons for my immediate Departure. That Night I arriv'd at my House, I wrote to *Lindamira*, that I would not fail to be in Town by that time our Nuptials were to be Celebrated, unless she commanded the contrary ; for my Uncle was then very ill of a fit of the Gout. I impatiently waited her Answer ;

but

but not hearing from her, I wrote again, and gave her an account of all my Defigns, begging of her, by all our Loves, not to fail writing to me. But having thus drill'd on a Fortnight, I became very Melancholy, not knowing what to Conjecture; and as ill as my Uncle was, I defired he would give me leave to go away; for I fear'd fome misfortune had bafallen *Lindamira*, that I had not heard from her. And, *Lyndaraxa* malicioufly reply'd, that fhe heard fhe had fo many Admirers, that fhe fear'd I fhould have the leaft fhare of her Heart. But however, I refolv'd to be gone in two Days: And, unfortunately, the Day before I affign'd for my Departure, two Gentlemen Din'd at my Houfe, that was newly come from *London*; and *Lyndaraxa*, who was always inquifitive after News, demanded of one of 'em, what was the beft News in Town. He replied, That the Marriage of Collonel *Harnando* and *Lindamira*, was the only Difcourfe at prefent. The other replied, that he had foon forgot *Elvira*, that could think of Marrying fo foon. The firft made Anfwer, *That the Collonel had a kindnefs for her in his Lady's Life-time, who was Jealous of her, and 'twas thought fhe laid it fo much to Heart, that it was the occafion of her Death.*

This Difcourfe (faid *Cleomidon*) was like a Dagger to my Heart; for knowing what excellent Endowments and Attractions the Collonel had, it bred fuch a Hurricane of Thoughts within my Breaft, that I was all a flaming Fire, which in my labouring Fancy was never

at

at eafe; nor could I tafte that Cordial Sleep,
that helps to eafe a troubled Mind: The
loaded Prifoners with Chains, fuffered not
fuch Torments as I did; but to imbitter more
my pain, the next Morning I received a confirmation of this News, from *Lindamira's*
Hand, and that, Sir, was the Letter you
have Read: Tho' now I am convinced it is a
Forgery, yet then I thought her falfe, and
the moft perjured of Woman-kind: Yet however, I intended to prefent my felf before her,
only for her punifhment, to obferve how fhe
could look on me, after the Vows that fhe
had broke; but as my Refentments were no
fecret, my Uncle faid all he could to appeafe
me; and perfwaded me not to complain to
Lindamira, fince her Fault could not be pardoned: And *Lyndaraxa* cunningly advifed,
to flight her Infidelity, fince nothing could
fo much gratifie the Humour of an Inconftant
Miftrefs, as to fee her Lover torment and
afflict himfelf for her fake. Thus was I
perfwaded to forbear my Refentments, which
if I had not delay'd, it would have fpared me
many a reftlefs Night; and had I followed
the Torrent of my Paffion, I fhould have
known the Truth, and then this Vail of Falfhood had been torn away, and *Lindamira*
had appeared as innocent as ever. But now
Martillo, What may I hope? Will fhe be
Deaf to all my Prayers? Will fhe forgive
my Silence, and impute my Fault to my moft
Rigorous Fate?

Thus

Thus did *Cleomidon* Complain, which mov'd
fo much Compaffion in *Martillo*, that he promifed to ferve him to the utmoft of his
power, and would prepare my Mind to hear
his Story. They appointed a Day to be in
London ; but *Cleomidon*'s impatience brought
him a Day fooner than *Martillo*.

My ignorance of what I have now related,
made me commit fo great an Abfurdity, that
I can hardly forgive my felf; but what I
have more to fay will make this Letter too
Voluminous; therefore I will conclude this,
with the Affurance of my fincere Love to my
deareft *Indamora*.

I am, your Faithful

LINDAMIRA.

The

The XXIIIth. LETTER.

CLeomidon was no fooner come to Town, (my deareſt *Indamora*) but he came directly to *Lyſidas*'s Houſe, and demanded if I were at Home ; and being told *I was*, beg'd the favour, to be admitted to me. This News was very furprizing, and I much admired, how he durſt approach me, after the injuſtice he had done me : But he being totally caſt out of my Favour, I ſent him word, *I had Company with me, and could not ſee him.* This Meſſage did not much furprize him, (knowing by *Martillo*, how great my Reſentments were) but he ſent a ſecond time, in the moſt fubmiffive Terms imaginable, ſaying, *He had ſomething of importance to diſcover to me, that related to us both.* But this I thought only a pretence to ſee me; and no excuſe could juſtifie his baſe Actions; that I ſent him word again, *I would never ſee his Face, and wonder'd how be could deſire to ſee mine.* Theſe laſt words made him almoſt Diſtracted ; and I had the pleaſure of ſeeing him in all the tranſports of Grief and Trouble (for there was a Window on the Stairs, that looked into the Parlor, that I could ſee any one, and not be ſeen.) Thus did I pleaſe my ſelf, in tormenting of him ; for at that
time;

time, no flinty Rock was more hardy and inacceffible than my Heart; and tho' *Iris* interceeded much in his behalf, and begg'd of me to fee him, yet nothing could prevail, and a third time I fent word, abfolutely to forbid him, ever to come where I was.

This laft Meffage was like a Thunderbolt to his Heart, which caft him into that Defpair and tranfport of Grief, that of a long time he fpoke not a word. At laft, faid he to *Iris*, *Will you tell the cruel* Lindamira, *that I will obey her; but 'tis Barbarous in her, not to hear my Juftification. I have fuch things to acquaint her with, that will ftartle her belief; but I will leave the reft to* Marrillo, *who perhaps may have more credit with her than I have.* As he ended thefe words, he immediately went away, with Looks fo dejected, and fo pale, as if his Grave he intended fhould be the place of his Afylum.

But he was no fooner gone, but I repented, and wifh'd I had but feen him, to have upbraided him with his Infidelity; but in this emergency I knew not what to do; for *Doralifa* was gone out, whofe Advice I wanted very much.

As foon as my two Coufins were come Home, I acquainted them with this wonderful News, which extreamly furpriz'd 'em; and they wifhed I had granted *Cleomidon* an Audience, believing it poffible for him to have appeafed my Refentments; and that perhaps he had been treacheroufly dealt by.

P   This

This Though made *Lyfidas* very induftrious
to find out his Lodging; (for he infinitely
efteem'd *Cleomidon*; and his Bafenefs to me,
was a great grief to him, as believing him
incapable of fuch an Action) but his endeavours were fruitlefs: That Evening, *Martillo* came to Town, and not meeting with *Cleomidon* according to appointment, came to
Lyfidas's Houfe, and acquainted him with
what had pafs'd between him and *Cleomidon*,
at *Byzantem*. He related all that I have already mentioned to you, which rejoyced
Cleomidon beyond what can be imagined.
And when *Martillo* told me this Adventure,
(which he did with fo much ferioufnefs, that
I could not doubt the truth) I was ready to
Faint away, and I found my felf difpirited ;
for I was fo extreamly affected with the Relation of *Cleomidon*'s Innocence, and vexed at
my own ill-nature, for not letting of him fee
me, that I wanted no other Accufer but my
own Confcience; but as I was ignorant of
what was paft, I did but ferve him as he deferved. But however, I excufed my felf to
Martillo, who told me, That the Hour of
their Appointment was come ; and demanded
of me, if I would not fend fome Words of
Confolation, to the unhappy *Cleomidon*. I defir d him to tell him, as being ignorant of his
Innocence, he could not expect a better treatment from me ; but fince he had not forfeited that Character that made me to efteem
him, he fhould find me as fincerely his Friend
as ever.

But

But Martillo, inftead of meeting Cleomidon, found a Letter Directed to him, and one for me Inclofed in it, which made him return with fpeed, faying to me, That I ought to Anfwer it ; for he found by his, that Cleomidon was Sick. I open'd it, and found thefe Words.

Cleomidon to Lindamira.

, You could let me depart, Madam, without bearing my Juftification, which is too tedious to Write ; but I have been inhumanely betray'd by my moft intimate Friends, which has made me appear a ftrange Criminal to Lindamira : But my Innocence is equal to the Love I bear you. I befeech you, permit me to make my complaint, that I may demonftrate the Treafon has been acted againft me : And nothing but the influence of your Eyes can revive me under fuch violent preffures I now fuffer. Deny not my Requeft to the moft paffionate of Lovers, whofe only Ambition is to Dye

Yours, CLEOMIDON.

This Letter wrought that Compaffion in my Soul, that I could not help fhedding Tears at the Reading of it ; which had fo mollify'd my Anger, that I accus'd my felf of Barbarity, and begg'd a thoufand Pardons of Cleomidon. But Martillo being in hafte to be gone, defired that I would Anfwer his Letter kindly, and that he might be the Mef-

fenger

fenger of it. I therefore wrote him thefe
few Words, as follows.

Lindamira *to* Cleomidon.

Your Innocence has defaced out of my Heart,
thofe juft Refentments I had againft you,
which were proportionable to the efteem I ever
had for you, and whilft I believ'd you guilty
of Infidelity and Ingratitude, I treated you
like a Criminal. I am impatient to hear your
Juftification, and to know who are thofe trea-
cherous Friends, that have fo unhumanely be-
tray'd you. Affure your felf that I am fin-
cerely,

Your LINDAMIRA.

Martillo loft no time, but went to *Cleo-*
midon's Lodging, where he found him Sick
in Bed, and his Phyfician with him. *This is*
kindly done, (faid he) *to come and fee a dying*
Friend ; and by this I find you have received
my Letter ; but what reception the Inclofed
found, I dread to hear. Fear nothing, reply'd
Martillo, *for* Lindamira's *Heart is not fo in-*
flexible as you had reafon to believe : The
Relation I have given her of your paft misfor-
tunes, has fo mollified her Heart, that fhe
gave me this Letter for you ; and does alfo
defire you to be careful of your Health. Cleomidon received this Letter with all the
tranfports of Love and Paffion, and thanked
Martillo for the good Office he had done
him. *But my kind Friend* (faid he) *the condi-*
tion

tion I *am in, will not permit me to fee my*
Lindamira, *who defires to hear my Juftifica-*
tion. I *will return to her,* (faid Martillo)
and acquaint her with your illnefs ; and I *am*
perfwaded that Doralifa *will prevail with her,*
to come and fee you. This officious Friend
fo well perform'd his part, as that Evening,
Lyfidas, Doralifa, and my felf, made our
Vifit to him.

But when I came into the Room, I was not
able to fpeak one Word to him, but ftood
like a Statue, with my Eyes fixed on him :
I look'd on him with grief and forrow ; for
his Misfortunes had fo altered him, that his
Colour was quite gone, and a dead Palenefs
diffufed all over his Face ; his Eyes looked
dull, and a deep Melancholy fettled in his
Countenance. Whilft I was in this Contemplation, *Lyfidas* took me by the Hand,
and asked me, if I would not fpeak to *Cleo-*
midon ? When I approach'd him, I was not
able to utter one word ; but fat me down by
him, and fell into a great fit of Weeping.
Cleomidon was much concern'd to fee me in
this Trouble, and faid to me the moft paffionate and tender things imaginable ; but I
could make him no other Anfwer but my
Sighs : For all our Misfortunes, fince our
unhappy Separation, came crouding into my
Thoughts, which ftopped the freedom of my
Speech. But Doralifa, whofe Soul was not
agitated with fo many different Paffions as
mine, begg'd of me to dry up my Tears, and
to fpeak to *Cleomidon,* and to know of him,
the

the Hiftory of his Life, fince the laft breach
between us.

That, Madam, cries he, will take up more
time than I fear your Patience will admit on,
or *Lindamira* will afford to hearken to.

No, my *Cleomidon* (faid I) I can never be
tired with a relation of your Innocence; and
tho' I know, partly by *Martillo*, you have
been betray'd, and that you fufpect the in-
humane. *Lyndaraxa*, yet I am ignorant how
you difcovered the Truth, and who were your
intimate Friends, that acted this perfidious
Part. If the Relation will not be too great
a Fatigue in the Condition you are in, let
me know this Night, how I have been de-
ceive.l, by the report of your Marriage with
Hermione, which has given me fuch juft
caufe to complain againft you.

My deareft *Lindamira* (reply'd *Cleomidon*)
then you may judge by your own Heart,
what I have fuffered, tho' in a greater degree; for the News of your Marriage with
Collonel *Harnando*, fo alarm'd all the fa-
culties of my Soul, and reduc'd me to that
extremity of Defpair, that I was not fit for
humane Society. But fyour Commands fhall
be obey'd; and I will contract this Narration
into as narrow a compafs as I can; and will
let you know how fortunately I made a difcovery of what I am going to relate.

As foon as I parted from *Martillo* from
Byzantium, I return'd to my own Houfe with
all the fpeed I could. I fent my Man to *Vo-
lifius*, a Friend of mine, that liv'd within
half

half a mile of me ; to him I oftentimes
imparted my Mind, and ask'd his Advice on
several occasions ; and in this Emergency,
wanted him to Communicate the most surprizing and most welcome News in the
World, that you were not Married to Collonel *Harnando* ; saying to him, This was
the most artificial piece of Treachery as
ever was acted, that could deceive us both
with a Report of each others being Married ;
and our Hands were so exactly counterfeited, as to lead us into these Mistakes, to
believe each other guilty of the highest Ingratitude imaginable. I am so much afflicted at it, said I to *Volusius*, that I should wrong
an innocent Person, that I would give an
hundred Guinea's to find out the Author and
Contriver of this malicious Plot. And affift me, my dear Friend said, (imbracing of
him) in the Discovery ; and tho' I have reason to suspect *Lyndaraxa*, yet I cannot prove
any thing against her.

Volusius harkned to me with the Countenance of a Friend, extreamly interefs'd in my
Misfortune ; and after a long time revolving in his Mind, whether he ought to own
the Treason, or seem innocent of it : But he
having some remorse of Conscience, he on
a sudden cast himself at my Feet, and the
Tears trickling down his Eyes ; in this sub-
missive Posture he besought me to hear him.

Sir, said He, your astonishment cannot be
greater than my Villany, in being an Ac-
complice in this treasonable Design, which
P 4   was

was to deſtroy the Satisfaction and Comfor
of your Life. Heavens forbid! (ſaid I, interrupting of him) Has *Voluſius*, my Friend, betray'd me? Oh! add not new Afflictions to
my Miſery; but tell me quickly, what you
know, and conceal not the leaſt Circumſtance,
that can juſtifie my Innocence to the injur'd
Lindamira. At theſe words, he roſe up, and
his dejected Looks wrought ſome Compaſſion
for my moſt cruel Enemy. Sir, ſaid he, The
Confuſion I am in, will not permit me to
make any Appology, nor can I offer any thing
to excuſe ſo unworthy, and ſo ungenerous an
Action: But not to keep you longer in ſuſ-
penſe; know, Sir, that *Lyndaraxa* came to
me one day, when you were in *London*, and
told me, ſhe had thought of a means, how
to raiſe my Fortune in the World, if I
would be rul'd by her. I thank'd her for
her obliging Care, and reply'd, I ſhould be
very acknowledging, if ſhe'd propoſe a way
how I may honeſtly advance my ſelf. Then
be rul'd by me, ſaid ſhe, and you ſhall have
two hundred Guinea's to morrow; and if the
Project ſucceed, according to my Wiſhes,
you ſhall have a hundred a Year ſettled on
you for your Life, which will raiſe you
above the Contempt of the World, and gain
you the Eſteem of all your Acquaintance.
Theſe were her Propoſals; and without
farther ſcrutiny into her Deſigns, I Swore
Allegiance to her, and an implicite Obedience
to all her Commands; and then ſhe explain-
ed herſelf to me, as follows.

You

You may ferve me (faid Lindaraxa) *and not be unjuft to you Friend* Cleomidon, *who is going to precipitate his Ruine with a young Girl at* London, *who has neither Wit, Beauty, nor Fortune ; and he defigns to marry her very fpeedily ; my defign is only, that you would write to him, that his Uncle lies a Dying, who is now ill of the Gout, and I know he will obey the Summons ; when he is here, leave me to finifh the reft ; for I will fo contrive it, as to break off this match, which will be the inevitable Ruine of his Daughter.*

I confefs, Sir, faid *Volufius,* that fhe had fo poffefs'd me with this Opinion, that I obey'd her without Reluctancy, hoping I might do you a future Service. But, Madam, faid I to her, 'tis impoffible to prevent *Cleomidon's* Marriage with *Lindamira,* for he Loves her paffionately, and thinks her not inferiour to the reft of her Sex : That is only his fond Opinion, faid this crafty Lady ; but do you write to him, and do afterwards as I fhall direct. I promifed her what fhe defired ; and my Fortune being at a low Ebb, (which fhe knew) I was unhappily prevailed with to comply with her.

That Night, Sir, if you remember that you come home, you wrote to *Lindamira,* and *Lyndaraxa* intercepted your Letter, and with great joy brought it to me, and thus delivered herfelf fmiling on me, telling me,

me, That now was the time, wherein she
expected the performance of my Promise.
Volufius (continued she) you muft not baulk
me of my Defigns; for if you do, I'll
fummon a Legion of Devils to be reveng'd
of you : Take this Letter, purfued this Malicious Woman, and practice thefe Characters; for there will be occafion to counterfeit this Hand. Thefe words made me ftart,
and I would have given my Life to have
been excus'd: But fhe held me to my Promife, threatning me with Shame and Punifhment if I betray'd her, or did not obferve
her Directions. She made me Swear a
fecond time, to be true to her Intereft, and
like an ungrateful perfidious Wretch, I did
agree with her for two hundred Guinea's, to
Counterfeit what Letters fhe pleas'd : And
I my felf went to the Poft-Houfe to receive *Lindamira's* Letters, and brought them
to *Lyndaraxa*: But it cannot be exprefs'd
the joy fhe fhewed, when fhe read the Melancholly Complaints of *Lindamira*, for
your filence. And fhe fhall have more reafon to complain, faid fhe, for *Lindamira*
fhall receive no more Letters from her Lover. My Heart relented at the reading of
this Letter; but I durft not difcover my
Sentiments, her Malice was fo implaca-
ble; and it was her Contrivance to have
thofe two Gentlemen at Dinner, who told
you the falfe News of *Lindamira's* Marriage with Collonel *Harnando*; and you
must

muſt know further, that there was a young
Agent of hers at *London*, who had a Lodging over-againſt *Lyſidas*'s Houſe. This
Creature had a Penſion from her, to ob-
ſerve what paſs'd there ; and by ſome means
ſhe came to know, that Collonel *Harnando*
had a reſpeἀ for *Lindamira* in *Elvira*'s
Life-time ; and this innocent Affeἀion ſhe improv'd to her own advantage. She was ſo
happy in her Deſigns, that this Report got
Credit with you ; and ſhe found it ſtung
you to the Heart, which made her very
pleaſant, when you were buried in your Melancholy Thoughts. But ſhe was no ſtranger
to what moſt concern'd you ; for her Maid
Julian, was an Eve-droper, and had often
over heard us Diſcourſing of *Lindamira*, in
Cleodora's Life-time. She was like a Mercury ; for ſhe was very expeditious in carrying to her Miſtreſs what ſhe heard us
ſay : And this with truth I can affirm, That
I never told her any thing you ſaid to me,
but what ſhe heard I could not deny. And
Julian, who always ſeem'd ſo very Civil
and Reſpeἀful 'to you, was a great inſtru-
ment in contriving this Miſchief : For ſhe
hearing you ſpeak of *Lindamira* with great
Affeἀion, related to her Miſtreſs, who had
ſworn a Revenge ever ſince you ſo happily
diſcovered her Plot with *Sabina* in the Garden ; She ſaid ſhe would croſs you in your
Love, and make you drag your Chains
heavily : This ſhe has effeἀually done ;
and

and I was fo unworthy to affift her in the management of it. That now, Sir, inflict what Punifhment you pleafe (faid *Volufius*) for I am too confcious of my own Treachery, to hope to efcape your moft fevere Revenge ; and if Repentance could expiate my Fault, or my Sorrow attone for my Crime, I may hope to find you merciful.

He ended his Narration with infinite of Tears, and I believe did truly Repent of his Perfidioufnefs ; but my aftonifhment would not give me leave to fpeak of a confiderable time ; but at laft being awaken'd from my Amazement ; *Oh Heavens !* faid I, *How am I crofs'd, and why am I thus unjuftly dealt by ? I have loft* Lindamira's *Favour for ever ; and tho' your Treachery deferves immediate Death, yet I will fpare your Life for your Punifhment ; and you fhall go along with me to* London ; *and if ever you fee* Lyndaraxa's *Face more, expect the heavieft Vengeance in the World to light on your Head.* I would not let him go Home to fetch thofe Neceffaries he pretended he wanted for his Journey, but furnifh'd him with Money, and other neceffary things, becaufe I durft not truft him out of my fight, fearing he fhould betray me a fecond time, and acquaint *Lyndaraxa* with my intentions. And two hours after Midnight, we departed for *London.* I only took with me two Servants and himfelf ; and I left *Cleander* (who Waits on me in my Chamber) to give me

an

an account of what paſſes in my abſence ;
And this day I received a Letter from him,
That my Uncle was ſurpriz'd at my ſudden
departure ; but *Lyndaraxa* is almoſt Diſtra-
ƈted at it : For knowing that *Voluſius* came
with me, ſhe finds ſhe is betray'd, and ſhe
knows not to whom to vent her Paſſion ;
that *Alcander* is in great trouble about her,
being ignorant of the occaſion of this Frenzy : She cannot Sleep, but walks about the
Houſe all Night ; and hearkens at every ones
Door, in hopes to have ſome Intelligence of
what I do ; that ſhe behaves herſelf ſo much
like a Mad-woman. that *Alcander* fears ſhe
will do herſelf a Miſchief.

This, my *Lindamira*, (ſaid *Cleomidon*) is
what has paſt ſince our fatal Separation :
And ſurely, Madam, I deſerve your Pity ;
for no Slave has dragg'd a more wretched
Life about him, than my ſelf : Tho' I believ'd you falſe, and thought you Married
to *Harnando*, yet I ador'd the Author of all
my Miſery ; and your Idea I could not baniſh from my Heart. *I* beſeech you, Madam,
hide not from me, how great a Progreſs
the Collonel has made in your Heart ; for
he has ſtore of Charms, to engage the moſt
inſenſible of your Sex : He is not only deſ-
cended from a moſt Illuſtrious Family, but
poſſeſſes all the advantages of a ſprightly
Wit ; and his bewitching Tongue never
fail'd of ſucceſs, where he deſign'd a Conqueſt.

But

But it being late, I told *Cleomidon* I would reserve my own Adventures for the next day, and make him Judge of my Actions, Whether or no I still merited his Affections. I left him to his Rest, and his Mind re-setled and satisfied, that he still held the chief rank in my esteem. Adieu my *Indamora.*

I am,

Your Affectionate Friend

and Servant,

LINDAMIRA.

The *laſt* LETTER.

THE next day, according to my promife, my deareſt *Indamora*, I was to
fee *Cleomidon*, whofe Indifpofition oblig'd
me to this Vifit: I found him much better,
and in a tranfport of joy, that there was a
true Reconciliation between us: For, 'Ma-
'dam (faid he) I can think with pleafure
'on all the Inquietudes I have fuffer'd, fince
'my *Lindamira* does permit me again to
'Love her. Therefore let us no longer tempt
'Fate, left we fhould meet with a new dif-
'appointment; for a fecond Separation will
'be Death to me; and tell me fincerely, if
'the Merits of Collonel *Harnando* has not
'defaced that impreffion I had once made?
I reply'd, That he Reign'd more abfolute in
my Heart, than ever; and being truly fenfible of his Sufferings, it had augmented the
efteem I had for him, which would laft E-
ternally. And at his requeft, I recounted
to him all that had paft between the Collonel and my felf, with the fame fincerity as I
have done to you, without omitting, or dif-
guifing the leaft circumftance; and fhew'd
him the Collonel's Letters, with the Cop-
pies of my own, which I brought along
with me for that purpofe. I told my *Cleomidon*

midon, That I thought it neceffary to write
to the Collonel, to acquaint him with his
Innocency, and to defire he would do me that
juftice , to acknowledge there was no Engagement between us, but only a Recriprocal Efteem and Friendfhip. To this purpofe I wrote to him, and fent my Letter to
the Poft Houfe by *Cleomidon's* Servant ;
and I doubt not but he was well enough
pleafed with my fincere way of dealing with
him, which immediately difplay'd it felf in
the effects ; for his Health return'd to him
in a fhort time after ; and in the interim
that I receiv'd an Anfwer of my Letter to
the Collonel , an unexpected deliverance
happened to *Cleomidon* ; for *Cleander* wrote
him word , That *Lyndaraxa* was raving
Mad by fits ; and when the Phrenzy was
in her Brain, fhe one Night defign'd to compleat her Character, of being a very notorious Woman, attempted the Murder of
Alcander ; but the Weapon fhe made ufe
of for this purpofe, was a rufty Knife fhe
found by chance in the Buttery , that
it being fo eaten up with Ruft, it would
not enter the Skin of *Alcander* ; and the
thruft fhe gave him, awoke him from his
Sleep, and laying violent hands on her, he
held her till his Servants came to his Affiftance, who taking of her out of her Bed
(when her Cloaths were on) fhut her into a
Clofet that had a ftrong Lock to it, where
fhe was to remain, till *Alcander* could con-
fult

fult with his Friends, how to difpofe of her.
But fhe had fo much Senfe remaining as, to
be fenfible of her own Wickednefs, and to
know that the ﹝Law could punifh her for
attempting the Life of her Husband. But
during the time of this Confultation, before Day broke, fhe made her efcape out of
the Window, by the help of fome new
Holland that lay in her Clofet, which fhe
faftened to the Bars of her Window, and fo
flid down. But when *Alcander* came with
his Friends to reproach her with her Villany, they found the Bird of ill *Omen* fled,
which was a great furprize to them. Di-
ligent fearch was made for her ; but no tidings could be heard, till the next Morning ;
and the Keeper of the Park brought word,
that he faw his Miftrefs floating in one
of the Ponds, but he durft not approach
her, fhe look'd fo dreadfully. Care was
then taken to have her fetch'd from thence ;
and her Funeral was performed with as
much privacy as poffible.

 Alcander began to fufpect, that fomething
extraordinary muft be the occafion of this
Difturbance in her Mind, and commanded
Julian to acquaint him, if fhe knew any
caufe for it. This Wretch feeing herfelf
deprived of her great fupport, and of *Volufius*, began to relent of what Villany fhe
had practiced, and made a fincere Confeffion of all I have related ; firft of *Lyndaraxa*'s defign of introducing a falfe Heir,
by the affiftance of *Sabina* and her Contri-

Q   vance ;

vance; and that *Lyndaraxa* has Sworn a
Revenge to *Cleomidon*, for making the Difcovery; and what fhe had Plotted with
Volufius, to render us both unhappy. That
finding her defigns difcovered, it was fo
great a torment to her Mind, that in her
Paffion would often fay, She fhould do herfelf a Mifchief. *Alcander* was fo much afflicted to hear this account of his Wife,
that it redoubled his Sorrow for her; and
was as much inrag'd at the Perfidioufnefs of
Julian, whofe fight, he could not' bear, but
order'd her to be difmifs'd, and fent back to
her Friends. The old Gentleman was much
afflicted at this accident, and wrote to *Cleomidon* a Letter fill'd with the Relation of
his Misfortunes; and alfo begging his
Pardon for the injury he had done him,
wifhing he would be fo kind to come to
him for a Fortnight or three Weeks; but
Cleomidon faid, he would not leave me till
he had ty'd the *Gordian-Knot*, that nothing
but Death can diffolve. And a few Days
after, I received an Anfwer from Collonel
Harnando, which was in thefe words.

Collonel Harnando *to* Lindamira.

Madam,

*What I fear'd, is at laft come to pafs, that
you would be convinced of* Cleomidon's *innocence*; *I knew the truth before I left you,
but had not the power to tell you fo my
Jelf. I muft not pretend to enter the Lifts*

with

with fo happy a Rival , who firft poffefs'd
your. Heart : But if you will leave it to the
chance of War, who fhall poffefs ycu, I will
meafure my Sword with him ; and fhall think
that Blood well fpilt, that can purchafe me
Lindamira.

In juftice to you, Madam, I do acknowledge,
you made me no Promife to be ever mine;
but you were cruel in refufing your Hand,
when you believ'd Cleomidon unfaithful.
But my too happy Rival (envy'd by all
Mankind) muft enjoy you, fince I cannot. This
unwelcome News has added much to my Indifpofition. If I recover of my Wounds, I will
fee you, tho' happy in my Rival's Arms.
You may fometimes think on an unfortunate
Lover, without violating your Faith to Cleomidon, who, I'm certain, has generofity e-
nough to pity a miferable Man. Ten thoufand Joys attend your Nuptials, and may
your wifhes be crown'd with Felicity ; and when
you hear of my Death, afford fome Tears to
the memory of your Conftant and Faithful

HARNANDO.

I fhew'd this Letter to *Cleomidon* ; and
when he had read it, feem'd very much
fatisfied ; and had goodnefs enough to pity the Collonel, and faid, he would Anfwer his Letter ; which he did in the moft
obliging terms he poffibly could.

And

And now, my Dear Friend, I am come to the period of all my Misfortunes; and my Conftancy is rewarded with the beft of Hufband's, whofe Affection to me, makes me infinitely happy. Our Sufferings has been mutual, and our Refentments were equal; and we have but too much experienced, what is in the power of Malice to do; that no Jealoufie or Sufpicion, is able to diffolve that Union that is betwixt us.

But before I conclude this tedious Narrative of my Adventures, I muft acquaint you with one thing that is material; That the poor Collonel fell ill after the receipt of my Letter; and as Relapfes are more dangerous, than the firft Illnefs, fo it is prov'd to him; for whether he became more carelefs of his Life, or that Succefs did not attend the Medicines he ufed, he fell into a violent Fever, and by fits was very Light-headed; and *Leander*, who never ftired from his Bed-fide, heard all his extravagant Expreffions of his Love and Defpair; and when he had any intervals of Senfe, he would be endeavouring to write to me, but had not ftrength to finifh his Letter; but to *Leander* did Communicate his Thoughts, and defired him to bring me a Ring, which he hoped I would wear in Remembrance of him. In a few Days after the Collonel Died, and I heard not of his Death, till *Leander* related it to me: I was moft fenfibly touched at this Accident; and I fhed many Tears upon this mournful occafion; and *Cleomidon* was fo
kind

kind to partake of my Sorrow; for he was
really concerned for his Death ; and was
much lamented by all that knew him. I
fail'd not of seeing his Son as long as he
stayed in Town ; and the great resemblance
he had of his Father, brought him often into my Memory!

Thus you see, my *Indamora*, I was deftin'd
to be a Mother-in-Law, which fide foever I
had chosen : And I hope, that the young
Hermilia will find no difference between me
and *Cleodora*; for I have the fame Affection
for her, as if she were my own; and where
there is a true Love to a Husband, an Affection naturally follows to his Children. I
have nothing more to add, that is material ;
and 'ts time to deliver you from the tedious Pennance you have endured ; tho' much
might be said to excuse my ill performance;
as not having Abilities to purfue fuch a Work,
that I inconfiderately undertook. I will not
trouble you with any tedious Appologies,
but will conclude my Adventures, with the
affurance of my fincere Affection , to my
dearest *Indamora*.

I am her faithful

LINDAMIRA.

FINIS.

Books Printed for R. Wellington, *at the* Dolphin *and* Crown *at the West-End of St.* Pauls *Church-Yard.*

Five Love Letters from a Nun to a Cavalier ; done out of French into English ; by Sir *Roger L'Etrange.* The second Edition, with the Cavalier's Anfwer.

De Re-Poetica, or Remarks upon Poetry, with Characters and Cenfures of the moft confiderable Poets, whether Ancient or Modern, Extracted out of the beft and choiceft Criticks ; by Sir *Thomas Pope Blount.*

Sir *Thomas Blount's.* Effays on feveral Subjects ; The Third Impreffion, with very large Additions ; befides a New Effay of Religion, and an Alphabetical Index to the whole

Of Education, efpecially of Young Gentlemen, in two Parts. The fixth Edition enlarged.

Cinque Letters, D'Amour D'une Religieufe Portuguife, Ecrites au Chevalier de C. Officier Francois en Portugal , Derniere Edition. Tranflated into Englifh by Sir *Roger L'Eftrange.* The Englifh being on the oppofite Page for the benefit of the ingenious of other Languages.

All

The Jilted Bridegroom

or London Coquet

Anonymous

Bibliographical note:

This facsimile has been made from a copy in the British Museum

THE
Jilted Bridegroom:

O R,

London Coquet, *&c.*

Treating of a true Intrigue betwixt a
Gentleman and Gentlewoman of this
City, within these twelve Months ; with
several Letters that past between them:
Sent in a Letter to a Friend in the Coun-
try.

LONDON.

Printed in the Year MDCCVI.

Price 1 s.

TO THE
READER.

THE *following* Letter *was* *fent to me,* 14th *of* December *laſt, and the Cha-racters and Accidents therein are not made up of ſictitious and fabulous* Tales, *but they are compoſed of clear* Matter *of* Fact, *tranſ-acted not in a diſtant* Age, *but an Intreague of the laſt Year, brought to its height the* 12. *of* July.

NOT only my ſelf, but above an Hundred Gentlemen *and* Ladies *have ſeen* Floria's *Original Letters , and we have very good Proofs of every Matter and Thing hereafter alledged : But I ſhall give the* Reader *ſome Reaſons, why this was publiſhed in this man-ner.*

THE Firſt *is, That* Hortarius *and his* Wife *have not been wanting to back their former Abuſes to my* Friend *in ſeveral De-grees, but particularly, they have given an extenſive Freedom to their* Tongues *, and privately and clandeſtinely have* traduc'd *and* reflected *upon him in ſuch a manner, that his Reputation calls for a* publick Defence, *they*

A 2 *all*

To the Reader.

all confidently affert, They never gave him
Encouragement, but upon Terms, and with the
moft hardned Affurance have declared him a
Cheat and Impofture with feveral other
Stories they have trimm'd up for their
purpofe, which have already (not a little)
prejudic'd him: So it is high time to ftop the
Current of their Malice, and oppofe their
Fury with naked Truth; for all the Reports
they with fuch Zeal have fpread abroad,
were form'd with a Defign to cover and fcreen
their unprefidented Actions, and to Cheat
the World into a good Opinion of a People,
That every Man who has any regard for his
Wellfare and Repute ought to fhun and a-
void.

THE Second Reafon is laid down as to the
Act it felf, which, without doubt, fhould it
be frequently practis'd, might prove as E-
pidemical as a Peftilence: For thofe Females
who are yet in a State of Innocency, will be
apt to take the fame Meafures, if they have
but a Poffibility of Practifing with Succefs;
therefore it ought to be detected; becaufe a
Prejudice may accrue to both Sexes therely.
Such Ladies and Gentlewomen, who are Miftreffes of the ftricteft Honefty, Honour and
Vertue muft defpife and abominate a Practical

To the Reader.

cal Coquet; *becaufe fome* Gentlemen *thus ufed* (*if ever there was a* Precedent *of it*) *in their* Warmth *and* Heat *of* Refentment *may be apt to reflect upon the* whole, *and injurionfly load the moft* deferving *and* ineftimable *Part of Womankind with the* Crimes *of one who has fpent Tears in abufing that Character , which all Women, who have the leaft value for themfelves, ought by their Actions to fupport and defend.*

AS to the ill Confequences *that may attend the innocent, undefigning Part of Mankind, we need not fearch Hiftory for Precedents ; for if a Woman may be allow'd to give Encouragement to any Man, carry on the* Amour *with* Promifes *and* Affurances *of* Love *and* Affection, *nay come even to the* Church-door, *yet upon more advantagious* Propofals, *carelefly and unconcernedly make void her former Promifes, and* abufe him, *if he infifts upon his Right , it may Prove a fatal Practice; fuch Ufage having caus'd the Ruin of many worthy* Gentlemen , *both in regard to their Perfons and Fortunes; fome have been put under the moft* diftracted Circumftances ; *others upon fuch* Extravagancies, *as have never ended but with their Fortunes and Eftates; and many upon this occafion have left their Well-Being, their beft*

Friends,

To the Reader.

Friends, and their Native Soil , to rub out the Remainder of their Days in a Savage Country ; for every Man has not the Conduct to retrieve himself : But allowing, that some are Masters of so much Reason, to Conquer their Paffion *, and forceably reduce themselves to their former* Tranquility *and* Peace ; *yet is that Eafe all owing to their own* Conduct, *and the* Woman *is equally guilty, as if they had mifcarryed, and been undone.*

THE Action *(as it appears in the following Sheets) is fo uncommon and* vile, *That it will call any Body's Reputation in question, who fhould appear in the* Juftification *of it.* Such Actions *as this (I say) fhould they become* common *, would give fufficient Reafons for the moft* deferving Part *of* Woman-kind, *to wifh there was a Mark of Diftinction fo vifible, That every Honeft Man might be affured to pitch upon One, as retains her* Primitive Honour *and* Honefty, *free from that Mixture and Allay of the moft* Modern Deception *and* Fallacy : *For 'tis morally impofsible any Man can be fecure of his Safety, if every Woman fhall think her felf out of the reach of Refentment, and have a General Difpenfation. If fhe* Entertains *as many Men as fhe pleafes,* Encourages 'em

firft,

To the Reader.

firſt, throws em off *at pleaſure, and never
deſigns, what ſhe ſeems to intend by her
Pretences and Aſſurances, till ſome ſingular
Gentleman of the Crowd, ſhall be thought
meritorious by the* weight *of his Purſe, and
the* Latitude *and* Longitude *of his Acres.
This with all due reſpects to the Honourable
and Deſerving* Females *is my Sentiment of
the Matter.*

AS to the following Letter, *it was wrote
in the Month after my Friend had received*
Floria's *Final Anſwer, and had reſolved upon no Account (ever after) to have any Concern with, or ſhew the leaſt reſpect either to*
·Floria, *or any of that Family : But how a
Man of Spirit could expreſs himſelf in ſuch*
ſweet Turns *of* Affection *to a Woman, who
had treated him with ſuch* Indecency *and*
Abuſe, I *cannot conceive ; for ſurely any
Man, but himſelf, who had been ſo* Brutal-
ly *handled, and Maſter of his* Qualificati-
ons, *would not have dropt ſo Noble and Im-
proveable a Subject ; but rather have made
a Preſent of it to the* Muſes.

BUT

To the Reader.

BUT as it came to my Hands, I Publish *it to the* World; *and as it was wrote in haste by a private* Person, *and not then defign'd to appear in this Order, I shall only fay, That what it wants in* Eloquence, *it has in* Truth, *and upon a slender Occasion, we can descend to* Particulars, *by way of* Exemplification.

THE

THE

Jilted Bridegroom:
OR.
London Coquet, *&c.*

Treating of a true Intrigue betwixt a
Gentleman *and* Gentlewoman *of this*
City, *within thefe twelve Months ; with
feveral* Letters *that paft between them :
Sent in a* Letter *to a* Friend *in the* Country.

S I R,

I Own I have given you the greateft Reafons
to fignify your difpleafure for by breaking off a Correfpondence, which I ought to
have fet the moft intrinfick value upon : But
fince Men are not always Mafters of their
Wills, being obliged to fubmit to Viceffitudes,
occafion'd by *Frailties* that attend Humane Nature, or fometimes according as the hand of
chance throws bufinefs in their way they may
be engag'd.

This indeed might be a juftifiable excufe,
were it us'd at fome certain junctures, but it
would carry an Air of Banter and Deception
along with it ; fhould I fhew that difregard
to a *Judgment* fo difcerning and in the poffeffion of a *Gentleman*, who has always fet me in
the firft rank of his Friends, to offer any Ex-

B   cufe

cuſe for *Six Months* Silence after receiving ſo many engaging and reſpectful Letters from your hand.

I have no other way *(Sir)* to clear my ſelf from the ſuſpition of Ingratitude, but by ſending you this ſlender Account of what I have been taken up with, ſince the *27th of May laſt*, from which as I take it you date my Neglect.

You know *(Sir)* there is a darling Paſſion which all Mankind at one time or another Eſpouſe and Cheriſh, tho' there is nothing upon Earth ſo enormous and deteſtible, but *Love* has been the occaſion of it : It ſeldom miſſes deſtroying of our Reaſon, and puts us upon a Million of Abſurdities, it ſteals upon us by degrees, and there are but few Objects that can effect the Soul, which don't give it birth : 'Tis the powerful and pleaſing bond of *Human Society*, without it there would be no Families, no Kingdoms, and yet on the other hand, we read of an *Alexander* that ſacrificed a whole City to the Smiles of his Miſtreſs : *Anthony* diſputed with *Cæſar* for the Empire of the *World*, yet choſe rather to be overthrown at *Actium*, than to be abſent from *Cleopatra*'s Arms. And Sacred Hiſtory tells us of the good King and Prophet *David*, who (notwithſtanding he was a Man fam'd for Proweſs as well as Piety) yet he baſely injur'd *Uriah*, the more freely to enjoy the Lovely Adultreſs.

But *(Sir)* the Fire is pure in it ſelf, 'tis the matter that ſends up all the Offenſive Clouds of Smoak, and if Nature were not deprav'd, *Love* would not cauſe theſe diſorders, 'twould

not

not mix Poyfon with Wine to deftroy a Rival, and thro' a Sea of Blood wade to its Object : *Love* is the moft formidable Enemy a Wife Man can have, and is the only Paffion againft which he has no defence, if anger furprize him, it lafts not long, for the fame Minute concludes as commenc'd it, if by a flower Fire it boyls, he prevents its running over. But *Love* fteals fo fecretly and fweetly with all into every corner of our Hearts, that it's abfolute Mafter before we can perceive it, when once we difcover it we are quite unman'd, he triumphs over our Wifdom, Captivates our Reafon, and makes 'em both his Vaffals to maintain his Tyranny.

The firft wound *Beauty* makes is almoft infenfible, and tho' the Poyfon fpreads thro' every part, we can hardly perceive we are in danger ; at firft we are only pleas'd with feeing the *Perfon*, or talking of them, affecting a Complaifance for all they fay or do. The very thinking of them is charming, and the defires we have are fo innocent, that no *Philofopher* could be fo rigid as to condemn us.

Hitherto 'tis well, but 'tis hardly *Love* for that like a Bee, forfeits its name if it has no Sting, but alas the lurking Fire quickly burfts out, and that pleafing Idea which reprefented it felf fo *fweetly* and fo refpectfully to us the moment before, now infolently intrudes upon our moft ferious thoughts, nay Perfidioufly betrays us in our very Sleep it felf, fometimes appearing haughty and fcornful, fometimes yeilding and kind, and that when there is no reafon for either.

The

The Infant Paſſion is now become a crue
Father of all other Paſſions, for he has no ſooner given birth to one, but he ſtifles it to
make room for another, whoſe Fate is the ſame,
and deſtroy'd the next moment its born, Hope
and Deſpair, Joy and Sorow, Rage and Fear
ſucceed each other.

Now (*Sir*) it ſurprizes me, for that moſt
or all Men (as I ſaid before) have been ſenſible
of this *Paſſion*, yet they don't readily own it,
or at leaſt ſeem very unwilling, when once
their more indulgent Fate has put a Period to
their *PASSION*. As for my own particular I ſhall (and it's the leaſt thing that I
can do to make you amends) gratify your Curioſity, I am not inſenſible the intreague has
been related with the moſt *Provoking* Partiali-
ty, and to vindicate my ſelf to you and the
reſt of my Friends; you ſhall be informed of
ſuch Particulars as may be neceſſary for my
Juſtification.

We have in Town various ways to diſpoſe
of our time, ſome part of it Buſineſs lays
claim to, and the remainder we give up to
thoſe Exerciſes or Diverſions that are moſt
agreeable to our Fancies and concurrent with
our Inclinations, you know (*Sir*) we always
admir'd walking abroad in ſeaſonable Weather, when time would permit, and either
pick'd out ſome *Author* for our Companion,
or choſe ſuch a Retirement as might furniſh
us with matter for Contemplation, of which
kind the Country affords many; but *Weſt-
minſter* can boaſt of one, that's not to be Rival'd by the Univerſe, for it will puzzle the
greateſt

greateſt *Geographer* to parallel it, eſpecially if you ſaw the *B E A U T I E S* that daily adorn it, *Beauties* which don't want Art to recommend 'em nor make the leaſt Addition to their *Charms.* In ſuch a crowd of Ladies, 'twas no great wonder if a Heart that was ſuſceptible ſhould find an Object worthy of its Aſſiduities: The Number of thoſe Charmers might have ſtagger'd any Man's Reſolution, and the Greatneſs of the Variety might likewiſe have obſtructed the Freedom of one's wiſhes for to confeſs the Truth ; an unbyaſs'd mind could not readily determine which of all thoſe Lovely Creatures ought to be poſtpon'd.

But as the moſt perfect that ever was, could not engage all Hearts to be hers, ſo I pitch'd at length upon the Lovely F L O R I A, I don't ſay the luſtre of her Eyes, the exactneſs of her Features, the Nobleneſs of her Deportment, or the readineſs of her Wit were ſuperiour to that of the other Ladies; yet I confeſs I found ſomething in her that was my *wonder* and *delight*, I check'd my growing Inclinations, but I ſoon found it too powerful to reſiſt, for the Commencements of *Love* are ſo very tempting, that we muſt renounce being Men to baniſh ſo agreeable a Paſſion.

As I did admire *her* above all the reſt, you may readily Conjecture that I was very Uneaſy 'till Methods were concerted to get a Letter to her hands. You may perhaps object and ſay you wonder I ſhould be ſo much in Love with *Floria*, and never convers'd with her, to which I anſwer, that an unfeigned Affection is without foreſight, and dictates more to us
in

in one Moment than all the Wit and Invention of Man can suggest in an Age.

Floria had nothing could displease, she was comely, in the bloom of Youth, and of an Incomparable Wit, so apprehending to be a Loser if I alter'd, I *devoted* my self entirely to her, and sent her the following Letter.

MADAM,

WIthout doubt the Receipt hereof may in some measure surprize you, but being 'twas the only means I could use to make my Affectionknown to you, I hope it brings its Excuse along with it, I have very often seen you accompany'd with your Mother, but had so tender a regard for your Ease and Tranquility, that I durst not make a verbal Discovery, tho my Love very often prompted me to reveal it, being unacquainted with the Temper of your Parent, who certainly would have been equally surpris'd with your self: The Boundaries of this Scrawl are too scanty to contain the various Circumstances of the Love and Affection I bear to you, so that what I have to Petition for, is the Happiness of a Moments Conference with you in Person, the Time and Place I shall repose in your unerring Discretion, only I must beg leave to tell you, that if there be any merit in a just and honourable Affection, mine has something to lay claim to; and further, were I to be seen in your Company, it could neither tend to lessen or disrepute you, so I shall conclude, and with the greatest Humility subscribe my self

Your Affectionate AMINTOR.

I gave

I gave this into the hands of a Female, who had known *Floria* from her Infancy, and was no Stranger to any Accident of the Family, indeed fhe told me fhe was cautious how fhe acted, but when I laid my felf and Station open to her and gave her affurances that my Pretences were upon *Honourable* and *Vertuous* Foundations, it removed the fcruple, and the Letter was fafe deliver'd to *Floria*'s hands the fame day. I had a Thoufand Rambling Cogitations and Sufpitions of the Event, but the next day I receiv'd *Floria*'s Anfwer in the following Words.

S I R,

YOur Letter furpris'd me mightily, it being from a Perfon I never heard of before to my knowledg, in anfwer to yours, as you defired, it obliges me to tell you, that I am in a great Confternation to think what you fee in me as looks fo loofely or carelefs of my Reputation, as to appoint a Time or Place to meet a Perfon I know nothing of ; as for my Parents Temper they are like other Peoples, they love to have a right underftanding : And you may, if you pleafe, and are in reality find ways and means with their Confents to fee me; 'till then I have no more to fay to you, but leave the reft to your Management, which is from your Friend

FLORIA.

The

The receipt hereof equally pleas'd and surpris'd me; for as I was not a little dash'd that I
should upon my first Applications give the
least cause for resentment, so where she pleased to put means into my hands and give me
liberty to improve 'em, it substracted from my
uneasiness and encourag'd me to make this following Apology.

DEAR MADAM,

*SInce I receiv'd yours, I have been extreamly
concern'd to find my self so unfortunate as to
fall under the Censure of the Person I prefer to all
the World: And where you seem to charge me
with thinking you loose or careless of your Reputation, you injure my Innocence; for what I wrote
was according to the Dictates of a sincere and well
grounded Affection, and notwithstanding any In-
advertency a Lover may be guilty of (for a Passion
so great as mine may discompose a Person much better
qualify'd than I am) I heartily declare to you, that
every Faculty of my Soul is entirely in your Interest,
and I could never forgive my self should I willfully
act any thing to disoblige one I so dearly respect:
You likewise are pleased modestly to resent what
I spoke of your Mother, when God knows, I had
no other design in what I mentioned but to acquaint
you, that I evaded every thing that might any way
tend to your dissatisfaction. The cause of my Con-
fusion at the time of Writing you may easily guess
at, and I hope you will excuse me for the Cause
sake, for I value both you and my self, above per-
swading you to any thing which may disoblige
your*

your Parents, and I never so much as conceiv'd *the Notion; but look'd upon it very odd to apply my self to your Father, 'till we have in some measure been satisfied between our selves; nay, I should deem it as a downright Affront to* you, *and an apparent Hazard and Uneasiness to* my self, *to make my Addresses there, before I have Establish'd an Interest in* your *Affection; for tho' I cannot remember many Years, yet have I seen several Misfortunate and unhappy Instances, occasion'd by that way of proceeding; I hope my Post and Character will assert my Honesty and Integrity, and I doubt not, if you knew how* dearly *I respect* you, *but you would give me the happiness of speaking with you, which with the greatest Impatience I shall wait for, whilst I am*

Your moſt Affectionate

AMINTOR.

This was Delivered by the ſame hand as my firſt, and with the ſame Caution and Reſervedneſs, but light of much better Fortune; for *Floria* now ſhew'd her ſelf too well bred, to be offended at the Continuation of my Addreſſes: I found, that if ſhe did not *deſire* my Sollicitations, ſhe did not *diſdain* 'em, and as for my good Will, ſhe would neither court it, nor ſcorn it.

Bu**t**

But (be pleas'd to understand) that two
days after my Letter was sent, I saw her upon
the same Spot where she laid the first Plat-form
of her Conquest; She appear'd surprizingly
Fair, and her Charms were in the Meridian of
their Glory, the greater Awe therefore was
upon me, and my Courage and Conduct both
diſſerted me ; Inſomuch that I was afraid to
attack her, tho' l had no reaſon to ſuppoſe the
leaſt Obſtacle in my way, which was confirm'd
to me afterwards, by what *Floria* confeſs'd to
my Meſſenger, which was , that ſhe and her
Siſter quitted the *Lady* who was with them, in
order to give me an Opportunity to ſpeak to
her.

Now (Sir) this laſt Circumſtance put me
upon all the Contrivances and Stratagems I
could invent, to ſee her as oft as poſſibly I
could ; in order thereunto, I was gratified
with a lofty Caſement, eminent for its Conveniency ; for that it commanded all the Garden, *&c.* which belongs to *Floria's Father Hortarius* : This I often viſited, and not without
Satisfaction, for whenever I paid her my re-
ſpeas, ſhe as civilly return'd the Courteſy, and
about the ſame time *Floria* ſent me a Verbal
Meſſage, wherein ſhe gave me Admittance to
ſpeak with her after her Fathers Doors were
ſhut at night, but we making no Improvement
of this propos'd Opportunity ; the next day
Floria ſent her Service to me, and deſired I
would write to her *Father* for leave to viſit her.
Here l began to contrive and lay down ſuch
Propoſals to my ſelf, as might be moſt conducive to bring this matter to a happy iſſue, when

in

in the interim, *Floria* anticipated my defign, produc'd my Letters, and broke the whole matter to her Father, which fhe took care I fhould be acquainted with.

Now *Hortarius* is look'd upon (by fome) to be a Man of a tolerable Fortune, having quietly reap'd the Advantages of a beneficial Employment in a moft *Aufpicious* and *Profperous* Reign; fo that according to *Zenophon's* Maxim, he ought to remember the Gods, and pay 'em his particular Devotions. It was not many days e're *Hortarius* made an Appointment to meet me, I was fo fearful of difappointing him, that I rather chofe to be fomething earlier than the Hour prefix'd, he nick'd the time directly, and after we had exchang'd a few words, and fuch common Compliments as are confiftent with good Manners and Civility, he defired we might choofe a more convenient Place for our Purpofe, which when we had fix'd upon, he gave me to Underftand he had feen the Letters, I have here inferted as fent to *Floria*, and really it was both an Act of Prudence and Difcretion, to let a Parent into the Secret; efpecially fince (as She told me afterwards) She was affured he vvould run parallel with her Inclinations.

I can't tell, whether *Floria* began to grow uneafie under Family Jars, or what made the matter go on fo harmonionfly between us; for it really feem'd to me, that there was fome latent Fortune was a kind of Friend to our Amour, becaufe upon all *Hortarius's* Enquiries backwards and forwards; as to any particular, there was but few fcruples, and thofe fo trivial and

C 2   foreign

foreign that they were immediately, banifh'd
and quafh'd, and he was not in the leaft harfh,
or difcompos'd in Converfe, Difpofition, or
Humour; but on the contrary, his Temper
feem'd to be fix'd in a Diametrical Oppofition,
to every thing that look'd like a Diffatisfaction,
fo at the clofe of our Interview, he told me he
would make a fmall fcrutiny into my *Character* and *Behaviour*, as, likewife would purfue that *Conjugal Precept* of confulting his *Wife*,
who ought to have a fhare in the difpofing of
her Child; after which, in a few days he would
let me know, whether I fhould be admitted by
Parental Authority to proceed in my Applications to *Floria*.

Here I was perfectly pin'd down, and durft
not make another ftep, 'till I had liberty from
the Oracle of his Will, for fear of unraveling
all I had done hitherto, fo I liv'd in a fort of
Exile, and apply'd my felf totally to the Enjoyment of my Friends. I well knew where he
laid the Foundation of his Enquiry, and that
he apply'd himfelf to no lefs a Perfon, equally
N O B L E, G O O D and G R E A T.
My Retirement did not continue long e're I
received a palatable Meffage, that *Hortarius*
defired to fpeak with me at his Garden-door, I
was furrounded with crowds of Ideas one upon the back of another, that Nature was fcarce
left ftrong enough, whether thro' Fear or Di-
ftruft, to fupport me in proceeding with the
fame Conduct I had begun, I hop'd for a *Fiat*,
but more fear'd a *Diffolution*: In fhort, I fully
determin'd to meet my deftiny, and luckily was
received with the *grandeft* Refpect and Decorum

rum, and as the Eyes are fometimes taken to be the Index of the Heart, by my Obfervations I found my felf exempted from danger, and received the kindeft Invitation; which I fhall give you in his own words. *Amintor* (fays he) *I have made my Enquiry, and fent for you, to tell you, that I have received fuch entire Satisfaction, that you are welcome to come to my Houfe as oft as you pleafe* ; *if I am not within my Wife will treat you civilly, and when my Daughter and you have agreed the matter between your felves, let me know, and I will proceed to the Settlement* ; the fame time he invited me to Dinner, and very kindly and freely introduc'd me.

It would be needlefs for me to give you a Bill of Fare, fo I fhall only tell you, that the Dinner was *Genteel* and *Decent*, and I as welcomly receiv'd, tho' had I din'd with Duke *Humphry*, and *Floria* had made a third Perfon, I could have been as well fatisfy'd as a Cardinal plac'd in the Center of forty well fill'd Difhes, provided by the Directions of the moft Notorious Epicure: The greateft *Rarities* could not have tempted me to Excefs, my Eyes were without Intermiffion fixt upon *Floria*, who look'd as Gay as the *Spring*, which adorn'd that Seafon of the Year ; and as the nearer we approach to the *Sun*, we muft expect to receive its more *powerful* heat, fo her Charms now appear'd fo *Perfect* and *Extraordinary*, that I now lov'd her, was beyond the Poffibility of any peradventure; Dinner was no fooner over, and a little vulgar chat made an end of, but *Floria* and my felf were left in the

poffeffion

poſſeſſion of the Room, I was conſidering with
my ſelf, whether our being left alone proceeded from Accident, or Deſign ; the Impreſſi-
on her *Charms* made upon me, ſuſpended my
Judgment for a time, but finding no manner
of Interruption, I made my Perſonal Addreſſes
to *Floria*, and acquainted her (with the greateſt ſeriouſneſs) how far her *Father* and I had a-
greed. That the matter was now Important,
I having entirely ſetled my Affection upon her,
and ſince her Generoſity had not only tolera-
ted my Endeavours, but adviſed and aſſiſted
me in the Proſecution of 'em ; I beg'd ſhe
would grant me Liberty to wait on her, in order to give her the greateſt proofs of my Conſtancy, and ſhew my ſelf worthy of her Favour, which was only wanting to compleat
our Happineſs.

  FLORIA anſwer'd : *That ſince her Parents had been pleas'd to give me Admittance, ſhe
had no reaſon to oppoſe my coming to the Houſe,
and were ſhe within ſhe would never refuſe my
ſeeing her.*

  I'll aſſure you (*Sir*) I found a vaſt delight
in her Converſation ; for ſhe is not only Miſtreſs of a ready Wit, but a ſound Judgment ;
as far as I was able to determin, the *Sun* therefore was not more conſtant to the Day than I
was to *Floria*, her Smiles had a Magnetick Quality in 'em ; for I could not go a day and not
Sacrifice ſome hours at her Shrine, and that
which highly added to the Pleaſure and Satisfaction of my Viſits, was her *Mother's* Condeſcenſion in giving all the Privileges young *Ladies* could deſire ; nay, as the greateſt Token
of

of her Kindnefs, fhe feem'd to be diffatisfy'd
that I did not freely Command any thing her
Houfe would afford, and generally *entertain'd*
me above my Expectation: Upon fuch numerous Friendfhips, and fuch a Scene of Prof-
perity, I had no room left for Doubts, or Suf-
pition, becaufe I did not queftion, but by a fe-
date ftable and *unalterable Love*, to bring *Floria* into an inviolable League of reciprocal Affection.

About this time I received a Letter, wherein I was advertis'd (*fince I ftand upon fo happy
a Bafis*) to make the quickeft difpatch in fecu-
ring *Floria*'s Affection, for that her *Mother* was
a perfect Weather-cock in her Temper, and
generally of an Irreconcilable Difpofition,
when fhe *fancy'd* to be fretful; I was not a
little fhock'd and diforder'd at the receipt hereof, but fearing there fhould be too much truth
in the Information; I did not think fit to go
about to difprove it. The very next day, the
moft proper Opportunity prefented it felf,
and *Floria* gave me her promife of Marriage, I thought us nearly ally'd by this time,
and fo was unwilling to proceed further without advifing with her; the matter confulted
between us, was, whether I fhould keep our
laft proceeding in Embrio for a certain time,
or whether fhe was willing that I fhould let her
Father know, according to his Order. *And
Floria agreed to the latter.* Thus (fince I had
her confent) it had look'd like coldnefs and inconftancy, had I not made her Father acquainted therewith, accordingly the next day afford-
ing an Opportunity of fpeaking with him, I
acquainted

acquainted him, how far we had proceeded, at which he feem'd very well pleas'd, and our time was in fome meafure taken up with Propofals for a Settlement, after our parting I had but little time for Confideration: Bufinefs intercepting, fo all things run in their proper Channel, 'till about fonr a Clock the fame day, about which hour I frequently vifited my *Floria*, I was admitted after the ufual manner, and entred the Houfe, expecting the fame freedom of accefs as all along I had been bleft with, when upon my Compliment to *Floria*'s Mother (which was cuftomary from my firft Vifit) I faw nothing but darknefs and difpleafure in her Countenance, which caus'd in me a fort of Confufion, indeed I had time to recover my felf, for that there was in Company a Relation of the Mothers, and at prefent not being oblig'd to demand Reafons for that ftrangenefs, thought fit to let the thing reft 'till the Gentleman's abfence fhould enlarge my Opportunity of enquiring into the bottom of fuch a negligent Reception. But in the interim *Floria* look'd at me, and I gazed as wifhfully at her, tho' the ufe of our Eyes was the extent of our Felicity, for it had been as dangerous an Experiment for me to have Saluted *Floria* (*notwithftanding fhe had promis'd me Marriage*) confidering the irregular and diforderly Paffion of her *Mother*, as 'twould have been to have gather'd the faireft Flower that ever *Egypt* afforded, in the face of a *Crocodile*. *Floria*, who could guefs at the infide of her *Mother*, by the difplacing the leaft wrinkle in her Face, faw further (you may judge) into the matter than
I could

I could pretend to do; fo *Floria* defired to fpeak with her, accordingly they withdrew into the Mother's Chamber, leaving the Parlour to the Relation and my felf, I all the while was wond'ring what Politicks could keep 'em fo long in Confultation, but, to my greateft Amazement, the Mother return'd without the Daughter; it was not long e're the Coufin withdrew, and then fhe fairly let me into a fort of a Secret, and in fuch a manner, as I believe no Man tho' never fo mean, was ever treated before (*except by a Woman of her Birth and Education*) but leaft I fhould judge wrong, and lay an injurious Opinion upon the Mother, which may be deem'd an Impofition, or a groundlefs Reflection: I will here relate the Paffage to you, and will reduce it into as decent Order as it will bear, exempt and free from Falfity or Antipathy. And to begin, you muft fuppofe her to look with a gruff Afpect, and to Attack me in thefe Words.

Pray, Sir, what bufinefs have you here? Why don't you get out of my Houfe?

This (*Sir*) was the firft Salutation, which furpriz'd me beyond a poffibility of fpeaking for a Seafon, and had any one been in my place, and ftorm'd at that rate, after a Series of civil Ufage, I don't at all queftion, but it would have ftartled him, tho' a man of the Politeft Capacity.

Pardon me for this Digreffion, for thus fhe went on: *Get out of my Houfe you forry Fellow, for if you ftay 'till Midnight you fhall not fee her.*

Here

Here I endeavour'd to appeafe her a little, and told her, I thought that way of Expoftulating was ill tim'd, becaufe *Floria* had promis'd to marry me the day before, and I was admitted by her and her Husband, and Encourag'd by both of 'em to Solicite for that Promife.

But fhe would not loofe an Inch in her part of the Dialogue, but proceeded in this manner: *Prithee tell me nothing of that, you have neither wedded her, nor bedded her, and I don't care a Fart for your Promife, but you carry the Devil in your Mouth inftead of a Tongue, and have deluded and enfnared my Child; for my Husband courted me three Years before he ask'd me the Queftion.*

I was here furpriz'd at her *Gallimofry* of Nonfence, and begg'd leave to fpeak ; in Anfwer to which, I urg'd, that if any body had deluded her Child (which I could not believe) it could be no body but her Husband and her felf ; becaufe I never addrefs'd my felf in Perfon 'till I had their *Unanimous* Admittance, and that without a *Referve* ; I likewife afferted, that my getting her Daughter's Confent fo early, was the *greateft* Argument of my *Love* to her, and I wondred how fhe could be difoblig'd, being it was the main end for which fhe and *Hortarius* licenfed me to Converfe with her, and that 'twas my Opinion a Woman might be told as much in three Weeks in our days as would be Proportionate to her three Years Courtfhip fhe was pleas'd to mention.

Her

Her Temper now began to grow rugged and tempeftuous without meafure, at length I ask'd her if fhe had any Reafons to give me for ufing me at this rate, whether I had in any particular misbehav'd my felf, or had fhe heard any ill Character of me; but having no reafon fhe could give me none, fo fhe took upon her felf an abfolute Defpotick Power, and when I mention'd applying my felf to her Husband, who I hop'd would give me a reafon for this courfe Treatment, fhe feem'd to undervalue my propos'd Application, and told me very haughtily : *I was miftaken, if I thought to get any thing by that way of proceeding, for fhe would have the difpofing of her Daughter, and bad me not to ftand prating there, but get out of her Houfe.* Upon which I bow'd to her, and took my leave, but her Paffion was fo great fhe could not return the Civility.

I was no fooner got out of her Dominions, but *Solomon*'s Woman came into my mind, with whom there was no living, tho' in a large Houfe ; fhe has all the Qualities but one, that can make her Husband miferable and her Children uneafy, fhe was rougher in her Anger than the Bay of *Bifcay* in the great Storm, being a Woman that no body can pleafe, few will ferve, and as few can endure, no Reafon could prevail with her (being compos'd of incorrigible ill-nature to thofe fhe can't gain by) and inflexible in her Opinion, efpecially when fhe is in'the wrong. You may judge *(Sir)* what a Perfon this muft be, when fhe had a fancy to be Exafperated, and

how

how *Floria* was documented after she had rallied me out of her Territory : I was somewhat
disoblig'd at this Unmannerly *Scoundrel* Treatment, and could not think but the Woman
took me for some *Chimney Sweeper*, or a *Pick
Pocket*, by the haughtiness of her mien, and
the disposition of her Language, which I believe I could not have bore with so much Patience and Condescention, but for the Ease, and
for the sake, of my *Floria*.

The day following I met *Hortarius*, and
with the greatest Concern I made him acquainted how roughly I had been dealt with
by his *Wife*, desiring he would use such means
as might immediately heal the Breach, and
set aside an Animosity which was grounded upon nothing but the *want* of *Reason*,
seconded by the *Arbitrary Passion* of a Woman; he seem'd very free, and to make way
for the Treaty, he advis'd me to *Write* to
his *Wife*, accordingly I was fond to lay hold
of any Opportunity that might bring me into
the presence of my *Floria* again ; so I wrote
to her with the submission of a Slave, and
own'd my self a Criminal for Acts of *Vertue*
and *Honour*, purely in Condescension to her
Ignorance and Irrationality, I told her that
'twas a great Affliction to me, that I should
act wrong in any Particular, which should merit her Resentment, and tho' the violence of
my *Love* and irresistible *Affection* carried me
beyond my Consideration to press *Floria* to a
Promise so soon, yet 'twas no ill Design in
me, nor Disobedience in her (strictly taken)
only an ill tim'd Action ; for we resolved to
make

make no further Progrefs without her Advice,
that I defired fhe would put no hardfhip upon *Floria*, for the guilt lay all upon my felf,
and *I was ready to make an Attonement for it*,
when fhe would pleafe to make me fo happy,
that I fhould patiently wait for the hour of
being reftor'd to her *Favour* once more, when
I fhould endeavour to eftablifh my felf in her
Friendfhip, with much more fuch Flattery
and Stuff.

This was fent to the *Mother*, and feconded
with one wherein I undervalu'd and leffen'd
my felf to a greater Degree than in this.
But I would not have ftop't at any thing
in this kind (tho' never fo much beneath my
felf) to have been reinftated in my *Floria's*
Converfation. She gave no Anfwer to my
Firft, and the Second fhe receiv'd with fuch
Indignation, that fhe order'd the Servant to
take in no more. Thus (*Sir*) did all my Endeavours prove *Abortive*, and the Advice of
Hortarius as unfuccefsful, for fhe feem'd as
deaf as an *Adder* to all my Sollicitations, and
as impenetrable as an *Adamant*, upon every
Application of mine.

In a day or two's time *Floria* fent a Letter
to me, which becaufe it feem'd to be wrote in
fome diforder, I fhall not here infert, but only
Extract a Paragraph or two ; fhe tells me therein, *That there is nothing certain in this Life,
and were fhe to fettle her Affections upon any
Perfon never fo Great, fhe muft carry it as nothing, if Parents don't like of it ; that I may
lay the blame wholly upon my felf, by being fo
hafty, that fhe did not dream in the leaft what
hung*

hung over her head, that tho' her Mother took no
notice to her of what she had heard, yet she mi-
ftructed there was something more than ordinary
by her looks, when I came in, which made her
defire to fpeak with her, (as I before have menti-
oned) that her Mother was pleas'd to reflect more
than ordinary upon her Conduct, which ftruct a
great damp upon her, &c.

Now the Parents had given me a Latitude of
proceeding *ad Libitum*, and the diflike of Parents *Floria* mentions. is nothing more than a
ridiculous Revolt of the *Mother*, who had (*by*
her frequent Encouragements) left her felf no
room for an Honourable or an Honeft Retreat; where fhe tells me I may lay the blame
wholly upon my felf : *I had before hand taken*
it upon me. Notwithftanding 'twas by *Floria*'s
Advice I acquainted *Hortarius* therewith, for
I made another Propofal to her, which fhe was
pleas'd to reject. My only Confolation upon
this Diffafter was, that *Floria* being a Woman who much overmatch'd her *Mother* in
Senfe as well as Judgment, would not fuffer
her felf either to be bullied or inveigled into a
difefteem of *Amintor*, no more than fhe would
be forc'd into a *Nunnery*, for now I liv'd fomewhat like a Camelion, becaufe I had nothing
but hopes to fupport me, and thofe but Airy;
and Imaginary Abfence in Love breeds Anxie-
ties, yet I was afraid to pufh too forwads for a
fight of my *Charming Floria*, leaft in fearching
for my own Felicity, I might hazard her *Re-*
pofe, fo that now I thought my Unhappinefs
to be compleat,

But

But the next Morning, meeting *Hortarius* in my Walk, and making Enquiry after the welfare of my *Floria*, his Answer shock'd me beyond the Power of a Description; as I remember, he told me she was well he hop'd, but she was above 20 Miles off, as soon as I could recover my self, I beg'd he would let me know the Place, but he modeftly refus'd it. This plunged me into the depth of my Misfortune, and I had only time to tell him, that I saw plainly into the bottom of his *Wife's Defign*, that she had sent *Floria* away to difappoint and abufe me, and brandish her Arms for a fresh Conqueft; but if I should hear of any Man who prefumed to make his Addreffes to *Floria*, upon any Grounds, Invitations or Encouragements whatfoever, I should look upon him as an Invader of my Property, and I would treat him accordingly: I should have proceeded further according to the direction of my *Paffion*, had not a Gentleman who had fome bufinefs with *Hortarius* feparated us; fo far as to what concerns the firft part of my Story.

Every place was now grown common to me, and no Curiofity either of Art or Nature could Entertain me with the leaft Delight the profpect of the Country in all the gaiety of a *forward Spring*, was even intollerable to me every thing appear'd Savage: The faireft *Towns* feem'd Wilderneffes, and the Critical-Adorn'd *Gardens* but fo many Defarts; I was like a diftracted *Marriner* who had no Compafs to Steer by, for I could not tell what Courfe to take, that might bring me fafe to the moft wifh'd for *Haven*, or *Port*, where my *Floria* refided,

and

and the greatest Disaster was, that I despair'd
of an Intelligence. But 'twas not many days
'ere my good Fortune (and *Floria*'s Directions)
presented me with the glad Tidings of her
wellfare, and the place of her abode, I was
altogether taken up with rejoycing within my
self, and was transported to that degree, that
the Message was as welcome to me as the appearance of the Dove, was to the Surviving
People of the *Delug'd World*; and since it was
extraordinary, as well as most acceptable, I
shall here give you a slender Account of it;
(*exclusive of the Persons*) because it may serve,
as an Introduction, to the second Part of my
Intregue. The day I received this great Satisfaction, a Person met me, who desired I would
walk along with him to a certain place, accordingly without asking the least question, I
yeilded to the Proposal, and was conducted to
a House with which I was altogether unacquainted (*being before a Stranger , both to the
Persons and their Habitation.*) Notwithstanding
this, I was kindly invited to sit down, and in
a few Minutes time a Stranger spoke to me in
these Words: *Sir, I am desired to let you know,
that if you have any thing to send to Madam*
Floria, *if you please to trust it with me, it shall be
safe deliver'd to her hands.* I could not tell
which way to proceed upon this strange piece
of unexpected Fortune, but the Person who
made the Proposal, had a Countenance promi-
sing so much Modesty, Innocence and Honesty,
that I was resolv'd to venture; in order
thereunto, I set Pen to Paper, and gave *Floria*
an account how much I had suffer'd, and of
the

the Methods I had purſu'd to bring her Mother
over to our Intereſt, that I had condeſcended
ſo low even to unman my ſelf, and ſubmitted
like a Slave,and yet I found the Mother's Temper was impenitrable, and too ſtubborn to be
reduc'd, I deſir'd ſhe would let me hear from
her ſpeedily, fearing leaſt ſome Peoples Uſage
and Endeavours ſhould work her to a Revolt,
I likewiſe told her, how I had argued the point
with her Father, who appear'd fixt in my Intereſt.

Three days before this, I had deliver'd a
Letter to *Floria's Siſter*, to give it a ſafe Con-
veyance to her hands ; but receiving no manner of Anſwer,I began to be more uneaſy than
ever I was before, tho' I did not in the leaſt
ſuſpect the fidelity of *this Bearer* : Indeed I
muſt confeſs my uneaſineſs in *Floria's* abſence,
had thrown myDiſpoſition off its Hinges;ſome-
times to my ſelf,I would conceive Aſſurances of
my *Floria's* unalterable Affection, but the next
Moment would adminiſter more Pain andCon-
fuſion than the Pleaſures of the former Aſſurances were able to ſtand againſt, which makes
me ſince be of an Opinion, that where Grief
has once got an Aſcendant over us, there is a
ſort of ſullen Pride in fomenting it,that creates
a Satisfaction, which makes us more violently
indulge it : But it was not above two or three
days 'ere *Floria* revived me with the Following
Lines.

E   SIR,

SIR,

YOURS came to my hands by Providence; for I was standing at my Prison-door, and a pretty young Messenger delivered it me, which was no small Surprize, when I saw your hand, by reason I thought by the distance and strictness over me, I could never hear, see, nor think any more of this Affair; but withal, I admire at my Sister——— I have never heard from her since I came hither; because (you say) you gave her a Letter on Thursday last, I am sure she has had Opportunities several times since, but I have received none; I am not a little concerned, That you should perplex and give your self so much Trouble about me, and at last, I am afraid, it is to no purpose; the Fault (I will assure you) shall not lye on my side; but I dare not say, my Soul is my own, if I had never been born, it would have been happy for me and you too; I am interrupted so often in the Writing of this, that I am ashamed of the Nonsense of it, by reason it has put a great deal out of my Head, which I did design to write in better order; which is from your Well-wisher, in haste

FLORIA.

'Tis

'Tis impoſſible to conceive my eager Joy
at the receit hereof, for (tho' Letters are but
a ſlender Diet for ſome ſort of Lovers, yet all
Obliging Commerce with the Perſon we A-
dore, makes the hours of Abſence leſs inſupportable) I read it over and over, ſometimes
kiſſing the Letter, and ſometimes thanking the
Meſſenger, to whom I ſaid every tender thing
of *Floria*, that *I*, or the Imagination of my Felicity could invent; when *I* went home *I* per-
uſed it an Hundred times, and as oft it gave me
a freſh Delight. Nay, *I* was ſo intent upon
conſidering it, that *I* could hardly find time to
anſwer it; but leaſt my Delay might be eſteemed a Defect in my Paſſion, after the Receit of
ſuch an *affectionate Letter*, where ſhe does not
only expreſs her *Concern* and *Uneaſineſs* under
her Confinement; but gives me a freſh Aſſurance of her *Love* and *Fidelity*; *I* fully deſign-
ed to begin ſomething, but could not preſently reſolve upon what, there being equal Matter for Sorrow and Satisfaction, for Concern and for Content. The Day after *I* received this, *Hortarius* and his Wife dined with
Floria, and at their Return home, *I* paid a Viſit to *Hortarius*, and deſired to know, what *I*
ſhould do in this troubleſom Affair; He was
extreamly civil, telling me, *he continued in the*
ſame Mind, and adviſ'd me to renew my Applications to his Wife; *I* mov'd to ſpeak with
her *then*, but he deſired *I* would omit that Opportunity, ſhe being a little indiſpoſed, and
I might take any other time, that was more fit
for my purpoſe, when he was not within : But *I*
knew all *I* could ſay, would but heighten her

E 2   Prejudice,

Prejudice, and not reduce her to Complyance;
fo *I* fcrawl'd over a few Lines to *Floria*; wherein *I* told her, That her Letter was as welcome
to me as the Day-light,by which *I* read it ; but
vvhy alafs! vvould fhe blaft the *darling Joy*,it's
Reception brought,by faying,fhe vvas not a little concerned *upon my Account* ; *I* begg'd , fhe
vvould let no Grief harbour in that *Breaft*,
vvhere fhe had fo kindly fecured me a Place;for
fhe could not conceive, vvhat an *Impreffion* her
Gratitude and *Conftancy* had made upon me;
fhe likewife might reft affured,that neither *Stra-*
tagem nor *Diftance* fhould hinder me from fighing out my tendereft vvifhes to her; vvhy therefore fhould one impetuous Paffion make two
Perfons thus miferable, if not to try our Sincerity by daring to be conftant, maugre every
Difappointment, That if vve had but Courage
enough to fupport our felves under thefe un-
kindeft fhocks of Fate; vve fhould triumph at
laft ; but vve muft either break thro' it or fall
under it ; for if fhe continued conftant, nothing
fhould make me love her lefs, yet fince *I* could
not be happy without making her thus wretched; *I* lookt upon the price of my Felicity to be
fomewhat exorbitant, vvith much more vvhich
I cannot remember.

This *I* trufted Fortune vvith, and had no
Point to purfue; but to fearch for, and endeavour to, influence fome Perfon, vvhofe *Intereft*
and Secrefy vvere likely to carry on my Affair
vvith Succefs. It vyas not long before *I* vvas
brought into the Acquaintance of a Female, to
whom *I* told vvhat had paffed between *Floria*
and *I* ; and how apprehenfive *I* vvas of the Mother's

ther's Difpleafure and *ill Temper*, withal intrea-
ting her to prefent my Service to *Floria*, and
tell her that (*fince her Affection had more than
once prevailed with her to make fuch obliging Promifes in my behalf*) I defired, fhe would not let
flip one Moment, but ufe the earlieft Means to
let me fpeak to her : For I am much an Enemy
to the Opinion of that Gentleman, who declared, that dreaming of his Miftrefs was a greater Tranfport to him than being with her in
Perfon ; Becaufe (fays he) in Dreams all the Fa-
culties of the Soul are intent upon that one
Object, whereas when awake they are diftracted by many various ones which interfere. This
" is (as *Plutarch* obferves) only Embracing of
" Non-Entities, and groping after what is
" Beautiful and Divine,

    " *Fallacious Dreams about his Temples flew,*
    " *But fuch as charm'd his Fancy tho' untrue.*

    Matters did not reft long upon this Bottom,
e're *Floria* declar'd her Complyance, and the
next *Sunday Evening* was the time fixt upon for
renewing my Correfpondence with my *Floria.*
The Hours mov'd but flowly, till theDay came,
but I was in hopes, this abfence might produce
a Love moft perfect and ftable, and hugg'd my
felf with the Apprehenfions of it : And when
Phæbus ufher'd in that Day, I thought my felf
in fight of my Felicity : For every hour admitted of fo many pleafant Ideas,that I had no reafon to doubt of a moft *happy* Interview. In
fhort, Methods were thus concerted, There was
a Tavern not above Twenty Doors diftant
                       from

from the Houſe, where my *Floria* was confin'd,
here was I to wait for the Meſſage of Admittance : And becauſe a true Confident, under theſe
Circumſtances, has allways been eſteemed an
acceptable friendly Companion, I at the Birth
of my Amour had repoſed my Truſt and Confidence in the Friendſhip and Fidelity of my old
Acquaintance *Alexis*. Inſomuch, that I had
hitherto made him acquainted with the minu-
teſt Paſſage through the vvhole Affair. *Alexis*
was therefore along with me at the *Tavern I*
have mentioned, where we had been ſome hours
full of Expectation, when about the hour of
Ten at night, a Meſſenger came who conducted me *Gradatim* into the Preſence of my
then *moſt endeared Floria.*

What Particulars paſs'd between us at this
Conference, you muſt excuſe my omitting : For
I vvas ſo raviſh'd to find her ſo *charming* and
conſtant, That about three hours time paſs'd a-
vvay in the moſt *innocent* Love and Amazement,
before I expected I had been there one. Since
I had been bleſt vvith her ſvveet Company thus
long, I fear'd keeping *Floria* out of Bed
longer, might in ſome meaſure indiſpoſe and
diſorder a Perſon, vvho, thro' the courſe of her
Life, had every way lived extremely regular, and
as there was nothing belonging to *Floria*, vvhich
had not it's peculiar Charm, I ſolicited her
for a Lock of her Hair, *which in a ſmall time
ſhe Conſented to cut off and gave me a Favourite
one.* Had not our Loves all this while diſpoſ-
ſeſt us of Fear, we might reaſonably have apprehended ſome Danger in ſuch an ungueſſed
at Meeting by *Floria's Guardian*, who little
dream't,

dream't, that *Amintor* was under the roof, or that any even the leaft Correfpondence could be between us at that Juncture unknown to 'em. *Floria* was fearful leaft a Difcovery fhould be made by any misfortunate flip or accident. In order therefore to remove all doubts or appearances of our Converfe unhappily coming to light; fhe advis'd me in thefe Words. *Amintor*, (fays fhe) *Your coming to fee me in this manner will be of dangerous Confequence, for we cannot evade at fome time being found out, fo I defire you would write to—— and ask leave to vifit me here*: I don't think *it will be deny'd you*: *You may, if you pleafe, inclofe two or three Lines directed for me, but let it be nothing you would fear fhould be feen*: But now, *Sir*, the time was come for the reafons before given for our parting : You may judge I was unwilling to feparate : For I now could have wifh'd, the Hours had mov'd as flow as they feem'd to do in the days of our Abfence. My good Friend had ftaid all this while at the *Tavern* in the fame room I left him, where he could find but little diverfion in fitting without Company: But he had fo great a value for my Eafe and Welfare, that his Looks as well as Expreffions fhew'd him much fatisfy'd, when I told him what had pafs'd at my Return. It being now two a Clock, we drank one Glafs to the Health, Happinefs and good Repofe of my *Floria*, and fo made the beft of our way homewards.

The

The next day, as I remember, I in complyance and a perfect refignation to the Advice
of my *Floria* (hoping to gain a Liberty to fee
her without fear or hazard) fent *per Penny-poft*
a few Lines ; wherein I gave a fhort Account
of the Freedom of my Admittance by *Hortarius* and his Wife, and moft Particulars I have
hitherto acquainted you withal , but never
own'd, that I had feen or heard from *Floria*,
fince the time her Mother confin'd her from
me, and tho' I had wrote three times to the
Mother, with the profoundeft Humility,yet never received the leaft Anfwer or Reafon for
fending *Floria* away, That I defy'd any one to
be laid down, which a Boy of Ten Years of
Age was not able to confute: And fhould the
Mother continue in her *Obftinacy*, and be fuffered to gain her Point, 1 was of Opinion, no
Gentleman hereafter would ever treat with
the Family, becaufe he might reafonably expect to be handed into the Depth of an *A-
mour*, and when they had led and directed
him *beyond* his Recovery, to be let fink, and pe-
rifh in their Undertaking, That I vvould oppofe any Body, vvho fhould be introduced to
make his Pretences, let the Experiment coft
me never fo dear, though at that rate the inconfiftent Paffion and Arbitrary Will of an un-
thinking Woman in *Power* may lay a Foundation for the Ruin and Deftruction of half a
dozen People.

The Letter thus fent (*according to Directions of Floria*) made vvorfe for us than all before; for not only vvhat I inclos'd to her vvas broke open before deliver'd to her hands; but the other vvas carryed to *Hortarius* or his Wife, or both; for a few days afterwards, I vvas paffing by their Door, and *Hortarius* very civilly invited me vvithin his Walls; but his manner of Salutation afterwards vvas the oddeft I have met vvith; for he began to fwear, and continued Curfing: I us'd all the Arguments I could to folten him, and bring him to reafon; yet all vvas in vain, and I might as vvell have prefumed to have appeafed a *Bedlamite*; for he raifed his Voice, and diftinguifh'd every Syllable he utter'd to that Degree, that every Paffer-by vvas fupply'd vvith Matter enough to difcover the Difference, and caufe of the Difference between us; he allow'd himfelf (*indeed*) fome Intervals for *fcurrilous* Nominations, fuch as *impudent Fellow* and *fawcy Rafcal* for daring to attempt a Vifit to my *Floria* vvithout his leave: He argued like a Child, and power'd a Parcel of paffionate indigefted Threats upon me, all which I bore (in refpect of my *Floria*) with a great deal of Calmenefs, though my Spirits were almoft funk, and depreffed at the fame time: For now I found the Temper of the Mother was Prodigious, and that fhe exercifed her *Will* over every body alike vvith an unlimited *Power*; And fince I received this fubftantial Proof of *Paffive Obedience*, I began to dread the unavoidable Confequences, that muft one Day attend

F   thefe

thefe fcurvy Proceedings, if *Floria* fhould ceafe to be juft and conftant (vvhich as yet I had no reafon to fufpeƈt) fo I no fooner vvas in a manner thruft out by *Hortarius* ; but I took my Pen in hand, and gave a true relation of this Brutal Jnference to my *FLO-RIA.*

It could never be fuppos'd, that any Man could bear and forgive fuch Dunghil Provocations, if my Love and Engagements to *Floria,* had not lain an Embargo upon my Fingers.

But to my greateft Satisfaƈtion, *I* receiv'd a Meffage (by a fecond hand) from *Floria,* and accidently fecur'd a Letter, vvhich is as follows :

Mr.

Mr.————

IT is *mightily against my Inclinations* to harbour *such Thoughts,* as I am going *to tell you, and that is to give your self the Trouble to inform* Amintor, *That I would speak with him about Ten* of the Clock this *Night* (at the Place appointed as was before) *but withal charge him, for his Life, not to divulge so great a* Secret *to the Dearest Friend he has, and I beg of you to Burn this* Paper *in which you will Oblige your Friend to serve you,*

FLORIA!

I can't tell what *Floria* meant by faying, this
was againſt her Inclination, where ſhe candidly
requeſted the favour of informing me with her
deſire : Nay, fixes the time and place ſo
punctually, and vvith ſuch a Caution for Se-
creſy, as you vvill ſcarce hear of in a thouſand
Intreagues ; eſpecially, when *Floria* was ſatis-
fy'd, that my Friend *Alexis* was to be truſted,
and depended upon, in regard he acted in her
Intereſt equal vvith my own.

But breaking off here, *I* ſhall proceed to let
you knovv, That *I* readily embrac'd this *Invitation* of my *Florias*, and as ſtrictly follovv'd
her Precepts, vvith a due Obſervation both of
Time and Place. *I* vvas at the *Tavern* before
the Hour of Nine ; vvhere time rowl'd on in
ſuſpitious and fearful Apprehenſions ; for
certainly Fear is as natural to a Lover as a
Coward, and 'tis impoſſible, any Man can be
fearful, unleſs he be diſpirited. Thus for vvant
of any Company, *I* doz'd away the time, 'till
I vvas releas'd from that Melancholy, and
Conducted once more into the Company of
my *Floria*.

Novv yvas the time, That *I* courted *Fortune* to
ſecond my Reſolutions, having fully determin'd
(vvithin my ſelf) to uſe all the Motives, that
Love and Argument could ſupply me vvith to
remove *Floria*, and fix her in my own Poſſeſſion, *I* vvas not inſenſible, that this vvas the moſt
ticklish Point to manage, and required an
Empire of Reaſon to lay the Deſign, and carry
it

it on vvith Succefs: For Virgins (vvhether through Fear or Modefty *I* fhall not prefume to determin) generally give Men the Trouble of *tirefom* Debates, and *dallying* Conferences before they make one ftep, vvhich may engage 'em beyond the Power of retreating : *I* gave her all the Affurances of faithful Love ; and urg'd the almoft innumerable and tediousHours vvhich had pafs'd, fince fhe promis'd to be mine, That even according to the Laws of *Reafon* and *Nature*, 'tvvas deem'd *In*juftice in the largeft Senfe to deprive a Perfon of the Poffeffion of his Property. Then *I* made a fmall Repetition of the *Abufes I* had received both from her *Mother* and *Hortarius*, vvhich *I* had eafily efcap'd, had *I* not fubmitted to her *Will*, and acted by her *Directions* : *I* vvas perfectly unskill'd in the Rudiments of Perfvvafion, but that Defect vvas fupply'd by vvhat my *Love* dictated to me, and vvhen *I* follicited her for her leave to procure fuch neceffary Utenfils as are convenient, and required in *Nuptial* Ceremonies : *Floria* faintly mov'd for a *Demurrer*, and blufhing told me, *I* had no reafon to be fo hafty, vvith other delatory Arguments ; but my *Love* back'd my Refolution, and being prepar'd for this Attack, fhe gave me a *direct Size for her Ring, and granted me her leave to take out a Licenfe for Marriage.*

By this time I heard a Neighbouring Clock ſtrike *One* , yet ſince night hitherto had been ſpent in nothing but Importunity and Solicitation, I could not without regret think of parting , 'till I had given Aſſurances to my *Floria*, how ſenſible I was of the encreaſe of my Felicity, occaſion'd by her Condeſcenſion, tho' ſhe might eaſily diſcover my Satisfaction ; for the Tranſport was as viſible as my Love, which grew perfect, as the *Charmer* diſtributed her Favours ; after which I thought it proper to ſeparate, for fear of clogging my *Floria* vvith thoſe uſual Repetitions a Captivated Senſe is frequently guilty of : And as it has been aſſerted, that the moſt ſacred things may become to loſe ſome part of their Efficacy by an immoderate uſe of 'em, ſo that Noble Paſſion may be apt to grow cold and loſe the Flame it boaſts of by an undue or untimely Application on either ſide : Therefore I took my leave of my *Floria*. But the Joy and Pleaſure, which conſequentially ſucceeds the uninterrupted Satisfaction , That a true Lover enjoys in the Converſe of a Woman he *adores*, was diſturb'd by a great Misfortune brought upon me by one of the Night-guard of our famous City of *London* ; who (for vvant of a Coach, that moſt excellent Conveniency the Town affords) I was obliged to make uſe of to conduct me to my Lodgings. The Watchman upon my Agreement to his Demand lighted me very near a Mile, where ſeveral of the ſame Order vvere carouſing in a Cellar, he ſtopt about two Minutes, but *I* had not ſo quick a gueſs to ſee

my

my felf in any Danger ; vve had not gone a-
bove 500 yards further, 'ere *I* was affaulted by
tvvo Ruffians, and my honeft Conductor joyn-
ed vvith 'em in the Re-encounter; they knock'd
me down twice, but by Accident getting my
Sword into my hand, *I* made way for my Deliverance, and by the Affiftance of a good old
Woman and her Crutch, *I* got to the *Bagnio*,
vvhere *I* vvas let Blood, and ftaid till about
eight a Clock the next Day : As foon as *I* was
tollerably vvell of Bruifes, *I* procur'd the
Ring and Licenfe, and the Sunday following
(at the old quoted hour of Ten) I vvas in Expectation of another Interview vvith my *Floria,*
and attended at the Tavern, but no Meffenger
came ; fo at Midnight I return'd homeward :
This Labour might vvell have been fpar'd, but
I made it a Punctilio to keep my Word; for
nothing can be a more fenfible Affront to a
Woman, than a feeming Neglect, and to
fail in an Appointment can't be conftrued
other than a flight. Suppofition upon Suppofition vvere employed to hammer out, or guefs
at, the reafon of my being difappointed, vvhen
in 2 Days time I vvas fatisfyed, That *Floria*
had acted that Part of Deception, vvhich vvas
ufually managed by the Servant, *viz.* To lock
the Door, vvith the Bolt out of the Staple, and
to carry the Key up to her Guardians, vvhich
gave 'em a reafonable Opportunity of moving towards a Difcovery of vvhat they really
fufpected before ; therefore as 'twas eafy to
make the matter prove it felf, the Door was
found open, vvhich caus'd them to carry a

ftricter

ſtricter hand, and a more vvatchful eye over *Floria* than before they ſeem'd to do. When *I* found hovv Matters vvere poſited, *I* ſent a Meſſenger at a proper time to knovv vvhen *I* might ſee my *Floria*; and, ſuppoſing her to be deſtitute of Pen and *I*nk, ſent therevvith my Pencil, vvhich *I* thought might perform the part of a Pen in a vvilling hand, and accordingly, *I* received a Letter vvrote therevvith in the follovving Words.

S I R,

S I R,

I Know no more how to order this *Affair*, than the Pope does ; as for my *see-ing you, I can fet no time, my Confinement is fo great* ; but to morrow Morning, if I can poffible fee you I will, *It will be with .fo much fear, that I had rather let it alone a thoufand times :* You are very of-ten pleas'd to tell me of my being too eafy to be work'd upon, you fhall never find me fo to your Prejudice ; *for what I told my Sifter, is no more than one Sifter will tell another, which is from your Con-fus'd.*

FLORIA.'

G   Upon

Upon the Receipt of this, I was oblig'd to entertain a Diflike of that Cruelty, which People generally exercife upon fuch as are put under their charge,upon thefe Occafions, making their Habitations a perfect Defart, a Nurfery of Inquietudes, and at the fame time, denying a Man the Liberty of Reproach; for had I fo much as mov'd, that Motion cou'd not have mifs'd interrupting and deftroying *her Peace*, and banifhing my own Quiet : So I was refolved to confine my Paffion in a Mediocrity, and where Power would in fpite of Fate be hurtful, lay it afide and ufe Policy. The next Morning by the hour of Five, I was under her Chamber Window, and gazed with fuch eager and wifhful Expectation, as a Merchant at the Arrival of a *Prize* of the greateft *Importance* to him. But the God of *Sleep* was more. powerful than the God of *Love*. So I thought fit to enter the Houfe, and fend up a Meffage, upon which in a fmall time, fhe came down to me, I fhew'd her the *Licence*, and mov'd that the Day might be fixt upon to put it in Execution.

In

In Anſwer to which *Flo-*
ria ſaid;

A Mintor, *what makes you ſo un-*
eaſy, you have no Reaſon to be ſo
Precipitate *in this Affair, for I will never*
Marry any body but your ſelf, and matters
may fall out much better than you ex-
pect, in a little time ; ſo pray reſt ſatis-
fy'd at preſent, and you ſhall hear from
me in two or three days. Here Sir we
parted ; and I ſhall likewiſe break off,
this being the ſecond Part of my Intreague.

G 2　　　　I gave

I gave my felf up wholly to thefe Directions of my *Floria*, tho' I had entertain'd a reafonable Opinion within my felf, that they were
all of a piece as *infecure* and ill laid, as her
former Advices, which not only threw the
Mother into the Vapours, but put *Hortarius*
upon Actions unbecoming a Man of Character and Honefty, which in fpight of that
Pride they are Poffeft of, were equally regnant
and prevailing. But not to hold you here, no
Letter came from *Floria* in four days time,
therefore I wrote to her, but fhe return'd mine
without opening it; this put me upon a pitch
of thinking, which grew fo ftrong by degrees,
that it prov'd a hard task to difunite and dif-
intangle that Complicated Plague which attended the return of my Letter, I thought 'twas
now time to dive into the reafon of her *care-
lefsnefs* and *ingratitude*, yet I refolv'd to avoid
heat, fuppofing this could proceed from nothing but fome *Whim*, which might effect her
Brain, and prompt her to make an Experiment upon me, tho' when I came to recollect
my felf, I could not believe fhe could be fo
great a *Stranger* to her Senfes, to impofe fo
incongruous, incoherent and *ridiculous* an Artifice upon me, with a defign it fhould take
Place; but if fhe did, and defign'd it, fo, it is
(in my Opinion) but a very flender and weak
evidence of her honefty and difcretion, becaufe the very procseding difcovers fo much
of Craft and Defign, that a Woman of the
leaft reafon muft think her felf laid open to
the refictions of *injur'd Love* and *baffled Affection.*

section. For it argues the Person so abus'd, to be the meerest Novice and the most abject Tool upon Earth, if he should want Spirit to exert his right, or be so remiss and disingenious to himself, to suffer a People *mean* in their Principles, *unfair* and *abusive* in their Language, *deceiving* and *premeditately jiltish* in their Actions, to triumph and insult, after being guilty of the most ungenerous Acts, without justly commenting upon 'em.

But to wave this Digression, 'twas not long ere *Floria* was releas'd from her Prison, recall'd home, and the Face of Affairs was alter'd thro' the whole Family. *Hortarius* thinking himself honestly, and well off the matter, *his Wife* having plaid the godly part, and religiously perswaded *Floria*, to make a solemn Vow to break her former Promises to me, and *Floria* who (together with the advantage of a good stock) wanted neither *Skill* nor *Practice*, in the knack of saying and unsaying, I find, was easily perswaded into the *Pious* Act. I know *Sir* you will suppose *Floria*, either to be very much in jest, or altogether out of her Wits; after all the Liberty of Nocturnal Conferences, such apparent Instances of Love and Affection, and by her own Invitations, without the Privity of *Hortarius*, or any body, who had any Power to dispose of her. The reason of all this came to my knowledg, about thirteen Weeks after she had made the Vow, which I shall here relate to you. Two days after, I shew'd *Floria* the *Licenfe*, the Mother whose

whofe Brains had been at work all the time of
her Abfence, had a Maggot took her to come
and fee her in her retirement: And propos'd,
that *Floria* fhould vow to differt me, after
which fhe fhould come home, be us'd with a
flacker Rein, and have her *fill* of Liberty,
and a certain Gentleman fhould be introduced
to Court her, who had a *GOOD ESTATE.*
Floria upon this Mercenary Propofition, righ-
teoufly made her Vows to be bafe and difho-
nourable, to a Perfon fhe had drawn in, and
bewitch'd with her *practical Allurements* and
Infiduous Invitations, and by the leave of her
yielding Confcience, quitted all former Engagements to *me*, for the Poffeffion of an Imaginary Joynture in *Nubibus*; for the very
Gentleman the Mother fixt upon, was never
invited but once, and then he fairly refus'd the
Offer, being a Perfon of too much *Weight* and
Management to be undermin'd and trick't, by
the *fallacious* Affurances, *frothy* Vaunts, and
empty Promifes of any Body: And any Woman
alive who could reafonably expect the Characters of *Vertuous* and *Honeft*, would upon
fuch a Propofal have frankly confefs'd, how
far fhe had been engaged; efpecially, fince
Floria did not want Senfe, nor the beft of Reafons to have laid the whole blame upon *Hortarius* and her Mother, for recommending me
to her, and giving me fo unlimited a Power;
but that great Eftate was prevalent and At-
tractive, tho' never to be catch't.

A Week

A Week had not pafs'd after *Floria* was *tranfplanted* into her Priftine Habitation, 'ere I met her and paid my Refpects to her, and (in the kindeft manner) with ferioufnefs and concern beg'd fhe would give me a Reafon, why my laft Letter was not as acceptable to her as thofe I had fent before fhe had fo firmly engag'd her felf to me ; all the Anfwer fhe gave me, was, that fhe durft not receive any more Letters, and defired me (*if I had any Love or refpect for her*) *to avoid being feen with her in Publick, and I fhould fee her elfewhere ; becaufe, fhould it be difcover'd, fhe was fure to be again confin'd.* I was afraid of expofing her to the leaft hazard, tho' fhe feem'd to have ten times more Liberty than before was ufually allow'd her, and every Man was welcome to her Company but my felf, I us'd feveral Opportunities and Means, to come to a Conference with her, but perceiv'd a vaft Coldnefs and Inconftancy in her, and for five Weeks I had no other than the fame Anfwer renew'd, and appointed feveral times of meeting me, but as oft fhe furely *fail'd* and *difappointed* me, which put me upon a new Method of Proceeding in order to correct her Errour, for by the extraordinary Liberty allow'd her, and the publick freedom fhe gave other People, of Converfing with her, I had almoft a demonftrative Proof, that *Floria* had commenc'd fome new Intreague ; therefore I thought it high time to give *Hortarius* a juft and impartial Account of the whole matter, which you have in the fecond part of this Letter ; but before I
would

would proceed. I told *Floria*, that since she had been so unkind to refuse my last Letter, and so Inconsiderate, Unjust and Ungrateful to persist in her Revolt, it would prove of lasting ill Consequence to her self, and a disgrace to the Family. *Floria* was uneasy under the Apprehensions of her Father's coming to the knowledge of the freedoms she had given me under her Confinement, and beg'd *I would forbear writing to her Father, and she would without fail give me the meeting the Sunday following*; but I found she never meant to perform any Promises she had made, I had much ado to contain my self; for I was quite tired with this shuffling Retraction, but the next time I met her, I found her lost to all Intents and Purposes, being destitute of the least Dram of Moral Civility ; for *Floria* discover'd a little of the Mother's Spirit, and her counterfeited Meekness and Sweetness of Temper, was turn'd into its Native Bluster and Bravado ;

She

She told me,

I Had put an insufferable Affront upon her, to assert that she contriv'd ways for me to write to her, and that it was as grand a Lye as ever was told; that I was pleas'd to express my Malice and Revenge to the Purpose, to say, that I would make known the whole Affair to her Father, that she gave me many Thanks for the Favour I was going to do her, which should never scare her into any Thing but what she thought proper and convenient for her Interest, that I might, for it lay in my Power, lessen her at Pleasure, but if I would do her Justice, I could never boast of her Fondness to me, or being in Love with me, with a great deal more of the same.

H   Now

Now any body that reads her third Letter will (without much Perſwaſion) believe, that 'twas by *Floria*'s own Contrivance, that I not only wrote to her, but viſited her, and by Conſequence I was not ſo great a Lyar as ſhe was pleas'd to call me : How *Floria* could look upon it to be Malice and Revenge, to give her Father the moſt convincing Reaſons, to compleat what ſhe with ſo much Induſtry and Toil had brought to ſuch a Pitch, I can't conceive ; for it was certainly the moſt conducive Means, if her *Honeſty* had not run Counter to her *Actions, Promiſes* and *Aſſurances*, ſhe diſclaims being *ſcar'd* into any thing, but what may be proper for her Intereſt, which in plain *Engliſh* is as much, as if ſhe had ſaid : *Do you think tho' I have made you never ſo many Promiſes, or Proteſtations, and have been with you at Midnight, and conſented to the taking out a Licenſe, that I'll be ſo great a Fool to marry you, if I can have any Man who has a better Fortune ; no, you are miſtaken in me.* And truly *Sir* (among ſome ſort of Women) a large Settlement and a better Eſtate, is always thought a very good Juſtification of the higheſt Piece of Perfidiouſneſs ; a larger Eſtate diſſolving all prior Engagements, and that they ought not to keep their word to their diſadvantage, as they call it : Then *Floria* ſaid, if I'll do her Juſtice I can't boaſt of her Fondneſs to me, or being in Love with me. Tho' any body who does not know her, muſt think ſhe ſpeaks in Riddles and Paradoxes, for if you make a Retroſpection into the Letters, Paſſages and
Interviews

Interviews of this Amour, you muſt look upon this frank Acknowledgment, to declare her ſomething that wants a Name.

But *Floria* had baffled and banter'd me thus for 7 Weeks, and by her Method of proceeding kept me under a perpetual Surprize, which made me grow weary and tir'd ; inſomuch,that I now reſolved to try the laſt Effort, by laying open our whole Proceedings to *Hortarius*, which I did with as much good Manners and Decency as my unactive Genius could direct me.

I gave *Floria* notice of my Deſign eight Days before, and told her, that this was the time to ſhew her ſelf Honeſt,by confeſſing and declaring her *Engagements*, and expreſſing her *Affection to me*, and ſhe had room enough, had ſhe not wanted Gratitude and Inclination ; for a ſudden Fit of Diſcontent well manag'd, has often extorted a Conſent from an Obſtinate Parent, *that never gave the leaſt Conſent for Addreſs* ; but now the Mask was pull'd off ; for when *Hortarius* had my Letter, and examin'd her, as to every Particular, ſhe inſtead of owning the truth, with a great deal of Aſſurance denyed the moſt material Matters of Fact,and the next Morning, as I take it, I receiv'd two Letters under one Cover, one from *Hortarius*, and the other from *Floria*, but they were compoſed of ſuch indecent and unmannerly Stuff, that it would taint my Letter to inſert 'em ; ſo I immediately wrote a few Lines in

Anſwer

Anſwer to each, and tranſmitted 'em in the ſame Order; but *Floria* intercepted them, and ſent them back by Penny Poſt. Three Days after this I received a meſſage, that *Floria* deſired to ſpeak with me at twelve a Clock the ſame Day, at her Father's Houſe; I could not tell what Concluſion to draw from this, and was indifferent, whether I ſhould believe the Meſſenger, 'till he told me he receiv'd his Errand from a Servant of *Hortarius*'s, I was yet very willing to be reconcil'd to her, upon the leaſt Promiſe of her Sincerity and Conſtancy; for there is nothing ſure more pleaſant than the Reconciliation of real Lovers, ſmall Jarrs, and Miſtakes being often neceſſary to quicken a languiſhing Affection. Acordingly at the appointed hour, *Floria* had plac'd the Servant ready for my Admittance, and I found her all alone, and enquiring into the Cauſe of my being ſent for, ſhe began very cleanly and artificially *to make her Apology, for being ſo rude in her laſt to me, aſſuring me that 'twas a Parental Conſtraint upon her, contrary to her natural Inclinations, and told me, ſhe had been much concern'd about it, ſhe likewiſe complained much of the rigour of our Stars, and the want of Poilcy in our Management*; notwithſtanding it was all her own Projection from the time of her Promiſe.

Floria begged I would not expoſe and ruin her, but have a little Patience, and deſired I would burn her Letters. I told her, it muſt be her own fault if ever they come to the Eye of the World, and I hop'd ſhe thought 'em very ſafe in the ſame hands

hands fhe had repos'd her *heart* ; for, notwithftanding all that happen'd, I heartily laid afide
all Prejudice, and had as great Value and Re-
fpeft for her as ever ; but fince the *Amour* had
been turn'd topfey torvy fo oft, and fhe had fo
many *Revolutions* in her Temper , I thought it
proper that fhe fhould renew her Promifes to
me before Witnefs, the next Opportunity we
fhould have of Meeting together ; and before
our parting , fhe gave further Affurances of
her Conftancy , tho' at the fame time fhe was
carrying on another Intreague unknown to me;
for not many days after I met *Floria* and a
Gentlewoman with her, when fhe refus'd my
accompanying her, and rejected every Offer of
Friendfhip. I fpent my Thoughts fome time
upon this Rudenefs and Difrefpeft, at length
I told her, if her Reafon and Juftice was both
debauch'd, 'twas my bufinefs to lye in the way
in order to *reinftate* her, and fecure her *Reputation*,for if fhe play'd faft and loofe at this rate,
I fhall never know what to make of her. fo I
defired fhe would once for all tell me plainly
and freely what fhe defign'd to do,but inftead of
giving me any Anfwer, fhe propos'd the Matter to be refer'd to the Gentlewoman that was
with her, and as I had not ftood out upon any
Propofal of *Floria*'s before , and finding the
Lady fhe put as a Referee, to be a Perfon of
difcerning Senfe and folid Reafon, I was refolv'd to purfue the Matter to the utmoft, tho'
I plainly faw what fhe was driving at, for the
Contrivance was all her own, and nothing of
Moment has been acted in that Family for fome

Years ;

Years ; but of *meer Necessity* the *Umpirage* has been repos'd in her.

But (*Sir*) the Plot was thus, I was to be lull'd and amus'd by *Floria*, 'till *Hortarius* and his *Consorts* could manage a Point to their advantage, and then I was to be left in the lurch. In the mean time, I sent a Letter to the Gentlewoman before mentioned, who at that time lay at *Floria*'s Fathers, I gave a special Messenger a Charge therewith, and got another to Superscribe it, fearing it might fall into wrong hands ; this Letter was taken in by *Floria* her self, who instead of delivering of it as it was directed to her *Confident*, very genteely communicated it to her *Mother*, and the Letter was broke open by them and read, you may Conjecture what attended *Floria*, who in diving into other People's Secrets, discover'd her own to her *Mother*: This is one particular Instance of the *Manners* and *Gentility* that Family boasts of.

I seeing the *Gentlewoman* about a Week afterwards, unfolded the whole Story to her, and upon the Result she frankly told me, that if she had acted *Floria*'s Part to any body, she should have believ'd her self so much engag'd in Honour, that it had not been in her Power to have receded. After which I press'd *Floria* for her final Answer, plainly seeing the end of her Dalliances, and being possess'd with a Confidence that she never meant any thing but *trick* and *deceit* ; so when she found I was bent
upon

upon it, and refolv'd to be releas'd from the Plague of Dependance, fhe boldly appear'd in her proper Colours, and after thirteen Weeks Shuffling, fince the *Licenfe* was taken out, fhe vouchfaf'd to let me know, that fhe would not have me Trouble my felf, for all I could do fhould have no effect.

This (*Sir*) is not fo full as I could have wifh'd it, but fomething muft be omitted, leaft to the better part of my Friends I fhould appear vain; tho' I have fince been inform'd more than once, that I have wrought a great Deliverance for my felf, by being quit of the Breed, and from henceforth, I fhall entertain an indifferent Opinion of the Family, and never think any of 'em worthy of the leaft Civility, which is due to People of Reputation and Honefty. And now *Sir*, I refer it to your felf, whether you don't think attending upon a defigning giddy Woman only at times of Leifure, a very full Employment, tho' I don't mean hereby to juftify my Neglect of fo good a Friend, yet I have fome faint Hopes, that this Breach of Friendfhip to a Gentleman that I am proud to be call'd his

moft humble Servant
AMINTOR.

Weftminfter
December 11th 1705.

F I N I S.